JACK TEMPLAR
and the
MONSTER HUNTER ACADEMY

Book 2

A NOVEL
By

Jeff Gunhus

Copyright 2013 by Jeff Gunhus

Printed in the United States of America

Cover design by Eric Gunhus
Cover Art by Nicole Cardiff

Library of Congress Cataloging-in-Publication Data
Gunhus, Jeff
Jack Templar and the Monster Hunter Academy: a novel /
Jeff Gunhus
ISBN-13: 978-0-9884259-4-1
ISBN-10: 0-9884259-4-7

Praise for Jack Templar Monster Hunter
The Templar Chronicles Book 1

Selected as a 2012 Finalist for the Book of the Year Award. – *Foreword Reviews*

"Gunhus brings young readers a monster-filled romp to read at their own risk. The tone is set--sarcastic, tongue-in-cheek and likable; rooting for Jack is easy...Gunhus masterfully introduces fully realized characters with whom readers can connect almost instantly. The pacing is quick but not rushed, and events seamlessly progress, complete with action, cliffhangers and surprise reveals. " - *Kirkus Reviews*

"The action starts right from the first chapter and doesn't let up until the book ends. This is the first book in a series, and I look forward to reading the rest of them." -*The DMS*

"Jeff Gunhus has made a terrific fast paced fantasy. I even wanted to bolt my doors and lock my windows! Five stars for the best book of the year." -*Elizabeth A. Bolt*

"Everything in this book was something a reader could love - action, adventure, mythical creatures, mystery and even a touch of romance." -*Sandy @ Magical Manuscripts*

"Move over Harry Potter and Percy Jackson, there's a new kid in town - Jack Templar, and he will take you on a wonderful adventure of good vs evil, with friends and enemies at every turn." -*Penny Brien* "

"This was a fun read with non-stop adventure.
Reminiscent of Percy Jackson and Harry Potter, Gunhus creates an interesting world and characters that are easy to root for. Already anticipating the next story!" - *M. Profant*

"This is a fantastic read!! Jack Templar Monster Hunter is full of adventure, twist and turns, and a couple of surprises also!! "Middle Graders" (as well as everyone else) will love this book!! Definitely recommend this read if you are a fan of fantasy!" - *MSRheinlander*

"I love this book...the character and action descriptions are so vivid. At times, the monster battles were so intense I didn't even realize I wasn't breathing! I would recommend this book to all ages." - *Tulip Bouliphant*

"Very rich and interesting characters. You get the feeling that there is much more of the story to unfold, so I am expecting sequels. Keep them coming!" -*Martha Biemann*

"I bought this book for my kids and found myself fighting them for time with it. From the first page you are drawn into Jack's discovery of a fantastic new world around him - a world he didn't know existed. It's a real fun, vivid read full of cliffhangers and non-stop action that will keep even your most reluctant reader interested." -*Jim Beard*

"Vivid imagery and tight, fast-paced narrative make this first book of a series a great read not only for middle teens, but for any reader who enjoys suspense a little on the darker side." -*Book Diva*

For my own little monsters:

Jackson, William, Daniel, Caroline and Owen

And for Nicole: who always smiles when she tells me to go write.

My name is Jack Templar and I am an orphan.

Just before my fourteenth birthday, I discovered that I came from a long line of monster hunters. You know, vampires, werewolves, zombies, you name it.

Not only that, but if monsters around the world could choose one human to kill, it would be me. Why? I haven't a clue. I'd like to find out some day, but for right now, I'm happy just to stay alive.

WARNING

Since I can't be certain that you read my first book about the night I found out I was a monster hunter, I should start out with a warning.

First, monsters are real. Vampires, werewolves, zombies, demons; you name it. In fact they are more common than you could ever imagine. Second, this book is not make-believe. This is a truthful account of my life as a monster hunter and the mysterious circumstances that seem to constantly surround me. Third, reading this book makes you fair game for monsters.

You heard me right: the simple act of reading this book will attract monsters to you and give them the go-ahead to attack. Usually, if you were under fourteen years old, you would be safe by the Law of Quattuordecim, an ancient truce between man and monster that protects non-combatant children on both sides until sundown on their fourteenth birthday. I blew it by attacking a monster that was trying to eat someone I knew the day before my birthday. You're about to blow it by reading this book.

If you're over fourteen, you are already at risk for monster attacks, but in reality they are few and far between. Still, by reading this book, you are guaranteeing they will come after you. So don't come crying to me if a rock troll chops off your feet or a harpy eats one of your eyeballs. The choice is yours.

However, *if* you decide to turn the page, you'll be reading about the Monster Hunter Academy, a place no *non*-monster hunter has ever seen or heard about before. What happened there is not for those with weak stomachs or for those who are easily upset. There is blood and gore and death and, like it or not, some kissing. But there is also an adventure unlike anything you have ever seen before.

So turn the page if you dare. The adventure starts now.

Jack Templar

Beware.
Here there be monsters!

*Label found on ancient maps
describing the lands beyond the known world.*

Chapter One

I leaned up against the ship's rusty metal railing, barely able to catch my breath. I took a pull from a water bottle as I looked out at the hundreds of miles of black ocean that stretched out in every direction, the full moon painting broad, glowing strokes across the surface that seemed to point right at me.

I always imagined that the middle of the Atlantic Ocean would be a violent place, filled with giant, rolling waves and massive storms, but the water that night was as calm as if we were on a lake. Good thing too, since the trawler we had been on for the last week was a creaky old lug of a ship whose best days were far, far behind it.

"Come on," said a girl behind me with a distinct English accent. "Break's over."

I was about to complain when I instinctively felt the attack coming. I rolled to my right and a sword sparked against the metal where I had just been resting. I held up my own sword in front of me and crouched down.

"Eva, we've been going for hours," I said. "Can't we relax just for once?"

Eva paced in front of me in the shadows of the main deck of the trawler. Her brown hair was tied back in a ponytail like every time we sparred. She held a sword in her right hand and had a nasty barbed hook screwed into the socket on her left wrist.

Even though it would seem that a lethal iron hook would attract my attention first, it was Eva's face that always distracted me when we fought. Even in the dim light, even though she was trying to run me through with her sword, she was just about the most attractive girl I'd ever seen. Every time I looked too closely at her face, I thought of the kiss she gave me right before my fight with Ren Lucre. As I pictured it in my mind again, Eva smiled, her teeth nearly glowing in the dim light. That smile wasn't good news.

She lunged at me, using a twisting combination to my weak side that I had to jump backward to avoid. I blocked a low blow from her hook, but felt a breeze as her sword swept sharply within an inch of my right ear. I reached up and felt a small patch of missing hair. I guess it was closer than an inch.

"You'll get more than a haircut unless you practice harder," she said.

I gripped my sword tightly and the two of us circled one another on the deck. Eva had been the first person to tell me that I was a monster hunter. She had been with me through that terrible first night, when the Creach horde had come to kill me. I had lost my Aunt Sophie that night, but I had also discovered that my father was still alive and held captive by the Dark Lord of the Creach—Ren Lucre.

Eva had been all business since we left Sunnyvale for the Monster Hunter Academy. Nothing but hour after hour of fighting practice. I didn't mind too much because she was an amazing fighter—much better than I was—and after coming face-to-face with the enemy I was eager to learn new ways to protect myself.

Not only was she a great fighter, but she seemed to understand how I had changed. She could sense the heightened strength and speed that had surged through me right before my fourteenth birthday. The change seemed to have either slowed or stopped, which bummed me out because I was hoping for full-on superhero powers. Or at least a body-builder physique. To look at me, you'd never imagine the strength I possessed. When I caught a glance of myself in the mirror, a skinny middle school kid looked back at me. Not only that, but I still thought of myself as Jack Smith, the name I'd been raised with my entire life. Jack Templar felt like a stranger's name to me and I wondered if it would ever feel like my own.

Still, my body was stronger, faster and more agile than I could have ever hoped for. Unfortunately, this didn't always help me when I faced Eva's superior skills.

"Brace yourself," she said. "This might hurt a little."

Before I could react, Eva was inside my defenses. I bashed into her using the hilt of my sword and I felt her fall back. I stepped up to take advantage of her misstep...only to find that it was a trap. The second I was off balance, she swept my leg and I hit the deck hard, my sword skittering across the ground.

She was right. It did hurt. Only I wasn't sure what hurt worse—my banged up knee, or my ego from losing to her for the hundredth time?

She lowered her sword, her green eyes showing her disappointment.

"See? You're on your heels again," she said. "That's why we can't stop practicing."

"I wasn't on my heels," I complained.

"She's right, Jack," said a voice, a bit garbled from a mouthful of food. "You were on your heels."

I looked over at T-Rex, one of my buddies who had come along with me on my adventure. He was in his usual deck chair watching the workout, a thick sandwich in his hand and a soda balanced on one of the armrests. After a rough few days of seasickness, he had since gotten his sea legs, found the ship's kitchen and was in the process of eating his way through everything the cook could throw at him. T-Rex had been round and heavy when we left

Sunnyvale, and he was only getting rounder and heavier as the journey went on.

T-Rex was back to being his usual cheery self, but I knew leaving had been hard on him. Mostly because he missed his grandma.

She had raised him most of his life, but in the last year she had started acting strangely. The doctors said she had Alzheimer's, which meant that her brain would slowly stop functioning and she wouldn't be able to take care of herself, let alone take care of T-Rex. Just as I was going to leave town, Child Protective Services had taken his grandma away to a nursing home and was looking for him to put him into a foster home. So, with no other family, T-Rex had decided to come with me. And I was happy that he had.

"Why don't you come out here and try?" I asked, glaring at T-Rex.

"Who? Me?" T-Rex asked.

He shifted uncomfortably in his chair, his hand creeping up from his lap. He then planted a finger firmly in his nose. Did I forget to mention that T-Rex was a world-class nose-picker? Every time he got nervous, he started digging for gold. That's how he had gotten his nickname, T-Rex, because we all wished he had itty-bitty T-Rex arms, so he wouldn't be able to reach his nose. The good news was that since our night battling monsters, his nose-picking had slowed considerably.

"Yeah, you," I said sternly. "You need to practice too. This isn't a vacation, you know."

T-Rex stuffed his face with another bite of a sandwich and said, "No, I'm fine right here, thank you."

"I'll do it." A shadow jumped down from a perch on the control tower in the center of the trawler. It was Will, my other friend from home. Both he and T-Rex had been drawn into my little monster problem on that terrible night. In fact, I owed them both my life. But that was where their similarities ended. T-Rex wasn't the adventurous type. He would have been perfectly happy staying at home if his grandma hadn't been taken away. As for Will... he was another story completely.

While I had been raised an orphan by my Aunt Sophie, Will had been raised by parents who were worse than the monsters we now fought. When my Aunt Sophie—who turned out to be a devil-wolf—was killed by Ren Lucre, Will felt the loss as much as I did. After that, there was nothing left for either of us in Sunnyvale, so it was a no-brainer that we left town with Eva, ready for anything this new world would throw at us. Three days later we were on a ship leaving New York harbor on the way to Europe. Destination: the Monster Hunter Academy.

Will strutted out on the practice area. He was short, but carried himself with a curled up tension that reminded me of a pit bull. Will loved it when people underestimated him because of his size. It made winning a lot more fun.

T-Rex cupped his mouth with his hands and made a sound like a stadium cheering a gladiator. I stepped back and let him into the training session. Will held a short metal rod in front of him. He pressed a button and both sides telescoped out, leaving him with a spear in his hand.

"Besides, I need to practice with the new toy you gave me," he said.

"You'll get your turn," Eva said, turning back to me. "Come on. Do it again."

I held out my hand to Will and he tossed me his spear. "Let's see how I do with this."

Eva flashed me a smile. The one I'd seen far too many times on the deck of the ship. It was the smile right before I got my butt spanked.

Will and T-Rex hooted at the challenge. T-Rex got out of his chair and joined Will on the railing like they were at a boxing match while Eva and I circled one another on the deck.

"Are you going to make a move?" Eva asked.

I didn't reply. I concentrated on her movements, moving the spear so that the tip created a figure-eight pattern like Eva had taught us.

Eva feinted to my side, testing me. But I didn't take the bait.

"Good," Eva said. "Better."

She made a run at me and we exchanged a flurry of blows, the sword and spear banging off each other. As we parted, I nicked the shoulder of her leather suit. It didn't draw any blood, but I knew Eva felt it.

"Yeah!" Will yelled. "That's the way."

"Get him, Eva!" T-Rex cried.

Eva and I circled each other again. Testing. Waiting.

"I'll admit, you're improving," Eva said. "You even look good doing it. Kind of cute, actually."

I felt my face flush at the comment. I paused, caught off-guard...and that was all she needed.

She lunged forward, smacking my spear to the side with the flat side of her sword, rolling her body along its edge until she was standing in front of me, my spear tucked under her arm. With a simple twist in the other direction, the spear flew out of my hands and skittered across the deck.

She spun and placed the point of her blade against my throat.

I gulped nervously, but nodded for Eva to look down.

Hovering right over her rib cage was my long dagger.

Will and T-Rex clapped. This was the first time I had even gotten close to beating her. Eva didn't share Will's enthusiasm.

Eva pushed me away and glared at us both.

"You all seem to think this is a game. It's not," she said. "Dying alongside your opponent still means you're dead."

"You're just mad because he almost got you," Will said.

Eva walked up to Will. She wasn't that tall but she still towered over him. She leaned down so they met eye-to-eye. Will, never one to back down, glared back at her.

"Wait until we get to the Academy. You won't last a day," Eva said. She turned on her heels and stalked off into the ship's cabins.

"What's gotten into her?" T-Rex asked.

"We're getting closer to the Academy," I said. "She's the only one who really knows what we're in for."

"So?" Will said.

"I think she's scared for us," I said.

"Oh," T-Rex said, rolling the idea over in his mind. "I didn't think of that. Do you think it's going to be that bad?"

"Nah, she's just trying to spook us is all," Will said, the certainty gone from his voice. "Don't you think, Jack?"

I shrugged. "I guess we'll find out soon enough."

We stared out over the water, each of us alone with our thoughts of what the Academy might be like. Eva had told us very few details beyond a brief history of the place.

Set up in the mountains near the border between France and Italy, the Academy was the last holdout of an ancient institution that had trained monster hunters for centuries. Even as recent as a few decades ago, there were several such places on every continent. But modern technology was making it harder and harder to remain hidden from the public eye. This mountain hideaway was the first Academy, and, according to Eva, it might be the last as well.

"Eva told me that there were real monsters kept in captivity there for the training exercises," T-Rex said. "Do you think that's true?"

I shrugged. "We've both known her for the same length of time. Have you ever heard her exaggerate about anything?"

"I guess not," Will said. "This is gonna be awesome."

I smiled. Will was always the eager one, ready for anything. While this often got him into trouble, I wished I could be more like him. When I thought of Eva's nervousness for us, all I felt was a twisting knot in my stomach. But I wasn't going to the Academy to participate in their little training program. The only thing I cared about was finding Ren Lucre's dungeons and then freeing my father. Eva had promised the head of the Academy, Master Aquinas, would tell me everything she knew when we got there. I was counting on it.

A soft bell chimed from up in the control tower, a deep, resounding clang that guided our ship safely to shore. I followed the tower's smooth, sheer walls upward, its top seemingly missing as it disappeared into a thick, swirling shroud of mist.

Three men walk along the balcony outside the steering house. The captain of the ship was one of them, noticeable because of the red glow from the tip of his cigar. These men were true sailors, paid off by members of the Black Guard back in America to take on three stowaways. Sure, a plane would have been more efficient, but try to leave the country when you're a kid without a passport. Not that easy.

I was about to turn to Will and suggest we head down to bed when I heard the first scream.

It came from a few stories above us. It was a man's scream, but high-pitched and filled with terror. A cigar hit the deck next to us. Instinctively, both Will and I crouched down to the ground, swords up as Eva had taught us, looking up to the balcony overhead. T-Rex just stood there, mouth open and gazing in the direction of the scream, clutching his sandwich to him. I reached out and pulled him to the ground next to us.

The fog descended further and covered the balcony in a thin, wispy haze. Through it, I could still see the dark shapes of the men on the balcony. They ran back and forth as if trapped. The captain cried out, his arms raised as if to attack something. He struggled with some unseen force, then tipped precariously over the railing.

"Watch out!" I cried.

The captain stood for a second, then stumbled backward as if forced by a strong shove. He fell backward over the railing.

"No!" Will shouted.

But just as the captain was about to hit the deck, a tendril of cloud bolted out from the mist and wrapped around his leg. He jerked to a stop just above the hardwood surface, held tightly by his one leg.

11

I breathed a sigh of relief, but it was short-lived.

Two other men tumbled down from the balcony, screaming. They were also caught at the last second by long wispy fingers of mist and held upside down off the deck. They struggled and kicked, but they could not free themselves.

The fog churned and swirled and I thought I saw bodies rolling just under the surface. Every so often an arm or a leg broke out from the cloud before dissolving into the night air.

"What is it?" T-Rex whimpered.

"I don't know," I whispered back. "But it can't be good."

Without warning, one of the tendrils of fog snapped back and forth like a whip being cracked. The sailor flew through the air, smashed into the wall, and crumpled to the floor.

"Definitely not good," I said. "Come on."

We ran, still low to the ground, staying as far from the ceiling of fog as possible. In front of us, the second sailor was tossed through the air, end over end until he smacked into the wall.

I lifted my sword over my head as I neared the captain, still hanging upside down. With a yell, I jumped onto a cargo crate and vaulted into the air, slashing the dense cord of mist just above the captain's foot.

But my sword went straight through it like there was nothing there.

I landed hard on the deck, rolled forward and ended back up on my feet. In seconds, Will and

T-Rex were at my side. Will brandished his spear. T-Rex still had a death grip on his sandwich.

"Impressive," Will said. "Now what?"

The mist churned and grew thicker directly above us. There was a swirling vortex, like the beginning of a tornado.

"Run!" I yelled.

Just as I did, the vortex above us transformed into wide, gaping jaws lined with horrific teeth.

We sprinted from the deck, T-Rex screaming as we ran.

The jaws descended on us, a thick neck of white fog behind it. Luckily, we were already on the move as the massive jaws chomped down on the deck where we had just been standing. Shards of wood exploded into the air from the impact.

We ran into the hallway connecting the two sides of the ship. It was open at each end so I could see the night sky rise and fall through the gap at the opposite side. I spun around and saw that the fog was still chasing us, its front end crystallized into nasty looking spikes. As we ran down the hall, we suddenly saw a thick white fog engulf our only exit.

"We're trapped!" Will shouted.

"This way!" I shouted back.

I opened a hatch in the wall and climbed in. Once on the other side, all three of us heaved against the thick metal door until it swung into place. I tried to spin the wheel to lock the door, when something heavy hammered in from outside. The force of the impact pushed the door open a few inches. We threw our shoulders into the door and slammed it back shut.

"Lock it!" Will yelled.

"I'm trying!" I said, lurching the wheel mechanism over, between the violent bouts of hammering on the outer side of the door. "Push harder! Both of you, on three. One...two...THREE!"

Will and T-Rex grunted and heaved against the hatch. It slammed shut just long enough for me to spin the handle and lock it tight.

There were a few more angry poundings against the sturdy metal door, and then silence.

We all rocked back against the wall and tried to catch our breath.

"Well, that was close," T-Rex laughed.

BAM! BAM! BAM!

Something slammed into the metal hatch again. Only this time we heard a voice as well.

"Let me in! It's going to get me... Please let me in!"

The three of us froze. It was Eva.

"Help me, please!" Eva cried. "I beg you."

"It's Eva," T-Rex shouted. "Open the door. Quick!"

"Come on!" Will yelled.

The door rattled even harder. I grabbed the wheel to spin it open but a hand reached out from behind us and stopped me. I spun around and saw Eva crouched next to me.

"Open the door! Help me," Eva's voice cried from the other side of the door. The fog creature was imitating her.

14

"It's called an Aquamorph," Eva whispered. "A powerful creature that can change shapes and shift from solid to mist in a split second. Usually they aren't this aggressive."

"Why won't you help me?" the voice that sounded like Eva cried.

"We almost opened the door for that thing. We would have been goners for sure," Will said.

"Please, Jack. It's hurting me," the voice whimpered.

"It knows who you are," Eva said to me. "That's not a good sign."

"Now what?" T-Rex asked.

Eva gave the wheel another tug to make certain it was secure and then motioned for us to follow her up the ladder. As she climbed, I noticed the apparatus screwed into the wrist of her missing hand—a short brass pipe tipped with the head of a spear. Before I could ask her what it was, she was already up the ladder and on the deck above us. Will and I followed fast behind.

We were now on the ship's upper level.

The lights flickered above us as we ran through the corridors. Twice we turned only to see a wall of fog billowing toward us. We had to double-back each time and find a new route.

"We have to get out in the open!" Eva said.

"And then what?" I asked. "Our swords do nothing to it."

Finally, we reached a doorway that led to the balcony where we had first seen the sailors attacked. The wind shifted and the fog cleared, giving us an opening. We ran onto the balcony and looked down at the fog swirling beneath us.

Even though the wind howled and bashed the ship, agonizing screams from the sailors reached us from the deck below. The raging wind was so loud that we had to yell to hear each other.

"OK, now what?" I shouted.

Eva stared into the fog, looking for something. "We need to find its center," she yelled back. "It's the only way to stop it." She looked up and pointed to an area above us and to the right, a point that was just off the ship's edge. I didn't see anything at first, but then I noticed that the fog swirled around it faintly in a circular motion—it was a giant version of the vortex we had seen earlier.

"It looks like a hurricane," T-Rex said, his hands held up to his face to protect himself from the wind.

"Is that it?" Will shouted.

"Can't be sure," Eva yelled. "We need to get closer and draw it out. That's the only way to make it vulnerable."

"Get closer?" I asked, looking up into the sky. "How do you suggest we do that?"

Eva nodded at the communications antenna on the roof of the bridge. It was constructed much like a ladder and stretched high into the sky. A red light flashed on and off at its peak, swaying to and fro as the ship rolled on the waves of the ocean. At first I thought she was kidding—then I realized she was just nuts.

16

"Come on," she shouted. "I need your help if it gets angry."

She clambered up a maintenance ladder that went from the balcony to the top of the bridge. I looked at Will and T-Rex, half-hoping they would try to talk me out of what I was about to do. But instead they both gave me a thumbs-up.

"Good luck," Will said, just as another round of screams came up from the lower deck. I couldn't help but wonder what this creature would be like angry.

I climbed up the ladder to find that Eva had already started up the antenna. She shimmied up the metal girder like an acrobat, despite the spear-tipped device in place of her left hand. She paused long enough to look down at me staring at her from below.

"Come on!" she yelled.

I sheathed my sword, jumped onto the antenna and climbed. As I did, the wind picked up, whipping my clothes against me. The higher I got, the windier it became. Worse, the antenna swayed dramatically from side to side with our combined weight. I felt like I would lose my grip at any second.

The vortex swirled out from our position about twenty feet both above and away from us. Hard to spot from the balcony, it was clearly defined now, pulling fog up from the deck on one side and spitting it back out from the other.

"Hold on," Eva said. "This might get tricky."

She leveled her arm that was tipped with the spearhead and took aim at the vortex. Timing the sway of the antenna, she waited until we were closest to it. Then, in the split second before we went the opposite direction, she pressed a button on her wrist and the spear shot from her arm, a rope trailing behind it.

Eva's shot was right on the mark. and the spear disappeared into the vortex. Eva pulled on the rope and it went taut, as if the spear had hit something solid just on the other side of the wall of fog. Then, things got crazy.

A terrific roar sounded, followed by an explosion of wind that blew out of the vortex, bending the antenna back from its sheer force. I lost my footing and clung to the metal girders with my arms as my legs flapped around in the hurricane force winds.

I heard a cry from Eva and felt her fall past me. I reached out and grabbed her, catching just enough of her shirt to divert her fall and swing her back onto the antenna.

I looked down and saw that her legs were wrapped around the antenna and she clung to the metal girders with her left arm. Her other arm was still holding the taut rope, which seemed to be trying to tug her off the antenna and onto the hard surface below. I looked back at the vortex, where the rope disappeared into an incongruous black shape, no more than a few feet wide. .

The hurricane blast turned into a twisting wind, bashing against us from all sides. The antenna swayed back and forth, Eva and the vortex locked in a deadly game of tug of war.

I managed to hook my feet to the antenna while I unsheathed my sword. I twisted almost upside-down, trying to reach Eva.

"What are you doing?" Eva yelled over the wind.

"I have to cut the rope!" I yelled back. "It's going to pull you off!"

"Get the center!" she yelled. "It's unprotected! That'll finish it! Get the center!"

I twisted back upright, sword in hand. The black mass in the center of the vortex was still a good twenty feet away, even after the antenna's sway tipped us toward it. There was no way I'd reach it.

I heard a cry from Eva. She still had herself braced against the pull of the rope, but I could tell she wouldn't last much longer. I knew what I had to do.

With my sword back at my side so I could climb with both hands, I worked my way up the antenna toward the blinking red light at the top. As if being buffeted by the wind howling around me wasn't bad enough, torrents of slashing rain began to pelt me from every direction, making it hard to see and even harder to climb.

Higher and higher I climbed, the antenna's mast, narrowing as I approached its tip. By the time I reached the red blinking light, I could easily wrap my arms around the whole of the metal pole. Good thing too, because the antenna bent back and forth so wildly that it felt like I was on the back of a bucking horse.

I followed the line of Eva's rope and saw the point where it was attached. If I timed the sway of the antenna right, I might be able to come close. Just as I pulled out my sword to get ready, a burst of wind blew me to one side. I scrambled just to hold on. As I did, I felt the handle of my sword slip from my fingers.

"No!" I yelled as it tumbled down and disappeared into the fog below. I felt a surge of panic. I lost my sword. There was no way I could stop the Aquamorph now. Everyone on the ship was going to die. And it was all my fault.

I searched my pockets for a weapon… anything! But I came up empty-handed.

"Hey!" A voice called from below. I looked down and saw Will standing on the roof of the bridge, my sword raised over his head. "You need this?" he yelled.

I waved at him and threw my weight into the momentum of the antenna's sway. As it dropped to its lowest point, Will threw the sword up into the air. He mistimed the toss and I had to dodge to the side to avoid being impaled. The sword clanged off the antenna, but I was able to still grab it by the handle with my free hand before it bounced into the murky waters below.

Below me, Will and T-Rex cheered.

The antenna reached the bottom of a giant sway, as far from the vortex as we were going to get. Eva cried out from the tension on the rope. I focused in on the black mass in the vortex as the antenna began its return trip in the other direction.

The wind and rain pelted me as the antenna sped toward the vortex. At the very last second, I jumped from the antenna, windmilling my arms through the air to get as much distance as possible, praying I would reach my target.

Sword out, I slashed upwards, severing the rope connected to Eva, then jammed the sword down into the center of the black mass.

BOOM!

The mass exploded and I was catapulted backward, head over heels into the night.

Luckily, I was thrown past the edge of the ship. I slammed into the water, the force of the impact knocking the air out of me. By the time I got my wits about me, I was deep underwater. I clawed and kicked my way to the surface.

Finally, I broke the surface and gulped down mouthfuls of fresh air. As I treaded water, I looked back at the ship. A brilliant white light shone where the vortex had been. The fog covering the ship was being sucked up into the light as a high-pitched whistle filled the air.

The moment the final traces of the fog were gathered up, the light shrunk to a mere pinprick. But the whistling continued to grow louder and higher-pitched.

The point of light exploded in a grand display of fireworks, ripping me from the antenna with an ear-shattering sonic boom. I crashed into the dark waves with a heavy splash.

Suddenly the waves calmed, and the night was again clear. Searchlights from the trawler were activated and in a short time they had a bead on me.

By the time they dragged me on board, Eva had made her way down from the antenna and was waiting for me on the deck with T-Rex and Will.

"Dude, that was crazy!" Will cried, high-fiving me. "I mean, I could have done it a little better, but still."

I smiled and looked at Eva. "Now you can't tell me the Academy is going to be more intense than that."

Eva smiled. "Yeah, I can," she said. "But that was a good warm up. You guys better get some sleep. We'll be there tomorrow." She turned and walked into the ship.

"A good warm up?" Will asked, shocked. "How bad is this place going to be?"

"Don't worry about it. She's just trying to scare us," I said.

Still, I couldn't shake the feeling that maybe she was telling the truth and that the Monster Hunter Academy was going to be more than I could handle. Try as I might, I couldn't get to sleep that night; my head was filled with images from the battle, and, worse, images of my father locked away in Ren Lucre's dungeon. I knew the Academy was the path to finding and saving my father. No matter how hard it was, I couldn't fail. I couldn't afford to.

The next day was going to be one of the most interesting and impactful of my life. Not only was I going to finally reach the Monster Hunter Academy, but I was going to find out a secret about my family that I never would have guessed, and, frankly, I still can't believe.

Eva was right. I needed a good night's sleep. Tomorrow was going to be a big day.

Chapter Two

In the morning, we spotted land. This was the first time in my life that I had been out of the country and I wasn't sure what to expect. I had images in my mind of Europe being filled with castles, ancient cathedrals and cobblestone streets. As we neared shore, all I saw was a broken-down harbor just like the one we had left behind.

Long buildings lined the wharf. Perhaps once the center of bustling activity, they were now rusting hulks with broken windows and caved-in roofs. Cranes to offload non-existent cargo sat perched at empty berths, slowly deteriorating from lack of use. There was a ship that had sunk in the harbor, just left there to rot.

Eva stood beside Will and me as the crew prepared to dock.

"Nice place," I said.

"It's perfect for us," Eva said. "No one will see us here."

"How about those guys?" Will asked, pointing to the hundreds of seagulls staring at us from the docks. "They're just birds, right?"

"Because they're looking at us like they're hungry," said T-Rex.

"Don't worry," Eva said. "No one knows we're coming."

I couldn't shake the feeling that Eva was wrong. I could feel the Creach's eyes everywhere, as though they could see everything we did. I could tell by how Eva squinted at the gulls that she had her own doubts.

"Come on," she said. "Get your gear. We have a train to catch."

We gathered our things and thanked the captain and crew for their help. Since the Aquamorph, they had kept their distance from us. Sailors were a superstitious bunch to begin with and having their ship attacked by a fog monster had made it even worse. They were nice enough, but it was clear that they were happy to be rid of us.

The four of us walked through the abandoned shipyard. I'll be honest with you, it was super-creepy. The dilapidated buildings all had shadowy openings that could hide monsters ready to attack us. I noticed that Eva had unscrewed the regular grasping hook she used for her missing hand and replaced it with a dagger. She had felt it too. Something was wrong. I followed her lead and put my hand on my sword.

"Don't," she whispered. "Just keep walking. Don't draw attention."

"What's going on?" Will whispered back.

"We're being followed," Eva replied. Will, T-Rex and I immediately scanned the buildings around us. Eva hissed at us under her breath. "You daft idiots. I said don't draw attention."

I faced forward, a little embarrassed. "What now?" I asked.

"Now we find out who it is," Eva said. She smashed her foot onto a glass bottle on the ground and spread out the pieces with her toe. We turned a corner and Eva shoved us into the empty doorway of one of the buildings. Then she crouched to the ground and waited.

In less than a minute, we heard footsteps approach us—soft at first, barely discernible. Then a loud *crunch* followed as whoever was stalking us stepped onto the glass. Eva whipped around the corner and Will, T-Rex and I followed right behind.

There was no one there.

Eva glanced around, searching the closest possible hiding spaces. A little rock pinged off the top of her head. We all spun around and looked up at the roofline.

There was a boy, probably sixteen, with stiff, spiky hair and intense blue eyes, standing on the roof, making no effort to hide. He was dressed in a black outfit similar to Eva's, but this one was more tight-fitting and showed off a muscular physique.

The boy broke out into a wide smile. Eva shook her head and slid her sword back into its sheath.

"Daniel, you're lucky you didn't get killed," Eva said.

"Are you kidding? Your vacation has made you soft," Daniel replied.

"You want to play it out?" Eva asked. "See how the actual fight would go?"

The boy jumped down from the roof and landed lightly in front of us, clearly pleased with himself. "No thanks. I know when to stop. I'm not stupid."

"The self-control is new," Eva said. "But the self-awareness is about the same as when I left."

Daniel leaned in to hug Eva, but she turned her body away from him. "Let me introduce you to the new recruits," she said.

This wiped the grin off his face. He looked like he wanted to say more but turned self-conscious when he saw Will, T-Rex and I watching him. He turned toward Will. "So, you're the great hope for the Black Guard. I'm Daniel. One of the instructors at the Academy." He shook Will's hand.

"Good to meet you. But the great hope, if you want to call him that, is this guy," he said, nodding to me.

Daniel turned and looked me over. I held out my hand but he didn't shake it. He looked disappointed. "Yes, well, if you say so." He turned back to Eva. "Come on, we'll just make the train if we hurry." He grabbed Eva's bag and walked on ahead of us.

27

I lowered my hand and picked up my own bag.

"He just left you hanging, didn't he?" said T-Rex. "That's not very polite."

"Don't worry about it," Eva said. "He's one of the best hunters we have, but he can be a real jerk sometimes. Trust me, I know. Don't let it bother you." She set off after him.

But Daniel did bother me. The way he had tried to hug Eva. The whole thing with the handshake. And there was something about the way Eva had looked at Daniel, too. *Trust me, I know.* What did that mean anyway?

"I thought he was kind of cool," Will said. I gave him a hard look. "To me, anyway. Come on, let's catch up."

We walked through the shipyard quickly, led by our new guide who busily chatted with Eva as we went. After a brief wait on a creaky train platform, an old-fashioned narrow gauge train chugged into the station and we climbed aboard.

The compartment had rows of seats like in an airplane, but they were metal-framed and covered with thin, worn fabric. There were a few other people scattered among the seats, but none of them even bothered to look up at us as we chose our seats. Eva slid into an empty row and took a place by the window. I decided to sit next to her to see if I could finally get her to give me some details about what to expect at the Academy. But just as I stepped into the row, Daniel shoved me to one side.

"This is my seat, hero. Trainees don't sit with instructors anyway," he said. "Might as well get used to it." He smiled but there was no humor in it. He squared his body to mine as though he were hoping I'd put up a fight.

Will pulled my arm and dragged me into the row where he was sitting. I looked back and saw Daniel still staring me down as he took the seat nearest Eva.

"Daniel seems cool," Will said.

"Yeah," I said. "Just great."

The train pulled out of the station and we were on our way.

The French countryside flashed by as the train made its way deeper inland. I looked back at the last sight of the ocean behind us and felt a little twist of emotion in my chest. The ocean was my link back home. A connection that led directly back to America even though it was thousands of miles over rough seas. Losing sight of it made me feel even more cut off and made the surroundings around me more strange and foreign. I knew it was just my mind playing tricks on me, but I couldn't shake the feeling that I was never going to see America again.

I tried to distract myself from these morbid thoughts by focusing on the scenery passing by me. Wide swaths of farmland stretched out around us, sectioned out by ancient, stone fences that kept sheep and milking cows comfortably in their own pastures. Every now and then, the fields would give way to lush forests of tall pines and firs.

The speed of the train was more noticeable when we passed these forests, as their trees whizzed by in a blur. Then the scene would abruptly open again into a wide vista, so suddenly that it gave me a sensation of falling forward out of my chair.

But most interesting were the small villages we passed. The ones nearest the port looked very much like small towns in America. A main street of shops surrounded by rows of houses, a few open parks, electrical and telephone wires snarled atop poles lining every street, and cars clogging everything.

But as we traveled deeper into the countryside, the make-up of these villages changed. Smooth, paved streets gave way to cobblestones and gravel. Building materials of iron and concrete became old stones held together by thick seams of plaster.

Slowly, the wires strung through the streets decreased too. As did the cars. It wasn't long before each village took on an archaic appearance, preserved as they had been for hundreds of years. Eventually, seeing a car became more like spotting something modern in a movie that was supposed to take place in a different time. You know, like seeing a jet plane fly by accidentally in an old Western movie.

For hours and hours, the train hurtled down its tracks. It made infrequent stops. When it did, Eva and Daniel would carefully watch any passengers who got on and take stock of whether they were a threat or not. Once the train restarted and pulled out of the station, they would get up and go together down the length of the train to inspect every compartment. Only then would they return and settle back into their seats.

Each one of these times, I tried to talk to Eva and ask her questions about the Academy. But she was like a different person around Daniel. She was formal and answered me in short, clipped sentences.

"We'll get there when we get there."

"You'll find out soon enough."

"Stay in your seat."

Daniel smirked at me every time, taking a little too much pleasure in my frustration.

While Eva had given Daniel a chilly reception at first, they were now sitting warmly together, talking back and forth in low tones that I couldn't hear. Every once in a while, Eva would laugh at something Daniel said. I made the mistake of looking at them once and saw Daniel's hand on Eva's knee. I turned my back to them and tried to block it out.

"Get a hold of yourself, Jack," I murmured. I resigned myself to staring out of the window at the passing countryside. The sun went down behind us, casting long shadows. I craned my neck to look forward and saw the distant silhouettes of massive mountains rise up ahead of us.

"I wonder what mountains those are?" asked T-Rex.

"The Alps," Will said.

I turned toward Will, surprised.

"What? Just because I got D's in all my classes doesn't mean I wasn't listening," Will said. "I bet that's where the Academy is. Hidden in the mountains so no one finds it."

Eva burst out laughing from something Daniel said. I looked over and saw he had his hand on her knee, laughing with her. I felt a tightening in my chest and heat on my cheeks. I didn't like what was going on between them one little bit. Will glanced over at them, smiling.

"I've never heard Eva laugh like that," he said. "I wonder if they're a thing."

"A thing?" I asked. I thought I might throw up.

"You know, like going out."

"You think so?" I asked, spinning in my chair. Eva was pretending to ignore Daniel as he whispered something, a wry smile on her lips. She certainly seemed to be enjoying herself. I hoped the guys couldn't see my flushed cheeks. "I guess it's possible. He's kind of a putz, though."

"A putz with enormous muscles and rugged good looks," T-Rex added.

"Come on, he's not that great," I said.

"Are you kidding? Did you see the way he got the drop on Eva? I wish I could do that," Will said.

"Yeah? Maybe you can get him to teach you how," I said.

"You think he would? That would be awesome."

"Yeah," I mumbled. "That would be awesome." I turned to look back outside. The landscape was turning into inky blues and blacks as the last glow from the sunset faded from the sky. I closed my eyes and tried to block out the sounds of Daniel and Eva's hushed conversation and their laughing. I focused on the thump-thump-thump of the railroad tracks as we sped onward, deeper into the night.

I must have fallen asleep, because the next thing I knew Will was shaking me, his face right next to mine. I jerked awake and sat up in the chair. The five of us were the only ones left in the compartment and the train was rumbling to a stop.

"Come on, get your things," Will said. "We're here. There's snow outside."

"Really?" I rubbed my eyes to clear the sleep out of them. The light from the compartment was strong enough to illuminate the area just beyond the edge of the tracks. There was a low bank of snow beside us that came into focus as the train slowed. A soft, floating snow filled the sky. In the reflection of the window, I saw Daniel staring at me. I turned and he smirked.

"Get your beauty sleep, hero?" he asked.

"Something like that," I replied, pulling my bag down from the overhead compartment.

Will stretched on his toes, but still couldn't reach his overhead bag. I went to grab it but he snapped, "I've got it."

"Alright. Just trying to help," I said. I knew Will was sensitive about being short, but he usually wasn't a jerk about it. I saw him glance over to Daniel and realized he was trying not to look bad in front of the older boy.

Will climbed on the chair, jumped up and hooked his hand through the handle on his bag and dragged it down.

"Well done," Daniel said to him, patting him on the shoulder. "Hunters always find a way. I hope you're in my squad at the Academy."

Daniel and Eva walked to the front of the train, leaving Will grinning from ear to ear.

"Oh please," I said. Will's little hero's worship of Daniel was starting to get to me.

"I notice he didn't ask the fat kid to be in his squad," T-Rex mumbled. "I hope there's a snack shack around here."

"Two middles," I said. "Middle of the night. Middle of nowhere. I'm guessing we're not finding snacks anytime soon, buddy."

"I'm going to starve," T-Rex groaned.

I reached into my backpack and dug around, pulling out my last granola bar. I handed it to T-Rex.

"Awesome! Thanks," T-Rex said.

He ripped off the wrapper, devouring it in seconds. With the last half of the granola bar in his mouth, he looked suddenly guilty. He spat the half-chewed bar into his hand and asked, "I'm sorry, did you want to share this?"

I looked down at the mushed up granola bar in his hand. "It's all you."

He grinned and stuffed the food back into his mouth. With my stomach growling, we followed Eva and Daniel off the train and onto a small wooden platform lit by a single old-fashioned lantern. The train gathered steam and chugged out of the station, disappearing quickly into a tunnel of trees. We all looked around. There was nothing in any direction. No village. No road. Nothing. I looked to Eva for answers.

"Was someone supposed to meet us?" I asked.

Eva looked at Daniel who seemed embarrassed. "We must be a little early," he said.

Eva shook her head and drew her sword. "We can't stay here. We're too exposed. Let's go."

"How far is it?" Will asked.

"Far," Eva replied.

Eva jumped off the platform and strode down a trail. The rest of us gathered our things and trudged after her. I didn't like the thought of a long walk through the snow in the middle of the night, but I admit I enjoyed seeing Daniel squirm.

I looked into the dark forest, filled with black shadows and strange noises. I swallowed hard and tried to push back the fear rising up in me. In my head, I conjured up all types of monsters that could be lying in wait for us among the trees. But nothing in my imagination could have prepared me for what happened next.

Chapter Three

The forest quickly turned dark as the little light from the train platform faded behind us. I hadn't seen it before, but there was a road that led away from the tracks. Covered with snow, it was hard to see, but once we were on it, it was clear to see the swath cut through the forest. A half moon slid out from behind the clouds and painted the snowy landscape a silvery hue. We walked in a single-file line with Eva in front, Will, T-Rex and I in the middle, and Daniel following in the rear.

It wasn't long before the bitter cold seeped into my clothes. I was without gloves so I stuck them deeply into my pockets to try to keep them warm. My sneakers were no match for the heavy, wet snow and soon I added my toes to the growing list of body parts I couldn't feel. Daniel walked up next to me, looking warm and smug in a fur-lined jacket, heavy gloves and moccasins.

"Are you all right? Want to borrow my jacket?" he asked, the mocking tone in his voice unmistakable.

"No, I'm fine. I grew up in the mountains, so I'm used to it," I said, trying not to let my teeth chatter.

"Sure," Daniel said. "If you say so."

Just then, Eva crouched to the ground ahead of us and took cover behind a tree. I followed her lead and hid as well. Daniel ran low to the ground to Eva's position just ahead of where the rest of us stood.

Eva indicated toward a spot in the road. There, barely visible in the shadows, was a dark, hulking figure positioned against the trees. I squinted, trying to make out what it was, but it was too far away. Whatever it was, it didn't belong in the forest. Then the shape moved and a soft neigh of a horse drifted through the air. With that piece of information, my mind put together that I was looking at a horse and carriage. I marveled at how Eva had been able to spot it from such a distance.

"That's a Black Guard cart," Daniel said.

Eva nodded. She and Daniel communicated in a flurry of hand gestures. When it appeared they had agreed to something, Eva slinked off into the tree line. I crawled up to Daniel.

"Where's she going?" I asked.

Daniel ignored me. "Stay here; this is a task for real hunters," he said.

He crossed to the other side of the road and picked his way along the edge. I saw the glint of Eva's sword through the trees. They were closing in on the cart from either side.

"We should do something," Will whispered next to me.

"I think they would have asked if they needed our help," T-Rex said.

"Just wait," I said. This was all about the element of surprise. I held my breath as they closed in on the cart.

I lost sight of Daniel. He blended into the trees and shadows, but I knew he had to be close.

Then, perfectly timed, two black shadows darted from either side of the road and converged on the carriage. Daniel and Eva moved silently, their swords flashing in the moonlight.

Arrrhhhggg!

A large, black shape arose from the carriage, its arms flailing about. The horse whined and took off with a start. Daniel jumped out of the way as the horse stampeded forward, the carriage bouncing along the rough road behind the frightened horse. It was coming right for us. As it came closer, I saw the dark figure on the carriage pulling hard on the reins to bring the horse to a stop.

"Come on!" I exclaimed to Will.

I dragged Will into the road with me, right in the path of the approaching horse.

"This isn't what I had in mind," Will said.

"I'll stay here," T-Rex called out.

I raised my arms up and waved them so the horse could see me. Will followed suit. As the horse closed in on us, it didn't look like it was slowing down. If anything, it was speeding up.

"Whoa!" I called out, arms waving.

"Whoa is right!" Will cried. "Whoa!"

The horse continued to charge at us. I was just wondering if getting in front of it was going to be the last stupid thing I did in my short life, when the animal dug its hooves into the soft snow and skidded to a stop. It reared back and churned its legs in the air, snorting wildly.

A low whistle from back down the road caught its attention. Its ears swiveled toward the sound and it lowered its hooves to the ground. Another low whistle echoed through the night and the horse jerked its head in its direction and swung the carriage around, trotting easily down the road. The figure, which I could now tell was a man in a heavy cloak and hat, pulled back on the reins, but the horse ignored him.

We followed behind the carriage and saw Eva standing in the center of the road, her arms spread wide. She whistled again and the horse grunted in recognition. It walked up to Eva and placed his muzzle in her chest, nibbling excitedly on her with his lips. Eva hugged the horse and kissed it on the nose.

As we walked up, we could hear Daniel talking to the person on the carriage in a low, angry voice. "Why weren't you at the station, you Ratling grunt?"

"Begging your pardon. I know I shoulda been. I know it. When Master Aquinas picked me for this, I was so proud. But I was so tired, though. A day full o' cooking, tendin' the garden." The man was almost in tears and speaking so fast I could barely understand him. "I cleaned over twenty rabbits today, I did. My eyes, they kept shuttin' on me. So I thought, sleep for five minutes, then you'll be fine."

"I don't know what Master Aquinas sees in you. You're a disgrace," Daniel said.

"That's enough," Eva said. "A mistake was made. Now it's over." She smiled and put a hand on the man's shoulder. "I've missed you, Bacho. I've been craving your rabbit stew all these months I've been gone."

Bacho's face lit up. "An' I made it jus' for you tonight, Miss Eva. Truth be told, I had plenty of it myself before I left."

Even dressed in a black, heavy cloak, it was clear Bacho never missed a meal. In fact, from his rather wide, thick waistline and his moonish face supported by no fewer than three chins, it was safe to say he probably had a few extra meals every day. I wondered how many of those rabbits he had eaten himself. He was older, maybe in his early thirties, but acted with deference to Daniel and Eva, like a servant around his masters. He obviously liked Eva and disliked Daniel. This made him a perfect fit for me.

Daniel spat on the ground at Bacho's feet. "No one cares about your rabbit stew. You're lucky you're not dead. You know what's in these woods, don't you?" Daniel asked.

"Beggin' your pardon," Bacho said, his head hung low in shame. "Beggin' your pardon."

"Bah," Daniel said. "Come on. Our things are scattered."

Daniel jumped down while Bacho carefully climbed down the ladder hanging from the wagon. I stepped toward him and held out my hand. "Hi, I'm Jack," I said.

Bacho's eyes went wide and he stooped low in front of me, looking at the ground at my feet. "Beggin' your pardon, sirc."

I still had my hand out so I reached out to grab his hand and shook it. He gasped and quickly withdrew his hand. He turned to help Daniel, but knocked into Eva, who was still petting the horse. "Beggin' your pardon," he mumbled as he finally stumbled away.

"That guy is totally weird," Will said.

"He's a Ratling," Eva said. "One of the lower orders in the Black Guard. They mostly cook and clean. And kill the rats, which is how they got their name. Bacho's been the Head Ratling since I was a little girl. He's one of my favorite people in the world." The horse whined and Eva turned her attention back to it, grinning. "I said he was one of my favorites, not my all-time favorite. That's still you, boy."

"Is this horse yours?" T-Rex asked.

"He belongs to the Black Guard and he's considered a monster hunter in his own right," Eva said. "But we have a bond. We've been through a lot, this horse and I."

"What's his name?" I asked.

"Saladin," she said. The horse whinnied at the sound.

"Pretty," I said, reaching out to rub his nose. Saladin bared his teeth and snapped at my fingers. I pulled my hand back. "Hey."

Eva grinned. "He's very particular. I'm the only one he'll let ride him. Isn't that right, boy?" Saladin nuzzled back into her neck. "Is that why they have you pulling this nasty cart?" The horse made a soft gurgle that sounded like he was telling Eva all about the mistreatment he'd received since she'd been gone. "I'm back, now. Not to worry."

"OK, I think we have everything," Daniel said as he threw their bags into the back of the carriage. "We'd best be on our way. Our scent will have carried half a mile by now." He took a whiff of Bacho and wrinkled his nose. "Maybe more."

The insult seemed to slide right by Bacho. He climbed up to the driver's bench and took the reins as the rest of us climbed into the back. Saladin snorted and pawed the ground, jostling us around. Eva climbed up next to Bacho and took the reins. Saladin immediately became still. Eva gave a click with her tongue and Saladin strained against his harness. The wagon wheel rolled forward through the heavy snow as we bumped our way down the road and into the forest.

Progress was slow. The cold air and repetitive forest scenery sliding by lulled all of us into a quiet trance. After a short while, a soft snore came from the front bench where Bacho was hunched over to one side, wrapped in a heavy blanket. Will also had wedged himself into the corner in the back and had fallen asleep with T-Rex snuggled up against him for a pillow. I looked over to Daniel to find him staring at me, a smirk on his face.

"Get enough sleep on the train, hero?"

"Do you have some kind of problem with me?" I asked. I was getting tired of his attitude.

"Hester was a good friend of mine. A top class hunter," Daniel said.

I felt a pit form in my stomach at the mention of the name. Assigned to protect me, Hester had hidden in plain sight as the school secretary at Sunnyvale Middle School. On that terrible night when Ren Lucre had come for me, she had appeared just in time to help us escape certain death. But she had paid for our escape with her own life. I had relived that moment so many times in my mind, always wondering if there was something else I could have done to save her. The words she uttered right before she slipped from my grasp and into the horde of zombies below continued to haunt me.

Just make it all worthwhile.
Do your duty, come what may, Jack Templar.
You are the One. I know it.

I still didn't know what she meant when she called me the One. I asked Eva once but she refused

43

to talk about it. I wanted to make her sacrifice worthwhile, but I hadn't a clue how to do it.

"I owe Hester my life," I said to Daniel. "In more ways than one." I fingered the medallion that hung around my neck. Hester had given it to me. It cloaked me from monsters being able to sense me. I was pretty sure that without it I would have be monster meat weeks ago.

"You're right about that," Daniel said, the anger in his voice clear. "And so far, I don't see anything that says her life was worth trading for yours."

I saw a flash of movement parallel to us in the trees. It was barely discernible, like a shadow inside a shadow.

"Did you see that?" I whispered to Daniel.

"Am I making you uncomfortable?" Daniel asked.

"No. There was something in the woods. Moving fast."

Daniel strained his eyes in the direction I pointed, but shook his head. "There's nothing there. If there were, I would have seen it before you. Trust me."

I ignored the comment and fixed my eyes on the woods. I saw it again. A shadow had moved between the trees, and then disappeared. Only this time I saw two of them. I looked to the other side of the road and saw more of them.

I reached over and tugged at Eva's arm. "Do you see that? In the woods?"

"I told you," Daniel said. "There's nothing…"

With a snarl, a massive black wolf broke from the tree line and ran at Saladin's legs.

Saladin erupted in a high-pitched whine, reared back and delivered a blow to the wolf's rib cage with his hoof. The wolf yelped and tumbled backward. Saladin bolted forward at full-speed, dragging the wagon behind him like it was no more than a toy.

Bacho, wide-awake now, clung onto the side rail for dear life. T-Rex yelled and hung onto the side. Will lost his grip and tumbled down the length of the wagon, hitting the wood gate at the back end. That seemed to stop him for a second, but then the gate broke open and he fell backward.

At the last second, Daniel grabbed his arm and held onto him. Will was half out of the wagon, his legs dragging on the ground.

Two wolves fell in behind us, running hard. They closed in on Will's legs.

I crawled forward and grabbed Daniel. T-Rex tugged the back of my jacket to try to help pull us back on. Together, we heaved Will back into the wagon, the nearest wolf snapping at his heels as we hauled him on board.

The forest was now alive with wolves. Black shadows on both sides of the road hurtled through the trees, keeping pace with Saladin's manic sprint.

Daniel pulled his sword. Will and I followed suit. Bacho grabbed T-Rex with one of his huge hands and dragged him forward onto the front bench by him.

"Are they werewolves?" I shouted.

45

"No. No this lot anyway," Daniel said. "If they were, we'd already be dead. There is one among them, though. A giant black wolf with a white cross on his chest. Watch for him."

In the front, Bacho pulled out a crossbow and a quiver of bolts from under his seat. He took aim at one of the wolves and fired. The bolt flew harmlessly above the animal. Not even close.

Eva leaned over. "Bacho, give me the crossbow," she called.

"Careful, Miss," Bacho said. "Them's poisoned bolts on there."

Bacho handed her the bow just as two wolves sped past the wagon, drawing even with Saladin. They nipped at his long legs, biting at his haunches.

With one smooth motion, Eva plucked out a bolt, slid it into position, cocked the crossbow and took aim at the nearest wolf.

Thwack.

The bolt caught him in the side and he rolled up in a ball with a yelp.

The other wolves pulled back into the tree line, but still kept pace with the wagon.

I looked up ahead and saw what they were waiting for. The road was about to get very narrow. Worse, the path had been cut into a hill so that the ground on either side rose up just a bit higher than the top of the wagon. The wolves tore through the trees and up the hill.

"Get ready!" Daniel cried.

As we entered the cut, the wolves were suddenly above us. One from each side jumped into the wagon. Out of the corner of my eye, I saw Daniel fend off the snarling wolf on his side with his sword. I felt the wagon sag from the weight of the creature as it landed. But my eyes were firmly fixed on the wolf heading my way. I raised my sword just as Eva spun in her seat and fired the crossbow. But a second wolf, twice as large as the first, jumped in front of the shot and took the bolt in its side in mid-jump.

The wolf's momentum carried it through the air and it smacked into me, a wrecking ball of fur and claws.

One second I was in the back of the wagon, my feet firmly planted in place and ready for battle. The next I was flying through the air, tangled up with the wolf.

With a thud, I landed in snowdrift with the wolf on top of me. Between the force of my fall and the weight of the beast, I sank deep into the snow, completely covered by the stinking body. This had probably saved my life.

All around me, I could hear the howls of the wolf pack racing past me, their paws scattering the snow around me. I silently thanked Hester again for the cloaking medallion she had given me. Without it I was certain that the wolves would have been able to sense my presence. A single, soulful howl seemed to come from right over me, perhaps a quick eulogy for the fallen comrade that lay on top of me.

I lay as still as I could, trying to slow down my frantic breathing. Even though I still had my sword with me, it sounded like there were dozens of wolves in the pack. If they discovered me, I was dead.

Luckily, Saladin's fast pace quickly drew the pack away from me and I soon found myself alone in the silent night. Silent, that is, except for the ragged breathing coming from above me. In the commotion, I thought for sure the wolf was dead, but I suddenly realized he was very much alive.

The wolf seemed to have the same revelation at the same exact time. I felt his body grow tense as a growl snarled from deep within his throat. He rolled back and forth to get out of the deep snowdrift we were in and scrambled to his feet.

I grasped my sword and clawed my way out of the hole as fast as I could. Before long I found myself in the open stretch of the road, facing the wolf. He was a giant black wolf with white fur on his chest that formed a perfect cross.

The wolf Daniel had warned me about.

One of Eva's crossbow bolts stuck out from the beast's front left shoulder. Not very deep, but firmly stuck there as if lodged into the bone. The wolf kept its weight off that paw, but seemed just as lethal balanced on the other three.

We circled one another in the middle of the snow-covered road, the distant sounds of the chase echoing from a distance deeper in the forest.

Close up, I saw details in the wolf I hadn't noticed before. He was larger than any wolf I'd ever seen, every bit as large as the devil-wolf form that my Aunt Sophie took the first night I became a monster hunter. He was stocky and muscled with thick tufts of black fur, except for the mark on his chest.

Under different circumstances, I might have marveled at how impressive a creature he was. However, since I expected an attack at any second and a fight to the death to follow, I found it hard to appreciate his good looks. He looked hungry, and, unfortunately, it appeared that I was on the menu.

But then I noticed the heavy trail of blood on the snow behind him as we circled one another. Soon, his other front foot gave out and he put pressure on his injured leg to keep from falling. He let out a yelp and nearly fell. He licked the wound, in turns whimpering and then growling at me.

Finally, whether too weak from the loss of all that blood or giving into the pain from the bolt, the wolf's legs gave way and he crumpled to a pile.

Sword raised, I edged up closer to him, careful that it might be a ploy to get me to lower my guard. But after a few steps toward him, he didn't even raise his head to look at me. He lay there, taking short, labored gasps of air.

I raised my sword over my head and prepared to strike a finishing blow.

This movement caught the wolf's attention and he tilted his head with all his might. He looked at me with enormous brown eyes and I saw an intelligence there that I hadn't expected. Even though it seemed like he knew what I was about to do, he just lay his massive head back on the ground and closed his eyes.

There was something about this simple gesture that took me off guard. I knew what I should do. Strike hard and fast, then move on to find the others.

But I couldn't.

I thought of what my Aunt Sophie had looked like in her devil-wolf form, waiting for death at the hands of Ren Lucre. Was I to be no better than him? Suddenly, I didn't have the stomach to kill the wolf.

I lowered my sword to the ground and put both hands out in front of me so the wolf could see them.

"All right, my furry friend," I said. "Don't make me regret this."

The wolf looked up at me with renewed interest. If I didn't know better, I'd say he looked genuinely surprised.

"Shhhh," I said. "The bolt is poisoned. We need to take it out." I eased closer, ready to jump back if the wolf made a lunge for me. But he didn't. He cocked his head on the ground so as to get a good look at me, but he stayed still. "That's it. Now, I'm working on the assumption that if I help you, you're not going to jump up and bite me. Can we agree on that?"

The wolf let out a huff of air. I couldn't be sure, but it seemed like an agreement to me.

I wrapped my fingers around the shaft of the bolt sticking out from the wolf's shoulder. It was in there solidly, right into the bone. The wolf whined from the pressure on his wound.

"OK, here we go," I said. "This might hurt a little." I yanked back as hard as I could and the bolt popped out.

I went reeling backward and landed flat on the ground.

Almost immediately, the wolf was on his feet. In the blink of an eye, he was on top of me, a paw on either side of my shoulders, his massive head directly over my own.

Hot blasts of air blew on my face as the wolf moved closer, inch by inch. His lips pulled back into a snarl, showing a row of sharp teeth that looked like they could chew off my head with one bite. That's when I considered that taking pity on the wolf might have been the dumbest thing I'd ever done.

Then, as suddenly as he had pinned me to the ground, the wolf jumped off me and ran toward the tree line, still favoring his injured leg but now at least able to put some pressure on it.

I scampered to my feet and grabbed my sword. When I turned back toward him, the wolf was looking over his shoulder at me, almost as if he were amused. He bowed low to the ground, his nose almost in the snow. Awkwardly, I returned his bow and added a little slicing salute with my sword as I had seen Eva do when we sparred.

A burst of howls exploded from the path that the wagon had disappeared down. I looked down the road and saw a faint silhouette of a rider atop a horse galloping down the road. When I turned back, the wolf was gone.

I looked back to the rider and recognized the unmistakable outlines of Eva and Saladin. As they bore down on me my heart sank. Behind them was a black wave of wolves chasing at their heels.

Eva leaned to one side, her arm outstretched.

I slid my sword back into its scabbard and climbed a rock to get a little more height. I knew we would only get one chance at this. If one of us missed, then I was going to be dinner for a pack of hungry wolves.

I tried to stay calm, but the rock had a thin layer of ice on it and my feet kept sliding from one side to the other. When she was only steps away, I nearly lost my balance entirely and had to swing my arms wildly to regain my foothold.

As soon as I did, I felt Eva's strong grip on my forearm as she lifted me up onto the back of the saddle. Not missing a beat, Saladin cut to the right into the forest, circled back through and charged right at the approaching wolves.

Eva dropped the reins quickly, grabbed the crossbow and immediately shot down the two wolves in the center of the road. The others hesitated just long enough for Saladin to find a weakness in their line. With a giant leap, he was over the two dead bodies, and had given another wolf a sharp kick to the head. Soon we were galloping down the road at a safe distance.

"Where are the others?" I yelled at Eva.

"They're safe!" she shouted back. "We're near the Academy."

I looked back and saw that the wolf pack was back on our trail, howling and snapping at their prey. Further behind them, I saw the wolf I had saved climb up onto a rocky outcropping, the cross of white fur nearly glowing in the night.

"There!" Eva shouted.

I looked ahead and saw a massive stone wall with an open gateway rise up ahead of us. It looked ancient and worn down, as if the forest were trying to reclaim it. Men stood in position along the battlements above the gate, swords and bows at the ready. Two other men on horseback charged at us from the gate, swords swirling in the air, a battle cry bursting like a song from their mouths.

A single howl rose up above all the noise. Strong and clear.

The pack of wolves slid to a standstill in response to the call.

Eva quickly closed the distance to the riders coming from the gate, and as they pulled up to us, she turned Saladin and lined up along with them. Now the three of us faced the wolves together.

"They're just out of range for the archers," the rider next to me said. I turned and was surprised to see it was Daniel. "Cheeky devils."

The wolves clawed at the ground, teeth bared.

The howl came again and this time I followed the sound up to the rock outcropping where the wolf I had saved stood like a general surveying a battlefield. The other wolves reacted to the howl, turned and ran away into the night.

Eva whispered to me, "See that one? The one with the white on its chest? That's Tiberon. As he commands, the others follow. We've been trying for years to track him down. He's too clever for his own good."

"Is he a werewolf?" I asked.

"No one knows," Eva said. "But—"

"But nothing," spat Daniel. "He's a werewolf all right, and I'll wear his skin for a winter coat soon enough. I promise you that, hero."

I felt Tiberon's eyes bore into me from his position and I returned the gaze. I decided it would be better if I didn't reveal my part in helping the wolf that night.

But then Tiberon bowed once again in my direction. The others looked around as if deciding whom the gesture was meant for. I tried to keep my expression blank but I must have done some small thing to acknowledge the wolf because Eva turned to look at me.

"Anything you want to tell me about?" she asked.

I glanced nervously over at Daniel. His eyes were still fixed on Tiberon, hate burning in his eyes. Luckily, it didn't seem like he had picked up in the connection between the black wolf and myself.

"You said the others are inside?" I asked, eager to change the subject. "Maybe we should go in."

Eva gave me a hard look, but finally reined Saladin around and trotted back into the fortified wall, followed by Daniel and the other rider.

We crossed through the large gates, revealing the sheer thickness of the outer walls. They must have been nearly twenty feet thick on all ends. Inside was an enormous courtyard lit by small campfires and torches. Wooden structures were pressed against the fort's massive walls, their roofs serving a platform for the bulwarks above. At the far end of the courtyard, nearly a hundred yards away, was another wall. This one stretched across the mouth of a massive cave that appeared to go deep into the mountain. This looked even older than the outer wall and bore signs of repair work done over time. I wondered if this second wall was the next line of defense, or if was built to keep things from getting out of the cave.

In the center of this second wall was another gate, set between two tall towers on either side. Eva noticed my interest and said, "That's the Citadel, the original Academy before the outer walls were built."

"And what's that?" I asked, pointing to a giant oak tree growing just outside the second wall. Its trunk was as wide as two cars and its gnarled, lower branches were the size of full trees in their own right. Intertwined throughout the tree was a series of balconies, stairways and walls that seemed almost part of the tree itself. Golden lanterns hung throughout its thick branches, giving it an ethereal quality.

"That?" Eva said, "That's the Templar Tree. Supposedly planted by Jacques de Molay himself."

"Who's Jacques de Molay?" I asked. Unfortunately, Daniel was near enough to overhear my question.

"Did you just ask who Jacques de Molay was?" he snickered. "Yeah, he seems like the One to me." He spurred his horse forward.

I was about to ask Eva about it when Will and T-Rex mobbed me.

"You son-of-a-gun," Will said. "You scared the crap outta me."

"We thought they got you," T-Rex blubbered.

I climbed off the horse and we all hugged each other, laughing.

Bacho rushed up and nearly knocked us over. "I thought you was a goner for sure."

"What? And let you guys have all the fun?" I asked. "Not a chance."

Several dozen people crowded around us in the courtyard, everyone talking over one another excitedly. I could only catch pieces of the conversation.

"Which one you thinks he is?"

"Canna be the little guy, can it?

"Thems both kinda little. I thought he'd be tall as a minotaur."

"I heard he was s'pposed to be the best fighter ever."

"He's friends with a Ratling?"

"Wolves can almost get him. Then how can he be the One?"

"Maybe he's not, right? That's what I heard the instructors sayin'. Maybe he's not."

Thud. Thud. Thud.

A heavy rapping echoed throughout the fort, immediately silencing the group. I followed everyone's gaze upward to the source of the noise, to a well-lit balcony perched on the second floor of the Templar Tree. An ancient looking woman stood looking out over the courtyard, a wooden staff clutched in her hands.

She pointed at us and curled her fingers in to tell us to come meet her. Then she went inside.

"Alright. Excitement's over," Eva called out. "Instructors, see to your students. Ratlings, finish your preparations for the breakfast meal." She pointed a finger toward Will, T-Rex and me. "You three, come with me."

As we followed Eva into the tree, I noticed faces stealing curious looks at me as they filtered back into doorways around the courtyard. There were a few people in their early twenties, but most of them were around my age, some of them much younger. But it wasn't hard to notice that even without knowing me at all, there wasn't a single face that looked happy that I was there. In fact, many of them looked outright hostile.

"Don't worry about them," Eva said, also noticing the cold reception. "After being in this place a while, it's hard to accept outsiders."

"Where are the adults? The instructors?" Will asked.

"Most instructors are my age. You don't find a lot of adult hunters," Eva said.

"Do I want to know why?" T-Rex asked.

"The average life expectancy for an active hunter is only twenty-five years. I told you, this isn't a game. This is life and death. Come on, Aquinas doesn't like to be kept waiting."

We followed Eva toward the giant oak tree. I noticed there wasn't a single electric light anywhere in the compound.

"No electricity?" I asked.

"A few generators for emergencies. But we're completely off the grid so this place can stay secret," Eva explained. "Aquinas prefers the old hunting methods anyway. You won't find guns here. Swords, axes, and crossbows are our weapons of choice."

"No electricity?" T-Rex moaned. "Does that mean no Xbox?"

"No Xbox. No Wi-Fi. No TV," Eva said. "Just training on how to hunt and fight the world's most terrifying monsters."

"More like how to hide and survive attacks by the world's most terrifying monsters," said Daniel, striding up toward us.

"There's some disagreement about how aggressive we should be," Eva said, giving Daniel a hard look.

"We're monster hunters, not monster hiders," Daniel said.

"But we are the Black Guard," Eva said. "We watch over the Regs and keep them safe."

"Regs?" Will asked. "What are they?"

"Non-hunters," Daniel spat. "Regular people. The ones who sit out there, happy in their ignorance of monsters. I don't know why we should bother protecting them. What have they ever done for us?"

"Daniel," an old, creaky voice said from above us. "That will be enough." It was Aquinas. "You four, come up."

Doing the quick math, Daniel replied, "Don't you mean five?"

"I may be old, but I can still count fairly well," Aquinas muttered as she walked away from the balcony edge. "Monster hiders, indeed."

Daniel looked to Eva who just shrugged. I couldn't help but suppress a grin. Daniel spotted it and looked furious as he stomped off.

Eva walked to the stairs, but then turned to us. "Just...just be careful what you say. Aquinas has a bit of a temper."

"That old bat?" Will whispered. "What's she going to do, throw her dentures at us?"

I shuddered at the phrase *that old bat*. The last time I heard that was when my principal had actually transformed into a giant bat creature right before my eyes. A chill passed through me and I tried to put it out of my mind.

"I'm warning you. Don't underestimate her," Eva said.

"We'll be fine. There are some answers I want from her anyway," I said, trying to sound braver than I felt. "Let's get on with it."

Eva continued up the stairs.

As we got closer, a pit formed in my stomach. The kind I get right before something bad happens. Eva had told me only the smallest details about Aquinas. She was the leader of the Black Guard, head of all monster hunters everywhere. But she was also the one who had made the decision to use me as bait to trap Ren Lucre on my first night as a monster hunter. Most importantly still, she was the person most likely to know the truth about my father's whereabouts.

I reached the top of the stairs, ready to finally get answers to my questions.

Chapter Four

We walked into a large room that glowed warmly from dozens of candles spread throughout. The trunk of the tree rose through the center of the floor and disappeared through the low-hanging ceiling above. Branches scrolled gracefully throughout the room, serving as dividers for the various areas.

In one section, a long table made of thick, rough-cut wood stretched out with enough room for twelve people. Another area was a clutter of comfortable looking couches and pillows laid out among stacks of old, leather bound books. Back in the far corner, unlit by candles but still visible from the glow of the rest of the room, was what looked like a mad scientist's laboratory. Glass beakers, weights and scales, test tubes, drafting tables with diagrams, and more rows of books filled the area.

The final quarter was empty except for several weapons lining the edge of a straw covered mat. A training room. I spotted a circular staircase in the back of the room that went up a level to what I supposed were the sleeping quarters.

Aquinas stood with her back to us as we stood on the balcony.

"Well, step in here, boy," she said. "Let me have a look at you."

I stepped closer and Aquinas turned to face me. I had been able to tell from below that she was old, but up close the word 'ancient' was the only one that came to mind.

Deep wrinkles crisscrossed her face, framed by shock-white hair. She hunched over as if just the act of breathing was a challenge. A dull, red scar wrapped around her throat and up one side of her face to her ear. She leaned heavily on the gnarled walking stick, even though she was standing motionless.

While her body language signaled nothing but a dull frailty, her eyes were an intense blue, almost to a point of being unnatural. They looked me up and down with focus, taking in every minute detail. It was a clear signal that there was more to her than her appearance implied.

Eva had warned me not to underestimate her. One glance at those eyes and I knew she was right.

"May I present Jack Templar and his companions Will Chacon and T-Rex Boyle," Eva said formally.

Aquinas approached Will and T-Rex first. "So, you are the unexpected additions. An unfortunate lapse of judgment by one of my best hunters." Eva lowered her head at the reprimand. Aquinas put her face very close to Will's. "Perhaps I will remedy this error and send you home?"

The threat of being sent away took Will by surprise. He stammered for the right words. "I...but I already...why would..."

"I'm afraid there is nothing but blood and pain here for you, young William Chacon," Aquinas said. "I do not want your death on my hands." Aquinas turned to Eva. "Send him home."

"Now, wait a minute," I said.

"What?" Will cried out. "No way."

Aquinas watched Will, waiting.

"I can't go back," Will said. "I have nothing to go back to."

"What of your family?" Aquinas asked.

"I have no one. At least no one who matters, anyway," he said. I thought back to the bruises Will used to come to school with. To the school counselors, he always had a good story, but the bruises didn't come from falling off a bike, or tumbling down a flight of stairs. They came from his father. Getting away to come to the Academy had been the best possible thing for him. Now, only minutes after arriving, he found himself about to be sent home.

"I won't go," he declared firmly.

Aquinas raised an eyebrow and studied him. "What did you just say?"

63

"I said I won't go. You're going to have to drag me out of here and it's going to take more than a few people to do it. And I don't care if you take me all the way back to America. The second I'm free, I'll start my way back here. And when I get here I'll just climb right over that wall and do it all over again."

"Just words," Aquinas hummed. "Easily said, but harder to do."

"Send me home and you'll see that I'm telling the truth," Will said, tears welling in his eyes now. "I swear on my life that I will just keep coming back until you let me stay."

Aquinas looked at Eva, who couldn't help but crack a smile. "You were right, Eva," Aquinas said. "He is a feisty one. And you vouch for him?"

Eva looked Will over and then nodded. "I do. I vouch for him."

Aquinas lifted her walking stick up and poked Will in the chest with it gently. "If you stay, you will follow every command given to you. You will do exactly as you are told, exactly when you are told to do it. You're loyalty is to the Black Guard if you stay. Nothing else. Do we have an understanding?"

Will beamed with excitement. "Yes, of course. Thank you. I won't let you down. I promise." He acknowledged Eva with a nod of the head.

"Yes, yes, we'll see about that," Aquinas said. "And what to do with this one?" she asked herself, sizing up T-Rex, who immediately stuck a finger in his nose. She knocked his hand away with her cane and then poked his belly with it. She shook her head disapprovingly. "What to do, indeed."

"Begging your pardon, ma'am," T-Rex said nervously. "But Eva told me there might be a fit for me in the kitchens. A Ratling, she called it."

Aquinas arched an eyebrow. "A Ratling? This is for hunters who cannot complete their training, either because of an injury or because they lack the courage."

"Oh yes, that's perfect," T-Rex said eagerly.

"It means not being a hunter and not going out to fight the monsters," Aquinas said.

"That sounds great!" T-Rex exclaimed before catching himself. He looked at Will and me. "Not that I don't want to fight...it's just...you know..."

"You'd just rather be around the food," Will said.

"Exactly," T-Rex said.

Aquinas broke out into a wide smile and placed a hand on T-Rex's shoulder. "Then so you shall. There is a bell in the central courtyard. In the morning, you will go to it and ring it three times. Only three times, mind you. Any hunter who wishes to stop his or her training may ring the bell at any time. Afterward, you will see Bacho and he will train you."

"Three times. Got it," T-Rex said.

"Only three," Aquinas said, her voice laced with warning. "Make certain of it."

"What happens if he rings it more than three times?" Will asked.

"The Trial of the Cave," Eva said. "It is..."

"...quite a long story," Aquinas interjected. "And the hour is late, Eva. Wouldn't you agree?"

Eva nodded and fell silent. If she was trying to stop us from wanting to find out what the Trial of the Cave was, she had just done the opposite. I made a mental note to ask Eva at the first chance.

Master Aquinas turned to me and I felt a small burst of adrenaline. While I was happy that both Will and T-Rex were being allowed to stay, I found myself battling a rising anger as I stood waiting for Aquinas to address me. I reminded myself that Aquinas had used me as bait for Ren Lucre. A dangerous game that resulted in the death of both my Aunt Sophie and Hester.

"This is all well and good," I said, unable to hide the anger in my voice, "but I came here to get answers."

Aquinas turned toward me slowly, sizing me up with those crystal-clear blue eyes. "Everyone wants answers, young Templar. Unfortunately, there's a shortage of them in this world," she said.

"Where is my father?" I asked. "Is Ren Lucre still alive? What are the Jerusalem Stones?"

Aquinas shuffled close to me until we were standing face-to-face. She reached up with a shaking, gnarled hand and placed it carefully on my cheek. "You look so very much like him," she whispered. "Is it too much to hope that your heart is like his as well? Tell me, what do you stand for?"

The directness of the question took me aback. Her hand cradled my face, holding it so that I couldn't look away from her piercing eyes.

"What do you mean?" I muttered.

"What do you stand for!" she said, her voice deep and powerful. This was no longer a question, it was a command.

I searched for an answer but nothing came to me. I froze, suddenly terrified of this frail, old woman who seemed able to see right through me. She searched my face, then finally exhaled, smiled and patted my cheek. "The day you can answer that question is the day you will find your true power. Sleep, young one. Tomorrow your training begins."

She took her hand away, turned her back and slowly walked toward the stone staircase in the back of the room. I stood there, stupidly, shocked by the sudden end to the conversation. Even though my hands trembled, I couldn't believe that she was walking away from me. "That's it?" I asked. "You're not going to answer any of my questions?"

Aquinas hummed quietly to herself as she walked, clearly meaning to ignore me.

"But I came halfway around the world looking for answers."

"Then, by all means, you must find them," Aquinas said.

"I don't understand. I came because Eva told me you had answers."

She slowly climbed the stairs, whistling a tune as she did, her cane thumping heavily on each step. Finally, she disappeared into the room above.

I felt an overwhelming urge to follow her and demand that she tell me what she knew. But I felt Eva grab my elbow and pull me toward her.

"Come on," she whispered. "There will be time for answers later."

Frustrated, I pulled my arm from her and marched out of the room and onto the balcony. The courtyard below was now empty except for the guards at the gate. Above, the winter storm had blown past and revealed a brilliant sky of bright stars. I pulled my cloak around me to ward off the chill and looked out of over the wall into the forest. A wolf's howl rose up from the trees, haunting and beautiful.

Eva, Will and T-Rex came up and stood beside me, each of us lost in our own thoughts. Finally, it was Eva who broke the silence. "Aquinas practically raised me after Ren Lucre killed my family. Without her..." she held up her left arm with the missing hand, "I would have been a Ratling. She means the best."

"Sorry, but it's hard to see that right now," I said. "I'm here to find out where my father is being held. Once I find that out, or if Aquinas can't help me, I need to go look on my own."

"Come on, I'll show you to your room. You need to get a good night's sleep. Even with the excitement tonight, the Academy is open for business at first light. You boys are going to need to be at the top of your game."

We let her lead us down into the courtyard and into one of the wide barracks built into the side of the wall. Rows of bunk beds lined the room and the soft sounds of breathing filled the air. Eva pointed to two empty beds at the end of the room. "It's not much, but it'll be warm in here."

"There are only two beds," I said.

"Ratlings don't sleep in the hunters' dorm. I'll show T-Rex to his bed," she said.

"Where are you sleeping?" Will asked.

"Instructor's lodging. Two buildings down," she whispered. "I might not see you at first. Just follow the others. You'll figure it out."

Eva turned to leave but I grabbed her arm. She looked at me, puzzled. "I don't think I ever thanked you for coming back for me. You saved my life."

"I like it better when you owe me one," she said. "Now get to sleep."

We waved at T-Rex as he left with Eva. Will and I climbed into our beds. After the craziness of the last day, lying down in an actual bed felt amazing.

I closed my eyes and felt my aching bones settle into the mattress. I then took a deep breath, and let sleep wash over me.

What felt like a second later, a great crashing sound filled the air. I leapt out of bed, ready to battle whatever monster was making such an outlandish noise. But instead of a monster, I saw three older boys walking down the middle aisle of the beds, banging swords on metal shields and making a racket. Pale strands of first light filtered in through the windows.

"Come on! Up and at 'em," one of the boys cried.

"Bunch 'a pansies. Sleep is for the weak. Let's go!" said another.

I swung my legs out of bed and was rewarded with Will's feet smacking the top of my head as he crawled out of the upper bunk.

"Sorry," Will mumbled. "Hey, did you get one of these?" He held out a folded set of black clothes. The same style Eva and Daniel had worn.

I searched my bed and found my own set underneath my blanket. "Yeah, I've got a pair."

"So cool," Will said. "So freaking cool!"

I smiled at Will's enthusiasm, thinking for the hundredth time how thankful I was to have him on this journey with me. I wondered how T-Rex was doing in the Ratling's dorm.

As if on cue, a deep bell sounded outside. Everyone stopped in mid-activity, then made a mad dash to the windows and doors to look outside.

"Who is it?" mumbled a dozen different voices. "Who's missing?"

"Strange; it's first thing in the morning," someone else said.

Will and I followed along and went outside just as the second chime reached our ears. Of course, we already knew who it was. In the distance, perched awkwardly on a boulder in the center of the training field, T-Rex struck a large bell for the third time with a heavy-looking, two-handed hammer. Bacho stood next to him and helped him down.

"Just what we need—another Ratling," a thin hunter with red hair mumbled.

"What'd ya think?" asked a squat, muscular boy with terrible acne. "That he was goin' for tha Cave 'a Trials? That's a lark."

"Makes sense," a hunter said nearby. "The fat one never would have made it."

"I doubt any of them will make it," said someone else in the crowd. The hunters nearest us looked embarrassed by the comment. Will stepped forward but I held him back by the arm. The last thing we needed was to get into a fight on our first day of school.

Within seconds of the last bell, the room was back to being a flurry of activity. Soon, there wasn't a single person left in their bed; everyone was busy putting on their clothes and stretching the sheets tight on their mattresses. Will jumped down to the floor beside me. "You've got to make your bed," he said. "Hurry up."

I made the bed quickly. It was easy enough because I had slept so hard that I don't think I actually moved once during the night. Will had found out from one of the boys that the bathroom was in the back, so we went there and waited in line. No one spoke to us, but there was no shortage of curious looks and sidelong glances. After we had our turn in the bathroom, we followed the migration of boys out of the barracks and into the courtyard.

The Academy looked completely different by day. While the flicker of campfires and torches the night before had made the courtyard seem mysterious and foreboding, the bright morning light made it look more like a working farm than a secret hideout for monster hunters. Well, a working farm with extensive fortifications and battlements, that is.

The layout of the fort was fairly basic and entirely built for defense. I could see the main wall better in the daylight. It looked like something out of a history textbook about the Middle Ages. Black boulders stacked high into the air with slits for shooting arrows. The wall was rugged and looked like sections of it had been repaired over the centuries. I wondered whether it had been time and the elements that had made the repairs necessary, or if those sections were the scars from long-ago battles.

The Academy's main wall curved in an arc from left to right, both ends terminating into the side of a mountain of black rock. In the dark, I hadn't noticed that the entire Academy actually rested on top of a small plateau with a massive, sheer mountain face behind it. I looked up to the top and felt dizzy from the height of it. It was a perfect defense, as it seemed climbing the face was impossible. I suspected that the opposite side of the mountain was just as steep, giving an attacking army no option other than an uphill assault on the wall.

And that was just the first line of defense. A second wall rose up on the opposite side of the wide courtyard, covering the mouth of a giant cave. I noticed there were two towers built into the wall on either side of the gate that I hadn't noticed the night before. This wall looked even older than the outer defenses.

At least twenty feet tall, it was covered with nasty spikes, blades and wires, making climbing nearly impossible. The roof of the cave towered over it and went back deep into the mountain.

I took a few steps backward to get a better angle and see how far back the cave went. The rock ceiling continued to rise, but the shadows were too dark; it was impossible to tell how big it was.

I was no expert in medieval fortifications, but this set-up seemed perfect. Any attack would first have to come uphill to the first wall, where the enemy would be completely exposed to the archers and defenders. An almost impossible task. But, if they were to succeed, the defenders had to simply pull back to the second wall and renew the defense. Again, the attackers would be totally in the open in the wide crescent-shaped space of the courtyard, an area that was about the length of a football field in the center and that tapered to a point at each end.

Meanwhile, the defenders would be holed up in the cave system protected by a thick, seemingly impenetrable wall. I imagined that there would have been food and water supplies in the cave that could last through any siege. Whoever had built this fortress must have known they would eventually be attacked. I wondered if the Black Guard had been the original builders and, if not, then who? I added it to my growing list of questions to ask Eva when I saw her next.

"Jack!" Will called out to me. "Come on, breakfast is over this way."

Just the mention of breakfast sent my stomach rumbling. I jogged to catch up with him. Boys and girls ranging in age from eight to sixteen poured out of the barracks and converged on a grassy open area near the top end of the crescent. Nearly everyone wore the same simple uniform— all black—including a heavy black cloak to ward off the cold. The only exceptions were the instructors, who wore blood-red cloaks, and the Ratlings.

The Ratlings stood behind the serving tables, hefting mounds of steaming food onto the hunter's trays. They wore stiff grey coats that went three-fourths of the way to the floor and covered their heads with knit caps. But their clothes weren't the only thing that separated them.

I remembered Aquinas saying that hunters became Ratlings if they were injured or couldn't handle the training. I noticed quite a few of them walked with a limp, or even had an arm, leg or foot missing. They ran the gamut from being so thin that a soft breeze could knock them down to someone like Bacho, who looked like he just might have eaten a couple of the skinny Ratlings for breakfast. Right next to Bacho, grinning like he had won the lottery, was T-Rex dressed in the grey Ratling uniform.

I waved at him and he waved back.

The distinctive smell of bacon wafted over the air and I realized how hungry I was. I grabbed a plate and watched as it filled with bacon, scrambled eggs, baked tomatoes and chunks of a white cheese. I reached Bacho and T-Rex's place in line and they gave me wide grin.

"Isn't this awesome!" T-Rex said. "We got to eat before you guys. All the bacon I wanted!"

Bacho smiled, happy with his new charge. "Don't ya worry, M'ster Jack," Bacho said. "I'll take care a' T-Rex 'ere. Come on, you can 'ave a lil extra. On the 'ouse." Bacho heaped a massive serving of thick porridge onto my plate.

It sloshed over all my other food and dribbled off the edge of my plate. Bacho looked so proud to have helped me out that I tried not to show my dismay that my entire breakfast was now going to taste like porridge.

"Thanks, Bacho," I said. "I appreciate it. See you later, T-Rex."

I followed Will through the rows of tables, trying to ignore the people staring at us. We took a seat at an empty table and sat across from another. No one had started eating yet, so we followed their example and waited.

I craned my neck to find Eva in the crowd. I spotted her sitting at a table filled with older hunters, all of them instructors, as noted by the ribbons tied around their arms. Someone blocking my view moved to the side and I saw that Daniel sat next to her. He was telling a story and the entire table was hanging onto every word. He must have told the punch line as the table erupted in laughter and the instructors closest to Daniel slapped him on the back.

"What a putz," I whispered.

As if sensing my stare, Daniel turned and looked directly at me.

I spun back around in my chair and pretended to play with my breakfast, forcing myself not to look over in that direction again. Even as more people filtered in and got their food, no one sat at the table with us. They just passed right by like we didn't exist and sat at the next table over. Soon, everyone had been served and every table in the room was crowded to over-capacity, but the ten open spots at our table remained empty.

"Geez," Will whispered to me. "I know we didn't take a shower this morning, but I didn't think we smelled this bad." He leaned toward me and took a good sniff. "It might be you."

I was about to comment that he didn't exactly smell like a flower either, when Aquinas walked into the room. Everyone stood up from their chairs and fell silent.

"Hunters and trainees of the Black Guard. May honor guide you, may truth comfort you, and may justice always be your goal," Aquinas intoned.

In unison, everyone put their right fist to their chest, then extended their arm forward. It was the same hunter salute I had learned from Eva. "Do your duty, come what may," replied the group.

"Enjoy your meal," Aquinas said.

The room exploded in loud conversation as students dug into their food. Famished, I hardly noticed the soggy porridge that covered all my food. Will and I barely said a word as we devoured our plates in a matter of minutes.

Good thing too, because no sooner had we finished than a high-pitched bell rang, very different from the deep tones of the one T-Rex had rung earlier. In an instant, all the hunters were on their feet and hustling out of the room, leaving their dirty plates behind.

Will and I followed along and jogged to catch up. A quick look back confirmed what I thought. The Ratlings were clearing the tables and cleaning up the mess left by the hunters.

The crowd jogged to the main courtyard and quickly assembled itself in organized rows with military-like precision, ten men across and fifteen deep. At the head of each row, facing the column of fifteen, was an instructor.

Everyone seemed to have an assigned spot. Everyone except Will and me, that is. Thinking it was first-come, first serve, we tried to stand in a column only to shortly have a hunter run up and claim the spot as their own. The bell kept ringing, adding a sense of urgency to find a place. We worked our way to the back of the formation and took our place there, making two columns an uneven length. A glance down the line confirmed I was in Eva's column.

"Get behind me," I whispered to Will. "We want to stick together."

But Will had a different plan. He spotted Daniel and jogged down the back of the formation to join his column.

The bell finally stopped ringing. Everyone snapped to attention and fell silent.

Daniel left his column and walked over to the boulder with the large bell on it. "Good morning," he started. "Despite the events of last night, today will be a normal training day on the regular rotation. But first, three announcements. Until further notice, due to the aggressive wolf activity, leaving the grounds will be by instructor permission only." Groans rumbled through the crowd. "Second, we welcome the return of one of our best instructors after a successful field assignment. She will be filling in for Instructor Saliba who is still recovering from his training injuries. Eva." Daniel pointed to her and clapped his hands. The assembly followed his example and gave her a rousing applause. "Third, we all heard the bell ring this morning." He played up the drama, shaking his head as if he were speaking of a great tragedy. "Not the five rings of a hero, but three. Only three." He strung out his delivery, pacing and shaking his head. "A person who was given the chance of a life of valor and bravery, and instead chose one made of potatoes and dirty dishes."

A low chuckle passed through the group. Eva stared Daniel down with a scowl.

"Every day, you must choose to be here," Daniel said. "We need you. We need all of you. But only if you have the commitment to achieve excellence. Because, after all, what is the Black Guard, if not excellence?"

I looked around at the young hunters near me. They were eating every word up, their heads nodding in agreement.

After a long pause, Daniel let go his near-hypnotic hold on his audience by clapping his hands together. "I wish that excellence extended to our weather." The group dutifully laughed. Daniel held up his hands and they fell quiet. "I should also point out that we have two new recruits who have joined us. Will Chacon and Jack Smith," Daniel said. "Welcome them."

"Templar," Eva corrected. "It's Jack Templar." She whispered something to Daniel who shrugged and grinned.

Everyone spun around to seek us out. A murmur passed through the crowd.

"I know I speak for both of them when I tell you they do not want, nor should they get, special treatment," Daniel said. "They must earn the right to be here just like everyone else. Or they can join the Ratlings like their friend and make our supper."

Laughter rippled through the crowd.

"We're on regular rotation," Daniel said. "Dismissed."

In a flurry of action, each instructor ran to a different section of the open area, followed fast behind by the column of hunters. Eva stood where she was, realizing that if everyone ran off, then the current area would suddenly be empty. I watched Will run over to where Daniel's group was meeting.

Daniel reached out and shook Will's hand generously, introducing him to other members of his group.

I turned back to see that the rest of my column had already moved up and gathered around Eva, sitting on the ground in a semi-circle. I was left out in the open, the only person not in a group. Suddenly, the hair on the back of my neck pricked upward as if someone were staring at me. I looked up at the giant oak and saw Aquinas hunched over the railing, watching my every move.

I took a deep breath and jogged to Eva's group. She was already mid-lecture, talking about the difference between rock ogres and forest ogres, and the most efficient ways to dispose of each.

I took a seat and tried to pay attention, but my thoughts were a million miles away. I couldn't help but wonder if I had made the right decision to come here.

Certainly, Aquinas knew some of the things I needed to know, but she didn't appear even close to sharing those answers with me. And the training we were doing was great if I had a couple of years to dedicate to study. But I didn't have that kind of time. My father's life was in peril, and every minute spent playing soldier was time that could be used to search for him and free him.

I decided to give the Academy a few days, but if Aquinas wouldn't give me some answers by then, I'd have no choice but to strike out on my own.

I looked back over to the balcony on the giant oak and saw that Master Aquinas had gone. I settled in for my first full day of class at the Monster Hunter Academy.

Chapter Five

Any hope that I would be welcomed with open arms by my new monster hunter family seemed to be just that, a hope. True to Daniel's introduction of me, everyone seemed to not only go out of their way not to give me any special attention, they appeared to go out of their way not to give me any attention at all.

I got it. I was the new kid in school. And in this school, everyone carried a sword and was trained to fight. There wasn't going to be a cookie and punch reception to welcome me.

Any idea that our "classes" were going to involve sitting in a comfortable, warm room at a desk with a book and a professor was quickly proven wrong. The groups met out in the open, even as a dusting of snow floated down on top of us.

I had a sneaking suspicion that if there had been a blizzard, we'd still be meeting outside. Obviously, this school was not interested in turning out academics. The graduates of this place needed to be tough and ready to survive, no matter the weather.

I wrapped my cloak tight around me and sat quietly in the back of Eva's group and tried to focus on the lessons of the day and not worry about the chilly reception.

I glanced over and saw a few of the Ratlings hand up a huge tarp in the center of the field with the list of classes in the rotation that day. The segment titles that would have sounded bizarre to me only a couple of weeks earlier now all seemed strangely reasonable.

Don't roll over and die for the undead. Defensive strategies against zombies and other undead creatures.

Here doggy, doggy. Trapping werewolves through trickery.

When less is too much. How the Lesser Creach can surprise you (and kill you) if you're not careful.

Demons. How to use their hellish anger against them.

Stakes in the heart and other false rumors about vampires.

At least it was better than World History and Algebra back at my normal school. I wondered how things were back in Sunnyvale and how the community had reacted to the sudden disappearance of three boys in the middle of the night without a trace. I wondered if—

"Jack," Eva said sternly, "do you have an answer or not?"

I turned my attention to Eva and suddenly realized that the entire class was staring at me. I had been daydreaming and I had no idea what Eva was talking about.

I shook my head. "Sorry, can you repeat the question?"

A few of the other kids chuckled at my expense. Eva didn't look happy.

"I asked, what is the greatest point of vulnerability of a rock troll?"

She wasn't going to let me off the hook. The other kids enjoyed my squirming.

"Well," I said, "I'm not exactly sure what the technical answer is..."

"Then I suggest you listen instead of—"

"But all the rock trolls I've fought had bad eyesight and a terrible sense of balance. Oh, and they were dumb as rocks too, which might be how they got their name." A few of the kids laughed. They were all leaning toward me, taking in every word. "All you have to do is give them an easy target and get ready to move when they lunge at you. They'll over-commit and you'll get a clear shot to finish them off. Either to the back of the neck or here, in the ribs, under the arm. But you don't even need to do that."

"What do you mean?" one of the kids asked.

I glanced at Eva. She nodded for me to go on. "Like I said, they can't see well and they're pretty dumb. Once you juke them, it's hard for them to spot you again. If you can keep out of their line of sight for ten or fifteen seconds, then they're likely to forget about you. Literally. They just stand there thinking, 'Uhhh...I was trying to smush something, now what was it?'" The class laughed at my rock troll impression. I was on a roll. Or at least I thought so until I saw Eva standing with her arms crossed, looking not nearly as entertained as my new classmates.

"And how about their other senses?" she asked. "Touch, smell, that sort of thing?"

"I guess they're about the same as their eyesight," I said.

"You guess?" Eva asked. "Anyone else here want to guess when it comes to fighting something that's trying its best to kill you?"

The class turned quiet, the mood getting serious in a hurry.

"Rock trolls are cave-dwellers, so they spend most of their lives underground. But what they lack in eyesight, they more than make up for in sense of smell. Like a shark in the water, a rock troll can smell fresh blood nearly a mile away. They may be stupid, but once they lock onto a blood-scent, they won't give up until they're dead...or you are." Eva locked me in a stare. "But you're right, their lack of intelligence is a rock troll's greatest vulnerability. Just don't make it yours too."

The class shifted uncomfortably as Eva and I locked eyes. Then a whistle blew and the class thankfully jumped to their feet and jogged to the next instructor.

After everyone had gone, I stopped by Eva and said, "Thanks for that."

She grabbed me by the arm. "Give this place a chance. You'll learn things here that could save your life, or the lives of the hunters you are fighting next to."

I took a deep breath. She was right. I nodded and said, smiling, "Pay attention and listen up. Got it."

"Or I'll kick your butt," she said.

"Yeah, like that could happen," I grinned. As I turned to follow my class to the station, I got a swift kick to the backside. I spun around and Eva gave me a wink.

"Don't get a big head. I'll always be able to do that." She turned and barked orders to her new class congregating in front of her.

I jogged to catch up with my group, already feeling better about the day.

The rest of the morning's training segments were fast paced and did not waste a minute. Each class started with a lecture and ended with a practical exercise, either weapons practice or some kind of physical activity. Everyone else was used to the exercises and knew exactly what the instructor wanted the instant he or she asked for it. Meanwhile, I was bumping into people, moving left when everyone was going to the right, going right when we were supposed to go left, and generally making a mess of the drills.

After Eva's class though, the rest of the group seemed to warm up to me a little. At least they stopped glaring at me every time I made a mistake.

On the last rotation, our group went to the werewolf class. As we jogged over, I saw that the instructor was Daniel.

"Great," I said to no one in particular.

"Yeah," a young boy, no more than ten, replied in a soft English accent. "Daniel's by far the most talented hunter here, but he's tough on his classes." I glanced over and saw that the boy had a freckled face and a shock of bright red hair poking out from under the hood of his cloak. "Xavier's my name, by the way."

"Jack," I replied.

Xavier giggled, "I know who you are. Everyone does."

"Yeah, that's why I'm making friends so quick."

"Don't you know?" Xavier said. "Oh, that's funny. Really funny."

"What are you talking about?" I asked.

"Don't you see? They're scared of you."

"What?" I asked in shock. "Why?"

"The Reg who defeated Ren Lucre in battle? With no training? With no help? Are you kidding me?" Xavier asked.

"I had plenty of help," I said. There's no way I would have survived that night by myself."

"Still, there's the whole Ren Lucre thing," Xavier pointed out.

"I got lucky is all," I said.

The boy leaned in closer to me so that our shoulders were nearly touching. "Tell me, is it true that you fought Tiberon in the forest on the way here? Did you really see him? What he was like?"

"Alright," Daniel's voice boomed over us. "Settle down or I'll feed your toes to the mugwumps and turn the lot of you into Ratlings."

Clearly, no one thought this was an idle threat because the group fell totally silent and scrambled to sit in a perfect semi-circle around Daniel. I sat on one of the far ends, hoping to stay out of his line of sight.

"Welcome to the most important class of the day," Daniel intoned. "Yes, all the classes here at the Academy are important in their own way, but what we discuss here most directly affects your chance of survival once you walk through those walls. While a small fraction of you might see a shaman-demon or a bone-wraith ever in your lifetime, every one of you will see a werewolf. Why? Because one of the most dangerous and malicious specimens in the world lives in the woods right outside our front door."

As if on cue, a baleful howl rose up from deep in the woods and echoed throughout the walls of the Academy. Daniel smiled, pleased with the dramatic effect.

Xavier leaned over to me. "I don't think he's right about that. Werewolves are kind of my thing and I think Tiberon isn't really a werewolf at all."

"Really?" I whispered back. "Then what is he?"

"I'm trying to figure it out. He's something different though. Possibly even unique. Aquinas lets me use her library and I found a book that…" Xavier's voice trailed off as Daniel's shadow suddenly loomed over us.

"Did you have something to say, little man?" Daniel asked. "Something more important than the lesson I'm giving?"

Xavier looked at the ground and shook his head.

"What? Sorry, I couldn't hear that," Daniel said.

"No, sir," Xavier mumbled.

"Not good enough," Daniel barked. "On your feet, boy."

Xavier started to stand up but I pulled him back down and stood up instead. "It was my fault. I asked him a question," I said. "Don't pick on him."

Daniel's eyes darted over to me. "Don't pick on him?"

"You might ask some questions from the class instead of just lecturing us. Xavier here has a theory about Tiberon," I said.

Xavier slinked down, trying to quietly sneak away.

"Is that right?" Daniel asked, a smile on his face. "I'm sure we'd all love to hear it. Come on, Xavier. What's your theory?"

Xavier stared at the ground. "I don't…I mean, I think…"

"Come on," Daniel said. "Out with it."

"I don't think he's a werewolf. Not in the classic sense anyway," Xavier's voice steadied as he gained a little confidence. "The journals describe a wolf with the white cross all the way back to the founding of the Academy, back when the Citadel was built. We all know werewolves never live more than a hundred years, usually a lot less. So knowing that, how could the same werewolf be here all that time?"

"Simple," Daniel said. "It's not the same werewolf. The white cross is just a genetic trait passed down the line."

"It's too perfect to be a genetic trait," I said. "I mean, it's like it was painted onto his fur."

Daniel stared at me, open-mouthed. In my eagerness to prove Daniel wrong, I'd let slip a crucial detail about the night before. "How would you know that?"

"I was as close to him as I am to you. Closer, really. I was touching him."

Daniel grinned, suddenly confident that he had caught me in a lie. ""Impossible," Daniel said. "And what were you doing touching him? Looking for ticks?"

"No, I was pulling out the bolt Eva put in him."

The rest of the class exploded in a new round of chatter. Daniel spun around and shouted, "The next one who speaks goes into the Cave of Trials. Understand?" This got their attention. Everyone quieted down and looked away.

"You helped a werewolf escape? If true, that would be grounds for a tribunal to consider your banishment from the Black Guard," Daniel said.

"You're missing the point," I said. "I think Xavier is right. Regardless, he certainly isn't the malicious monster you're making him out to be."

"No, he's a werewolf," Daniel spat, his face turning red. "And, like all werewolves, they're evil and can't be changed."

"You don't know what you're talking about," I said, raising my voice.

"How dare you challenge me in front of my class?" Daniel shouted. "Especially when you know nothing about the subject."

"I know enough."

"My family has hunted werewolves for over four hundred years," Daniel shouted. "How could you possibly know more than I do?"

"Because I know," I shouted.

"How?"

"Because I was raised by a devil-werewolf," I shouted. "And she died trying to save me from Ren Lucre."

I'd gone this far, so I decided it was too late to turn back now. I got up and pointed my finger at Daniel.

"So don't stand there and tell me they're all evil and can't be changed because you're wrong. You're dead wrong."

I suddenly felt the stillness all around me. I spun around and saw that all the groups on the field had stopped what they were doing and stared. A hundred pairs of eyes bored into me. They had heard everything. I turned back to Daniel. "That's how I know," I whispered.

I felt tears well up. No one moved and there was no place to hide. I tried to hold it in but I knew within seconds I was going to cry in front of the entire Academy.

Just then, a bell sounded from the meal area, bright and cheerful, completely opposite of the mood on the field. Still no one moved.

"All right, you lot. You heard the bell. Lunch time, on the hustle." It was Eva who broke the spell and sent the young hunters in training scrambling toward the lunch tables.

As the crowd ran by us, Daniel continued to stare at me as if I were a foreign object that he couldn't understand. Something about his bearing stirred a new emotion in me. I wiped away the tears that had been right on the edge of rolling down my cheek and took a step toward Daniel. Gone was the pain from thinking about my Aunt Sophie's sacrifice for me. Instead, all I felt was anger. And, from the look on Daniel's face, he felt exactly the same way.

I felt a tug on my arm and saw that it was Will. I disengaged from Daniel and let Will pull me away. As he did, Eva stepped in front of Daniel and blocked his path as he moved toward me.

While she talked to him in hushed tones, Will and I walked to the tables filled with food.

"You're making friends quick here," Will said.

"You seem to be doing OK," I replied, sounding harsher than I intended.

"What's that supposed to mean?" Will said.

"Nothing," I said, feeling miserable for myself. We stood at the end of the line in silence. By the time we reached the food, the trays of chicken, vegetables and pasta were picked over fairly well. T-Rex was in the kitchen, away from the serving line, so we weren't able to talk to him.

Bacho stood behind the younger Ratlings, barking instructions to them. When he saw me, his face lit up and he stepped forward, knocking the Ratling server out of the way with his hips.

"Hey Bacho," Will called out.

"Hey yer'selves," he leaned in conspiratorially. "Hope yous didn't mind none me ringing the bell a few minutes on the early side there. Seemed like you boys might be a bit hungry."

"You did that?" I asked.

The big Ratling beamed with pride. He reached under the table and pulled out two full plates of food and handed them over. "Right, 'ere you goes. Pulled out some of the best pieces, I did."

Will grabbed his plate and ate a piece of meat hungrily. "You're the best, Bacho."

"Thanks," I said. "I really mean it."

A crashing of pots erupted from the far end of the serving line. "These young'uns," Bacho groaned. "They give me the ones with nothin' but thumbs. Go on. Enjoy yer lunches."

Bacho hurried off to berate a poor Ratling on his hands and knees picking up the mess he had made. We turned and looked for a table.

Will noticed a group of hunters that had been in his morning group. They waved him over to come sit with them. When I looked over, the waves disappeared and the boys looked away. Will was right. I wasn't making many friends.

"Go on," I told Will. "You can sit with them. I won't mind."

Will gave a tell-tale look toward the table even as he shrugged the comment off. "Who, them? Nah, there's an empty table over there. Let's grab it so we can spread out."

Even though I knew he was just being nice, I was happy to have the company.

We walked through the lunch area, some hunters doing better than others at hiding the sidelong glances in my direction. We sat at the table and dug into our food.

"You know what?" Will asked. "The guys in our group were pretty cool. Maybe you could join us after lunch in the next rotation."

"Yeah, maybe," I said, not meaning it.

Will put his food down and leaned in. "Look, I know we just got here, but I really like it. I've never, you know, belonged anywhere before. I feel like this is my chance to really be part of something."

"I agree."

"I guess what I'm saying is, could you try a little harder to fit in?" He lowered his voice even more. "I mean, screaming in the middle of the practice field that you were raised by a devil-werewolf on the first day? A little much, isn't it?"

I put down my fork, suddenly not hungry. "What should I have done, just let him say those things? Not defend her? Are you forgetting that she basically raised you too?"

"I know. I'm just saying you could sort of ease into things a little."

"Ease into things, huh?" I snapped. "Yeah, I'll see what I can do about that."

Will backed off a little, my tone taking him by surprise. "Hey, I'm like one of three friends you seem to have here...four with Bacho over there. All I'm asking for, as your friend, is that you give this place more of a chance. For me."

I took a deep breath and forced myself to settle down. Will was right. I was letting this place get to me. I needed to have a little bit of patience and see what I could learn, especially from Aquinas. Once I found what I needed, then I could get back on the road and go find my father.

I nodded at Will. "You're right. I'm sorry I snapped at you."

"And you're sorry for being such a jerk?" Will added, smiling.

I returned the smile. "Yeah, that too."

"C'mon, say it," he said.

"I'm sorry you're such a jerk."

"Oww! Boom, right in the heart," Will joked. He put his knuckles out and I gave him a fist bump. "So you'll chill out a little?" Will asked.

"I'll chill out," I said.

"Good," Will replied.

"Because tonight we're sneaking into the Templar Tree to see what we can find."

Will stared at me, then finally shook his head and grabbed my plate of food for himself and started shoveling it in.

"What are you doing?" I asked.

"I figured this might be my last meal. I want to make it a good one."

As he ate, my eyes wandered over to the second floor balcony of the great oak tree. Even though the opening was black with shadows, I could have sworn I saw an inky shape dissolve back into the room. I squinted but saw nothing more. I wondered if Aquinas had been watching me the entire time.

"What do you expect to find anyway?" asked Will, following my line of sight.

"The only thing I came here for," I said. "Answers."

The rest of the day passed by without incident. While the classes continued into the afternoon, there was more of an emphasis on weapons training and physical fitness. The groups rotated through stations of exercises, including sprints, agility courses and strength conditioning. It felt like gym class back in school, except for the little fact that if we failed, we were most likely going to be food for something big and nasty.

I enjoyed these sections because the physical activity helped work off the tension and stress that had built up through the morning. My body, which had gone through the 'Change' right before my fourteenth birthday, felt stronger than ever. I was still getting used to my new strength and was pleasantly surprised to discover I was by far the fastest hunter in the training session. I wasn't about to try to draw even more attention to myself after what had happened earlier that day so I made sure to dial my performance back and come in second or third in all of our races and competitions.

Throughout the entire afternoon, the young red-headed Xavier stuck close to my side, pressing me with question after question about Tiberon and the pack of wolves in the forest. While it was clear that Xavier was some kind of genius, the strength of his mind did not carry over to his muscles. The poor kid could barely keep up with the exercises and each station found him more and more winded. At least this made him pause his relentless questioning.

At one station, we were supposed to climb up a heavy rope nearly twenty feet tall, scamper across a narrow wooden beam, then dive off into a pile of hay down below. The idea was that we were being chased by a werewolf and needed to utilize a quick exit. I stood next to Xavier as the others in our group went first. Even the strongest hunters were having trouble with the rope. I imagined that Xavier would be getting nervous, but when I looked at him, he seemed fine, eager for his turn.

"Do you want to go first?" I asked politely. "That way if you fall, I'll try to catch you."

Xavier smiled. "I'll go first, but I'm not going to fall."

I respected his confidence. After watching him all afternoon on the other exercises, I wasn't sure where it was coming from, but I liked it.

"Xavier, you're up!" the station's instructor, Darter, shouted. He was a muscle-bound teen with a square jaw and a Marine buzz cut who ran his station like basic training. "Go, go, go!" he yelled. "That werewolf's gonna chew you up, Xavier. Probably spit you out for being too bony."

Xavier strode up to the rope, looked up its length as if measuring the distance to the top.

"C'mon hunter," Darter shouted. "Gotta moooove!"

Xavier whipped back his cloak and revealed a metal contraption attached to his belt. It looked like a small fishing reel but tipped with a metal hook.

He pressed a button and the hook shot upward, dragging a fine, silvery line behind it. The hook reached the post at the top and dug into the wood.

"What are you doing, shooting my apparatus?" Darter yelled.

"Accomplishing the objective, sir," Xavier replied. He pressed another button and the fishing reel on his waist turned into a winch, pulling him quickly up into the air.

We all cheered as he ascended and he waved at us like a rock star.

"Watch out!" I yelled.

But it was too late. The winch pulled him up so fast that he didn't have time to slow down before reaching the top. Xavier smacked his head into the crossbar and the hook tore loose from the wood. The young hunter, arms and legs flailing, tumbled back down.

I reached out and grabbed him the best I could to break his fall. He landed hard on top of me and we both ended up sprawled together on the ground.

Darter walked up, his hands held together at the wrists and making a chomping action as if they were jaws.

"And the werewolf eats you," said Darter. "Fail. OK, who's next?"

As the next hunter struggled up the rope, Xavier and I picked ourselves up off the ground. "Are you OK?" I asked. "That was totally cool."

"I really thought it would work this time," Xavier said.

"This time? How many times have you tried it?"

"I think this is version eighteen," Xavier said. "Experimentation is the centerpiece of invention."

Overhearing, Darter added, "For you, it's the centerpiece of getting yourself killed."

Xavier shook the snow off his cloak. "These guys are locked in the past. We're using the same weapons our ancestors did out of some idea of nobility and honor," Xavier said. "I'm not saying we need to carry machine guns around, but a little technology can go a long way when it comes to monsters."

"So, you have other inventions?" I asked.

"Oh yeah, tons," Xavier said eagerly. "Nothing that really works quite yet, but some things are close."

"So, you're a scientist," I said.

I hit a nerve with the comment and Xavier beamed. "I like to think so. My parents were both scientists, so it's in my blood."

A little cheer rose from our group and we turned to see that one of the hunters had successfully reached the top of the rope and was now straddled on the beam and inching along.

"That werewolf's coming!" Darter yelled. "Don't you think they can climb ropes too? You better get on your feet and run on that beam, boy. Or you ain't gonna make it!"

I turned back to Xavier. "Where are your parents?"

Xavier turned to me. "You really don't know anything, do you?" He pointed across the field. "Orphans, every single one of us."

"I had no idea."

"Most come from hunter families who can trace their membership in the Black Guard back through the centuries. Not as far back as you, of course," he added. "But far. Some, like myself, were Reg orphans found by Master Aquinas. Throwaways who were destined to be lost in the system until she brought us into our new family."

"How did they die, if you don't mind..."

"No, it's OK. I was really young. It was pretty ordinary, really. Just a car crash. No monsters, no swordfights, just a slick road on a stormy night. I had

100

no other family; without Aquinas, who knows where I'd be."

"And what does Aquinas think of your experiments and inventions?"

"Are you kidding? She's the one who encourages it. In fact, I use the lab in the Templar Tree as my workshop. I'll show you some time if you want."

"Yeah," I said. "I'd like that."

"Templar," Darter growled. "You're up. Let's see if you can do any better than your wiz-kid friend there."

I gave Xavier a nod. "Gotta run. It seems that there's a werewolf chasing me," I said. I gave him a slap on the back. "Don't worry, version nineteen is going to be awesome."

"You think so?" he asked.

"Absolutely," I replied. I ran over to the rope and scampered up as Darter yelled instructions at me from below.

By the time dinner came around, I was famished. Will had already grabbed his food so I stood in line by myself. T-Rex was on the serving line this time and beamed at me when I reached him.

"I'll take a slice of Pappagallo's pizza with pepperoni and pineapple, please," I joked.

"Man, I wish," said T-Rex. "I'm trying to convince Bacho to let me make pizzas, though. I'll see what I can do. Until then..." he heaped an extra portion of mashed potatoes and pot roast onto my plate.

"Thanks, buddy," I said. "Are you doing OK?"

"Are you kidding?" T-Rex beamed. "These guys are great. We eat all day when you guys aren't around. And we don't have to do any of that nutty running around and exercising. I love it."

The next hunter in line nudged me forward. "Looks like I've got to go."

"My public waits. I'll catch you later, Jack," T-Rex said, happily scooping food for the next hunter.

I walked back to the table where Will and I sat for lunch. A group of five boys huddled around Will, laughing and kidding around with him. I took a deep breath and walked up to them.

"Hey guys," I said.

The boys stopped talking and said their good-byes to Will and moved away to another table. Will looked their direction and, even though he worked hard to mask his emotions from me, I knew he wanted to join them. He was just too good of a friend to show it. I decided it was about time to return the favor.

"I'm beat," I said. "If it's OK with you, I going to hit my bunk and rest."

"Yeah," Will said excitedly. "That's fine. No worries. I'll catch you later, OK?"

"We're on for tonight, right? The Templar Tree?"

Will was already on his feet and headed toward the group of his new friends. "Of course," he called back. "You can count on me. You know that."

He gave me a wink and jogged over to the group of guys. He was soon laughing right along with them. I watched, a pang of jealousy in my chest, but happy to see Will fit in so well. That's when I decided I needed to do my extracurricular activities that night on my own.

"Looks like you're a million miles away," a voice said, startling me. I turned and saw Eva. "Busy day, huh?"

I nodded. "Yeah, I was about to hit the sack."

A group of instructors walked past and I saw Daniel in the middle of them. One of the other instructors called out, "Come on, Eva. Let's go."

Eva waved them off and turned back to me. "You want to come along?"

"I thought instructors couldn't hang out with trainees," I said.

"You look like you could use a friend," she said.

I eyed Daniel in the group waiting for her and shook my head. "I'm good. Thanks though."

Eva turned to leave, but stopped. "You know, it'll get better. These are good people here. They just need a little time. Don't give up on this, OK?"

I nodded. "Thanks. I mean it."

"Besides, I'm looking forward to kicking your butt during drills tomorrow."

"I'll be there," I said. "But I'm pretty sure I'll be doing the butt kicking."

The instructors called out for her again. Eva flashed me a smile and took off, jogging after them.

I glanced over to the oak tree and saw a small light flickering inside. I imagined Aquinas sitting there reading through her dusty old books, filled with the information I needed. Nighttime couldn't come fast enough. I was ready to find out the answers to my questions, even if I had to break into Aquinas's library to do it.

Chapter Six

Hours later, when I rolled out of bed, the rest of the dorm was filled with the sounds of fifty sleeping boys. Snores, grunts, heavy breathing and even a few whimpers from nightmares about the monsters they were training to hunt. It created a perfect cover for the sounds of my creaking mattress as I carefully got out of bed.

Will was fast asleep on the bunk above me. I second-guessed whether I should wake him or not, but I decided it was better to do this alone. He was right that the Academy was going to be great for him. I didn't want to mess up his chance to finally belong somewhere, even if I never would.

I peered out the door, looking for sentries. The grounds were empty but I saw shadows pacing along the tops of the main wall. But these hunters were all looking out into the forest. If there was going to be a threat to the Academy, it was going to come from that direction, not from inside. Satisfied that I was in the clear, I set off on a sprint toward the tree, keeping to the shadows as much as possible.

I reached the base of the tree without any trouble and stood with my back against the massive trunk. I glanced around nervously, certain someone would sound an alarm any second. But no alarm came. I was safe. So far, anyway.

The stairs were open and unguarded but I decided they were too exposed. Anyone on the wall who happened to turn around while I was climbing them was sure to see me.

Instead, I worked my way around to the backside of the tree, searching for another way up. The first level of branches were twenty feet off the ground. If I could just reach those, I'd be able to easily climb to any part of the structure.

Finally, I spotted what I was looking for. A series of gnarled knots that formed a path up the trunk. I grabbed onto the first knot and pulled myself up. I worked hand over hand, trying not to grunt from the effort, scrambling with my toes to find a foothold. I was halfway up when I heard someone cough nearby.

I froze. My fingers dug into a good handhold, but my feet dangled beneath me. The sound had come from just round the bend in the tree. Close enough that I wondered if they had already heard my climbing and were coming to get me. I clung to the side of the tree about fifteen feet off the ground, not daring to move.

Two hunters walked around the tree, talking in low voices to one another. I recognized Darter as one of them, but didn't know the other's name. He was tall, scrawny and wore his hair long, down to his shoulders. He had a beaked nose that gave him a vulture-like appearance. They walked right beneath me and stopped.

It took all my self-control not to move. I hung there with all of my weight supported by my fingers. I was wondering just how long I could hold on when I overheard the conversation going on below me.

"I don't know, Midge. Maybe he is the One," Darter said.

"D'ya believe 'im today? Devil-werewolf? Bah!" the vulture-looking hunter called Midge replied.

"They say it's true. Said he faced down Ren Lucre, too."

"Faced down? What d'ya mean faced down?"

"In battle, you idiot. They say he won."

"An' who says that? Templar?" Midge spat.

"No, Eva said so to Daniel. I've never known Eva to make something like that up."

"If Templar beat 'im, then why's Aquinas gettin' us ready for Ren Lucre's war, then? Don't make no sense, does it?"

"I guess not. Still, if he is the One..."

"Ha! The One? Scrawny kid like that? Not inna million years. Better chance I'm the One than 'im."

"I had him in drills today," Darter said. "He's stronger than he looks. Real strong."

At that moment I didn't feel that strong as my muscles were starting to ache from clinging to the tree. I tried to shift my weight a little from one hand to the other but I wasn't sure how much longer I could last. The hunters below continued to talk, oblivious that I was directly over their heads.

"How about the wolf? How about that? I was there at the gate. There was like...a connection between the two of them," Darter said.

"Tiberon? Only connection with humans that one makes is with 'is teeth to our throats. You're startin' to worry me, you know that? Daniel says we're not to make it easy on the kid. You got that, right?"

Even though hearing Daniel's name gave me a surge of adrenaline, my arms still felt like they were on fire. My fingers were cramped up and I didn't know how much longer I could last. But if I let go, I would literally fall on top of the two hunters beneath me.

I carefully slid my toe back and forth across the tree, looking for anything I could use to prop up some of my weight and relieve my burning muscles. I found something and pushed down on it.

For a split second, it felt great. Then, suddenly, the piece of bark my foot was on broke off. My body dropped and my muscles screamed as I caught myself by digging my fingers back into the knots over my head.

My legs swung wildly as I tried to get back in control. Once I did, I peeked over my shoulder at the two hunters. The piece of bark must have miraculously landed behind them unnoticed because they were still locked in a low conversation.

"D'ya hear Daniel's plan for 'im? First time Master 'quinas goes on one 'uv 'er trips, he's got a somethin' real good going for 'im."

"What's he going to do? Is it really good?" Darter asked.

"I'm not tellin' you."

"Come on, Midge. That's not fair."

"See, Darter? That's your problem, ain't it? Thinkin' things gotta be fair."

The vulture-looking hunter called Midge walked away and I imagined the smug look on his face as Darter continued to beg him for information. I breathed a sigh of relief as they walked away, their voices disappearing into the night.

I didn't have time to wonder about the plans Daniel had for me at the end of the week. I wasn't sure if I would even be around by then anyway.

I scraped my feet against the tree and finally found a solid foothold. I grabbed the next highest knot in the tree and quickly made it to the lowest branches. Flexing my sore hands, I waited until some of the feeling came back. As I looked up, I pondered just how massive the tree's branches were, each one the size of a tree themselves. Looking around, I spotted a high balcony another thirty feet up and climbed toward it.

When I got there, I saw that the balcony had an open section in the railing that would let a person walk out of the structure and straight onto the tree on a wide branch. Or, as in my case, made it easy to sneak into the tree house.

I cautiously climbed onto the balcony and peered around the corner into the room.

I recognized the area. It was the space just behind where we had met Aquinas the night before. The walls were covered with bookshelves filled not only with old books, but stacks of loose papers, maps, binders and various knickknacks being used as paperweights.

I walked in slowly, testing the floor with each step to see if it would creak under my weight. But the structure was as solid as the tree itself and the floor didn't make a sound.

I approached the first row of books and scanned the length of them, not sure what I was looking for. The books were so old that their titles had worn completely off their spines. But one book drew my attention—it was set back a little deeper into the shelf than the books around it, as if it were hiding from me. I pushed aside the books on either side of it and saw that it was a tall, leather-bound tome with straps wrapped around it to keep it closed. That, combined with the fact that it was somewhat hidden from view, made me think it was as good a place as any to look for secrets. Besides, in some inexplicable way, the book seemed to be calling to me.

Not a voice. Not even a sound, really. It was a feeling that this was the book I should open. Giving myself over to instinct, I pulled the book off the shelf.

A thick coat of dust covered it and a cloud puffed into the air as I laid it on a table to examine. The straps were an intricate design of looping material, passing over and under like in a weavers loom. I found the end and set to work unraveling it. My hands moved quickly, as if I had unwrapped the book a hundred times before. If I had stopped to think, I might have realized something was off about the whole thing. But something had a hold on me and I was completely focused on getting that book open.

Finally, I got to the end of the binding and removed the last of the straps. I carefully opened the book, angling it to the moonlight streaming in from the door. It looked like some sort of ancient text, handwritten in a flowing style, perhaps in Latin. I turned the page and nearly dropped the book when I saw the picture printed within.

Ren Lucre!

Exactly as I had seen him only weeks before, glaring at me from the page.

I looked more closely, unable to take my eyes off of him. My hands trembled and in my mind I decided to close the book. But my body wouldn't respond.

My trembling hands pulled the book closer to my face.

I couldn't stop myself.

Then Ren Lucre's cold, dead eyes changed.

Right on the page, they started to glow.

Like two pinpricks of fire, right in the center of his eyes, growing steadily brighter, burning a hole in the page. A tendril of smoke rose up in the air.

I tried to turn away, but I couldn't.

My hands pulled it closer and closer to me.

"Enough!" cried a voice.

Something grabbed the book from me and threw it to the ground. It burst into flames and Ren Lucre's cackling laugh filled the air.

Then, as if the oxygen had been sucked out of the room, the fire was snuffed out, leaving behind a smoldering pile of ash.

I regained control of my body and staggered backward, holding on to the cloaking medallion around my neck as if that would somehow protect me. Strong hands grabbed me and guided me into a leather armchair.

A lantern flickered to life and I saw Aquinas with her back to me, poking the ashes with her cane.

I seized the chance and jumped from the chair to make a mad dash for the balcony. Before I could move one step, a sword whipped through the air and blocked my path. It was Aquinas. And she had moved impossibly fast, with all the agility of a fighter.

I glanced at the door leading into the tree structure, the only other way to escape.

"I hope you don't try that," Aquinas said. "I already know you have poor judgment. I'd hate to find out that you're stupid as well."

"What now?" I asked.

"You sit. I get tea," she replied.

"Tea?"

"You do like tea, don't you?"

"Yeah," I said, "I guess. That's it?"

"What? Did you think I was going to have you marched out of here in chains and locked up in the dungeon?"

I shrugged. "Something like that."

"Sorry to disappoint you. But the good news is…" Aquinas turned her back on me and struck a match, tossing it into the fireplace. The logs whooshed into a high flame that threw the room into a dance of light and shadows. "Depending on how tea goes, that still might happen. Be right back."

I swallowed hard and awkwardly stood in the center of the room, not quite sure what to do with my hands.

"Oh, and Jack," Aquinas called from the other room. "Be a dear and don't touch anything else in there, all right?"

I looked at the bookshelves that surrounded me and shook my head. After what just happened, there was no way I was touching anything.

I backed up slowly and settled into the armchair. With my heart still beating hard in my chest, I waited for my cup of tea.

Chapter Seven

I sat down next to the fire, the crackle of the flames the only sound in the room. As the seconds ticked by, I found my gaze drawn to the ancient, intricately carved wood table in front of my armchair.

Each corner was carved with a grotesque face looking outward. The two nearest me seemed to be a vampire and some kind of demon—both with their mouths pulled back in a silent scream. Along the length of the table, carved into the flat panel of wood, were dozens of soldiers with swords and spears, locked in battle against dark shapes that swirled around them. I leaned in closer and saw that many of the men were not holding their weapons in their hands. Rather, the weapons stuck out from their bodies, swords pierced through chests, pikes stuck into thighs and necks. It was a gruesome scene of suffering and defeat.

I looked up when Aquinas walked back in carrying a tray with two cups and a small white teapot scuffed on the sides from ages of use.

She set the tea service down and poured out two cups of hot liquid. An intense mint flavor filled the air.

"This teapot is from El-Fishawi," Aquinas said. "Have you heard of it?"

I shook my head as I took the hot cup from her.

"It's a coffeehouse in old Cairo. Been around since before your war of independence in America. Right in the middle of the Khan el Khalili souk."

"What's a souk?" I asked, taking the cup from her.

Aquinas walked over and stoked the fire with a metal poker. "A souk is a market. Buyuk Carsi in Istanbul is the oldest, but Djemaa el-Fna in Morocco is also amazing. These places are of the ancient world. They have long been gathering places for our kind. For Regs, they can be filled with wonderful mysteries. For hunters, they are filled with information and people helpful to our cause."

"I have enough mysteries, thank you," I said. "Respectfully, I'd prefer to have some answers."

"And you thought breaking into an old woman's house was the best way to accomplish that?" Aquinas asked, sipping her tea.

"I do think the answers I seek are here," I said.

Aquinas waved a hand at the bookcases surrounding us. "And you thought you would just break in and grab a book. Maybe one that said, 'Answers to Jack's Questions'?"

I shifted uncomfortably in my chair. "It was better than just sitting around. Even if I didn't find anything, it was better than not trying."

Aquinas beamed. "That's the first sensible thing you've said all night. Are you going to try your tea? It's quite good."

I humored her and lifted the steaming cup to my lips. It was a strong mint flavor mixed with flowery notes I didn't recognize. As much as I didn't want to admit it, it was really tasty. I looked up and Aquinas smiled, knowing I was trying to hide how much I enjoyed it.

"Perhaps I was wrong to wait," Aquinas said. "You are every bit as impetuous as your father was." I felt a surge of pride to be compared to my father. Aquinas noticed and squinted her eyes at me. "You do know what impetuous means, don't you? Rash, prone to act without thinking it through…"

"I guess it's just in my blood," I said.

A dark sadness came over Aquinas, both on her face and in the way her shoulders drooped forward. "Yes," she agreed, "perhaps it is."

"So will you tell me? Will you explain where I came from? Eva told me only bits and pieces. She said I would learn the rest here. I'm ready."

Aquinas arched an eyebrow at me. "Ready? How could you possibly know if you're ready?"

116

I leaned in close and fixed my eyes on hers. "Try me," I said.

Aquinas nodded and closed her eyes as if reading a book only she could see. Then she started to speak:

"The war between Man and Monster is as old as Man himself. Since the days when humankind first descended from the trees and began to group together in tribes, the Creach have hunted them as prey. In the earliest of days, when Man only existed in small pockets of the world, we were of no special significance to the Creach. We were simply another animal on which they feasted. But over time humans rose to prominence and became, for better or for worse, the organizing force on the planet.

Even then, the Creach ignored the rise of Man and continued to hunt him for sport and for sustenance." She pointed to the rows of books around her. "As evidence, the earliest writings in literature the world over contain references to monsters. It's a wonder that the modern world is able to wash away these facts as mere coincidence, to avoid facing the truth. Think of it. Ancient writings from every continent describe demons who shift their shapes from man to wolf, tell of monsters who drink the blood of their victims, of corpses that rise from the dead, harpies and centaurs and trolls. All from humans who had no communication with one another for literally centuries after these accounts were written. And yet the modern world calls this simply a coincidence, a shared universal imagination. When the war comes, it will be looked

117

back upon as the greatest collective state of denial in the history of the world."

"When what war comes?" I asked.

Aquinas waved her hands in the air. "I'm getting ahead of myself. You want to know the whole story. More tea?"

I shook my head and waited for her to continue.

"Man turned out to be an organized and social creature. It wasn't long before the simple tribes and villages turned into towns and bustling cities. Pretty soon, we had become hopelessly entangled in all the trappings of modern civilization."

"You mean like laws?" I asked.

"Laws, yes; but also the ability to wage war," Aquinas said. "Whether living beside the Nile in Egypt, the Euphrates in Sumaria or the Yangzte in China, Man used his energies to create weapons, form armies and set out to conquer lands through force."

"What does that have to do with the Creach?" I asked, feeling like I was back in one of my classrooms at Sunnyvale Middle School. I guess the difference was that this history lesson promised to teach me things very few people knew about.

"While Man organized himself into complex and organized forms of society, the Creach did not. Instead, they preferred to stay alone or in small groups, unwilling to cede control to any centralized power.

"You see, they were too slow to realize the true nature of men and severely underestimated how quickly he would expand his footprint upon the Earth. He would never be content to share the world, his drive to dominate was more than simply a desire; it was his single organizing principle. Nothing would stand in his way and stop him from building greater cities, damming the rivers, cutting down the great forests and asserting dominion over all the creatures of the Earth. But beyond this insatiable desire to control the world, men also wanted to control one another. Soon, all of their energies turned to developing better weapons and waging larger wars.

"Once able to choose their human prey at will, the Creach found themselves relegated to the dark corners of a world made for and controlled by men. To appear in the open risked becoming the hunted instead of the hunter. Where once they controlled the world with fear, they were now made to live in shadows, by necessity becoming more myth than reality."

"Until someone organized them," I said.

"Not someone," Aquinas intoned. "Some*thing*. A dark power rose up in the form of a vampire, one you have already met, I think."

"Ren Lucre," I whispered, shivering at the sound of his name on my lips.

Aquinas nodded. "Yes. Ren Lucre. In the year 999, he was a French nobleman with a bold future ahead of him. A brilliant mind, he was well-educated and sophisticated, experienced in the courts of Europe which were a front row seat in the practical application of power. This was an age of turmoil and superstition in all of Europe, but especially in France.

Everyone, from the leaders of the churches to the peasants in the fields, feared that the year 1000 marked the end of the world. Chaos and violence raged as the date grew closer. Society broke down, threatening the aristocracy of which Ren Lucre was a part.

"Fearing for the lives of his family both from the End of Times and the hordes of peasants roving the countryside, Ren Lucre turned his intellect to the study of the dark powers, especially in anything to do with the secrets of immortality. With the turn of the millennium fast approaching, he discreetly put out word of an enormous reward for a live vampire specimen. He didn't have to wait long."

"People were able to capture one?" I asked.

"No, of course not. But, hearing of this strange lord's reward, a powerful vampire appeared at Ren Lucre's castle one day, curious as to what kind of man would seek out a vampire so aggressively. The old vampire had come with every intention of killing Ren Lucre; instead they sat and talked for three straight days. As is often the case with important moments in history, Fate played a role in what happened next. On the eve of the old vampire's visit, Ren Lucre's wife gave birth to their sixth child, a boy, finally after five daughters. But the child struggled and died in his father's arms hours after birth, breaking Ren Lucre's heart forever. As if this weren't enough, his wife was on the edge of death herself. It was under these conditions, wracked with grief for his son, his wife lying on her death bed and surrounded by a world headed to chaos, that Ren Lucre made the most horrific of decisions."

"To become a vampire," I said.

"Yes, but not only for himself. He knew he could never again survive the heartbreak of losing another child."

"He turned them all turn into vampires," I whispered.

"And gained immortality for the simple price of their souls. His wife and five daughters never had a choice in the matter."

"And what of the old vampire, the one who turned them into vampires in the first place?"

"His name remains unknown and there is no further reference to him in the written or oral histories of the time. We assumed he was killed, perhaps by Ren Lucre himself during his rise to power. Perhaps by the first members of the Black Guard: your ancestors."

I felt a stir of excitement at the words. It seemed too distant and incredible to be true, but Aquinas said the words with such certainty that I suddenly felt that they must be. "Tell me about them. The first Black Guard."

Aquinas looked at a clock on the wall and glanced outside at the lightening sky. "It will be morning soon and you have a full day of training ahead of you. Why don't you come back tonight and we will continue?"

I started to object but Aquinas was already on her feet and walking away from me. I got the sense that this wasn't a subject up for discussion. "Thanks," I called after her. "Thank you for taking the time."

She turned to the side so that her face was in profile. She gave me a little nod, then kept walking. I turned to leave.

"Oh Jack," she called out. "You can use the stairs next time. It's a bit easier that way."

I smiled. "Will do. Goodnight."

I left through the front door and walked down the wide staircase that zigzagged back down to the ground level. The Academy was stirring. I saw steam and smoke coming from the kitchens where the Ratlings were preparing the day's breakfast. I stretched and considered going back to my bunk to catch the last few minutes of sleep but decided against it. My head was too full of images from the story Aquinas had told me. I was desperate to know the next part of the tale but knew I needed to get through the day first.

I walked up to the battlement wall and walked up the rough cut steps to the sentry positions on the top. From here, I had a great view of the forest, where wisps of fog drifted lazily among the pines. Somewhere far down the valley, a lone wolf howled. I wondered if it was Tiberon. So many mysteries surrounded this place that I wondered if I would ever get to the bottom of them.

The breakfast bell rang behind me and I turned to see the young hunters come out of the dorms to start another day of training. I looked back out to the forest and wondered if we were really any kind of match for the enemy we were training to fight. I hoped we would never have to find out. But in my heart, I knew this was a false hope. The war was coming, just as Aquinas had said. That much was certain. The war was definitely coming. Somehow, I could feel it in my blood.

"Hey, why didn't you wake me up?" Will complained to me the second he saw me in the breakfast line.

I thanked the young Ratling who scooped a heaping mound of eggs on my plate and drew Will away from the other hunters who stood there. "Not so loud," I murmured.

"Did you go without me?" Will demanded. "You did, didn't you? Why would you do that?"

"Because you were right yesterday when you said this was the perfect place for you," I said. "The last thing I wanted to do was have you get caught and get you kicked out."

The image of being sent packing out through the Academy front gate was enough to settle Will down. We found our table and hunched close together over our breakfast. "So, did you find out anything?"

"More than you could imagine." I told him everything from the night before, going over every detail. I wanted to share it with him but I also wanted to say it all out loud so I didn't forget anything. The entire night had the fuzzy feeling of a dream and I didn't want it to start to fade away in the morning sun.

When I finished, Will was awestruck. "So, you're going back tonight?"

"Absolutely," I said. "I mean, she's obviously using this as a way to keep me in line, but this is the reason I came here."

"The reason *we* came here," Will corrected me. "Let's get one thing straight— I'm here to help you find your dad. Yeah, I like it here, but if it comes down to it, I'm with you."

"Uh oh," said a voice behind us. "This sounds serious."

We both spun around and saw Eva standing there.

"How do you do that? You're so sneaky," said Will.

"If you had paid attention in my class yesterday, you would have learned how," Eva said.

"Are you allowed to be over here? I thought instructors don't mingle with us little guys," I said, coming across colder than I intended.

Eva nodded at our empty table. "Speaking of mingling, I can see you're doing a great job making new friends."

"I'm not here to make friends," I said.

Eva stared me down, not liking my tone. "Then I guess you don't need my help, because you're doing great."

"Eva!" Daniel called from the instructor's table.

I looked away. "Speaking of friends, you have great taste in them, by the way."

"Yeah, well, I thought I did," Eva said, looking more angry than hurt.

Will looked back and forth between us like he was watching his parents fight. "Whoa, c'mon guys. What's going on here? Will the two of you stop acting like a couple of babies? What is this?"

"No, it's OK," said Eva. "Jack's right. Instructors aren't supposed to socialize with newbie hunters who don't know a damn thing about hunting. By the way, great job yesterday, Will. The other instructors said you really stood out."

"Really?" Will asked, beaming.

"Yeah, you're obviously here to learn and get better. I wish I could say the same about the both of you." Eva walked away.

When Will turned back to me, he tried to stifle his smile that had been pasted to his face since receiving Eva's compliment. "Why were you so mean to her?" he asked. "She was trying to be cool by coming over here."

I felt a little pang of guilt but it quickly went away when I glanced over and saw Daniel drape his arm around her as she sat down at the instructor's table.

"Oh, I get it," Will said. "Holy crap. You're jealous."

"I don't know what you're talking about. Jealous of what?" I asked.

But Will just grinned. He had just solved a major puzzle. He stood up with his now empty plate. "If you want to play it cool, that's fine with me," he said. "But I've known you since before we could ride bikes. You can't pull one over on me."

"I really don't know what you're talking about," I said. Unconsciously, I glanced over at Eva and Daniel. I really did hate seeing them together. Will stuck his hand in front of my face, cutting off my line of sight.

"Then you won't mind if I do this," Will said. "Or maybe go over and tell Eva you're sorry for being a jerk and that...ouch!"

Will rubbed his shoulder where I had just punched him.

"All right, enough," I said. "Come on, let's get a move on. The class bell is going to ring any second."

Just as I said that, the bell rang and the hunters all around us sprang to the their feet. They ran toward the practice field, leaving their mess behind for the Ratlings to clean up. Will and I took our plates to the counter, scraped off the leftovers and placed them in the dirty dishes bin.

A young, rather big-bellied Ratling looked at us wide-eyed, uncertain what to make of two hunters going out of their way to help. T-Rex walked up.

"Thanks guys," he said. "Hunters sure are a messy bunch, aren't they, Simon?"

The big-bellied Ratling named Simon looked horrified that T-Rex would say something bad about the hunters. He grabbed the plates and scurried away.

"A little skittish, isn't he?" Will asked.

126

"He's alright," T-Rex said. "They're all scared of the hunters. I keep trying to tell them they shouldn't be. I mean, we're just as important as you guys. Without us, this place would grind to a halt. Let's see what happens if we stop cooking for a couple of days."

"You tell them, T-Rex," I said.

"Come on," said Will. "We've got to get into formation."

We said good-bye to T-Rex, jogged to the field and got in line.

That night, I was halfway up the front steps of the Templar Tree when Aquinas appeared on the balcony and walked down toward me.

"Come," she said as she passed by me, "I think you should see something."

We circled back around the tree and then walked along the base of the outer wall. I wouldn't say Aquinas was sneaking around, but she was certainly choosing pathways that minimized the number of eyes that might notice our little midnight stroll. We reached the point where the wall met up with the granite mountain and turned to follow the second, more ancient wall of the Citadel that ran the length of the massive cave that loomed over us.

I squinted up into the night and saw dark, black shapes flying in and out of the caves. Bats. Thousands of them. A chill passed through my body. When I looked down, Aquinas was staring at me.

"Sorry, the last bat I met tried to kill me...a whole bunch of times," I said.

Aquinas moved on and I had to jog to catch up to her.

Soon, we reached the arched gate at the center of the Citadel wall. I had only seen it from a distance since I'd been at the Academy and had thought it was a just a small opening. But now, standing in front of it, I saw it was much larger than I had thought. It was tall enough to admit men on horseback, even if they were riding four or five side-by-side.

A massive iron gate hung suspended above it with nasty-looking teeth along the bottom that would sink into holes in the ground below. The heavy gate was poised, ready to drop down when needed to close off the mountain stronghold from the outside world. I cringed at the idea of walking under it, like passing under the blade of a guillotine or in front of a loaded gun. All I could think about was how incredibly fast and effective it could squash anyone or anything unfortunate enough to be under it when it came crashing down.

Aquinas noticed me pause before walking under it.

"The gate weighs nearly two tons. It's never been breached in a battle," Aquinas said.

"I'm not so worried about it being breached," I replied. "I'm more worried about it dropping down and cutting me in half."

"That's good. A hunter ought always be aware of the dangers around him," Aquinas said. "Not to worry, though. The gate's suspended by thick chains.

It takes two people to operate the mechanism to lower it. Come along," Aquinas said.

We passed through the thick walls of the Citadel and entered the cave. I noticed the chains holding up the gate and the complex pulley system for opening and lowering it. The chains were covered with dust and cobwebs as if they hadn't been moved in years. I turned and looked around the cave as my eyes adjusted to the dark.

Looming directly in front of us was a battlement with dozens of narrow slits in the rock face where archers could fire directly at an enemy that had breached the main gate. Now they were cold, dark eyes that seemed to follow us as we walked deeper into the cave.

"Almost there," Aquinas called out.

Before us, a heavy metal door rose up out of the darkness. It was studded with sharp points and a heavy chain crisscrossed in front of it with eight or nine padlocks attached in various places. Whatever was behind the door, the hunters didn't want anyone to get in. Or, I considered, they didn't want something getting out.

"What's that?" I asked.

Aquinas glanced at the door quickly, as if not wanting her eyes to linger there too long. "That's nothing for you to concern yourself with."

"I keep hearing other students talk about this. Is something locked up inside?"

Aquinas turned and I felt her eyes bore into me. "It is a relic of the past and has no place in our world today. It is forbidden. Some things are best left in darkness, my boy. Just you remember that."

Then it occurred to me what I was looking at. "That's the entry to the Cave of Trials, isn't it? Why is everyone so scared of it?"

"Because they have every reason to be," Aquinas said. "No hunter has ever returned alive. In the old days, many good hunters, driven by the promise of great glory, made the attempt. But they all failed. That foolishness ended over a hundred years ago with the last attempt."

"What's behind the door?"

"Death," she whispered. "Now, before we go on, before we enter the room where so many of your questions can be answered, I have a proposal for you. A bargain, if you will."

"I don't like the sound of this," I said.

"We both possess things the other wants. You want answers. I want you to stay at the Academy and complete your training before the final battle is upon us. I'm willing to bargain one for the other. If you stay, I will give you what answers I can."

"How long are we talking about?" I asked.

"Until you become a first level monster hunter."

"But Eva says that can take six months, if not longer," I complained.

"And in return, I will explain to you the history of the Black Guard and your ancestors, the Knights Templar."

"Will you tell me where my father is being kept?"

"I will answer all your questions to the best of my ability," Aquinas said.

"And my mother. What do you know about her?" I asked.

"Ah, your mother. Eva told me that she came to you in a dream," Aquinas said.

"It wasn't a dream," I replied. I thought back to when I had seen the vision of my mother. It was after I'd drowned in the river and before T-Rex found me and performed CPR. "I think I was dead," I stated.

"Hmm..." Aquinas said. "Most unusual."

"Yeah, for me anyway," I said. "She asked me to forgive her but she wouldn't say what I was supposed to forgive her for. Do you know what she meant by that?"

Aquinas stared at me, her face completely unreadable. She could have known everything about my mother or nothing at all. It was impossible to tell.

After a few moments of silence she said, "In time I will answer all your questions to the best of my ability. But only in exchange for your solemn oath that you will continue your training here until you become a full hunter." Aquinas leaned in toward me, her eyes narrow and intense. "Think on it carefully, boy. Do not enter an oath with me lightly. It is unbreakable and cannot be reversed."

Aquinas held out her hand. I hesitated. Six months. Maybe longer. I hadn't planned on being here for more than a couple of weeks. Just long enough to find out where my father was being held, or at least a clue to send me in the right direction.

Still, the prospect of having all my questions answered was exciting. Maybe it was worth the time. Besides, Eva was probably right. I could stand to learn something from the classes and the fighting drills. Slowly, I reached out and shook her hand.

As I did, a spark passed between us like a massive discharge of static electricity. I flinched, but Aquinas didn't move. She grasped my hand and looked into my eyes. "The oath is made," she said.

I nodded my head.

"Good, now that wasn't so bad, was it? Now come along." She spun away from me and walked toward a solid, rock wall of the cave, and, without breaking stride, disappeared straight into the mountain. Or at least she seemed to. With one last look at the door, I walked to the spot where she had disappeared and saw a layer of thick brown vines covering a fold in the rock. I would have missed it completely except for a glow of light that barely penetrated through to the far side. With one last look at the forbidden door, I pushed my way through the vines.

I found myself in a narrow passageway, rough cut and hewn out of the solid rock of the mountain. A burning torch disappeared down the shaft ahead of me.

"Come along," echoed Aquinas's voice. "We don't have all night."

I hustled to keep up. When I reached her, she was unlocking a heavy wooden door studded with metal. Cobwebs and dust covered the door.

Wherever she was taking me, it didn't look like anyone had been there for a while.

Still, the door swung open soundlessly on smooth hinges. I followed Aquinas into another passageway, this one even narrower and with a low ceiling that made us both stoop over. Above us, I noticed the ceiling of the passageway glittered in the flame of the burning torch. I reached up and touched the surface and my hand came back covered in gold dust.

"Is this—"

"Pyrite," Aquinas said. "Fool's Gold. It has its uses. But certainly, a band of solid gold would have been preferable. OK, we're here."

The flame fluttered as we entered what felt like a much larger space. I say 'felt' because the small torch was no match for the intense darkness that surrounded us.

"What is this place?" I asked, my voice echoing through the dark chamber.

Aquinas held the torch up close to the nearest wall. Carved directly into the solid rock face was a beautiful image of an ancient walled city, surrounded by a siege army of medieval soldiers.

"This is our history," Aquinas intoned. "Different from what they taught you in school, I'm sure."

"The city is Jerusalem and this is the Crusades, isn't it?" I asked. "Eva had told me—"

"Eva told you what?" Aquinas snapped.

"Not much," I said carefully, curious about her reaction. "Just that my name, Templar, has something to do with the Knights Templar. From the Crusades."

"Yes, of course," said Aquinas. "And what do you know about the Crusades?"

"I—I—not much, to tell you the truth," I said.

Aquinas shook her head. "Technology has made intelligence more accessible than ever and yet the outside world just gets more forgetful. The ultimate result of forgetfulness is ignorance. And that is the most dangerous weapon of all."

She handed me the torch and indicated toward the wall. I explored the carving as she spoke. "There were many Crusades through history. All were efforts from the devout Christians of Europe to battle against what they perceived to be the threat of the growing Islamic power of the East. The centerpiece was the liberation of Jerusalem and the Holy Lands. Unfortunately, these lands were holy for both sides, ensuring that the fight would continue for centuries and, well, they continue to this day."

I walked further along the wall and the scene changed from a siege to a massive battle scene. Thousands of men were depicted in the carving, many of them lying dead in gruesome piles of mutilated bodies.

"But in 1099, the First Crusade saw the successful recapture of Jerusalem with great loss of life on both sides. Although they held the city, the lands around the city were lawless. Pilgrims traveling from Europe regularly found themselves attacked; sometimes hundreds of them were slaughtered at the hands of these bandits.

"Twenty years after the capture of the city, a French knight named Hughes de Payens was granted permission to set up a small protective order in Jerusalem to watch over the pilgrims. He and eight other knights set up camp on an ancient site called the Temple Mount, inside the Al-Aqsa mosque, which was believed to be above the old Temple of Solomon from biblical times. De Payens decreed a vow of poverty for his knights. For his insignia he chose the image of two knights sharing one horse. He called his order the Poor Knights of Christ and the Temple of Solomon. But soon they became known simply as the Templars."

"But how does any of this relate to the Black Guard?" I asked.

"Everything I've told you is in the history books," Aquinas replied. "What isn't there is the real reason why de Payens started the Templars. Yes, it was to protect the pilgrims, but not from bandits. It was the Creach. Commanded by an aggressive new leader, Ren Lucre. Under his leadership, monsters were attacking in broad daylight. This was not for sport. Nor was it for food. This was something different. It was as if a war had been declared by monsters against Man himself."

I moved my torch further down the wall and the carvings of grotesque monsters feasting on helpless pilgrims covered the wall.

Aquinas's voice came out of the dark behind me. "De Payens knew of Ren Lucre. He and his men did battle on a small scale against the Creach back in

France, but this new war with the monsters was to be on an unprecedented scale."

"But there were only nine of them," I said. "How could they make a difference?"

"Ah, but it's the power of the cause that builds an army, not the number of soldiers," Aquinas said. "While the Templars did indeed protect pilgrims from bandits and fight in the wars against the armies of men who tried to recapture Jerusalem, their true mission was carried out in secret by a group within the Order."

"The Black Guard," I said.

"Precisely," said Aquinas. "Led by de Payens himself, the Black Guard was committed to the defense of mankind against the rising power of the monsters. The history books call it one of the great mysteries of the medieval world, that, within only a few years of forming, the Templars had integrated themselves as a leading financial and political power in the world, rivaling kings and leaders of the Church. You can Goggle it on the Interwebs; it's all there I'm sure."

"I can what?" I asked, taken back.

"Isn't that what it's called?" Aquinas asked. "Goggling?"

I chuckled. "Oh, you mean Google. You mean Google on the Internet."

"I'll never get a handle on the modern world," Aquinas mumbled. "In any case, what you won't find on Google," she paused, waiting for me to acknowledge that she had it right, "is that once word of the Templar's true mission reached the secret corridors of power in Europe, money and men flowed into the young order."

"But I thought they were called the Poor Knights, and took a vow of poverty."

"They did, so men joining to fight would hand over their wealth to the Order. But what really gave the Black Guard within the Templars their power was what they discovered in the ruins of King Solomon's Temple."

The next carving showed brilliant streaks of energy, like beams of light exploding from underneath the Temple Mount.

"What was it?" I asked.

"The answer to defeating the Creach. A weapon so powerful that the ancients had buried it safely away, not entrusting it to either Man or Monster. The Jerusalem Stones."

"Ren Lucre mentioned the stones to me when I faced him," I said excitedly.

Aquinas appeared out of the darkness, suddenly very close to me. "What did he say about them, exactly?"

"He...he...it was like he was mocking me. Once when I was tied up as his prisoner, he laughed and said there wasn't a Jerusalem Stone in sight. And the other...it was during my battle with him..."

"Yes...yes..." Aquinas pressed in closer to me.

"Just that he would defeat me; even if I had the Jerusalem Stones, I was no match for him."

"He said that? Those exact words?" Aquinas demanded. "It's important, boy."

"Yes!" I exclaimed. "Just like I said."

Aquinas took a step back, her face furrowed with worry. She mumbled to herself. "A ruse? A simple boast? Or something more? Not good. Not good at all. I must find out for sure."

"Are you all right?" I asked.

Aquinas seemed to snap out of her thoughts, as if just remembering I was there. "Yes, of course. I'm sorry. The fate of all of us rides on this one thing. We mustn't get it wrong, you see. We can't afford to get it wrong. No, not this time."

I swung the torch back around to the next carving. An army of Templars rode through a sea of werewolves, trolls, ogres, demons and every other type of monster I had encountered. Beams of light shot out from the sword of the man in the lead position. "But it looks like we defeated the Creach."

"Won the battle, but immortal beings can afford to take a longer view. Ren Lucre retreated and reorganized. Much as he is doing at this very moment."

"So, I didn't really kill him," I whispered.

Aquinas studied me. "No, but I think you already knew that, didn't you?"

I nodded. Since that night, I had felt Ren Lucre's presence. He was out there and I knew we were somehow destined to meet again.

"No, he allowed the Templars to grow in strength and number, knowing it was only a matter of time before the Order's success made enemies out of the wrong people. It finally happened on October 13, 1307; King Phillip of France, under the sway of a curious advisor who never seemed to age, had hundreds of Templars arrested, including the last Grand Master—Jacques de Molay, your ancestor and the man who you are named after."

"What happened to him?" I asked.

"See for yourself," Aquinas said.

I waved the torch down the wall and saw a life-sized rendering of my namesake. He was old and bearded but had the regal bearing of a man accustomed to giving orders and having them followed. His hands were tied in front of him. Ropes wrapped around his torso and tied him to a thick wooden stake. Below him, flames engulfed a woodpile. He was burned alive.

"It was a dark day in our history," Aquinas said. "And perhaps on some unconscious level, the rest of the world knew it too. I told you he was killed on the 13th of October. That was a Friday. Have you ever heard of Friday the 13th being a bad omen?"

"Of course," I said.

"This is where that belief originated. Even the Reg world knew something terrible had happened. Seven centuries later and they still take pause on Friday the 13th even if they don't know the real reason why."

"And what of the Jerusalem Stones?" I asked.

"Good. Very good. That's exactly the right question. What about the Jerusalem Stones? It's clear Ren Lucre was the strange advisor who had the ear of King Phillip. Phillip, in turn, controlled the Pope at the time, a weak fool who disbanded the Order on threats of invasion from Phillip. Certainly, Phillip expected to acquire the Stones and use them for his own purposes. But he was never able to move forward with his ambitions."

"So he didn't get the Stones," I said.

"No, but neither did anyone else," Aquinas said. "After his death, they disappeared from history. They are our best chance in the upcoming fight against the rising army Ren Lucre is mustering. The Jerusalem Stones must be found if we are to stop him."

I looked back up at the face of my ancestor, Jacques de Molay. Even with the fire consuming the lower half of his body, he stood there bravely, a slight smirk on his face as if in some twisted way he thought he had pulled one over on his enemies. "Did he hide them? Keep them safe from falling into the wrong hands?"

"We can only hope," Aquinas said. "But it was long ago prophesied that a direct descendent of Jacques de Molay would be the one to find the Stones and restore them to the Black Guard."

"Wait, you're talking about me, aren't you? You want me to find the Jerusalem Stones," I said.

"It doesn't matter what I want," Aquinas said. "If I had my way, you would be back in your small American town living a normal life. But it is what the world needs. If the world of Man is to survive, we must have the Jerusalem Stones to fight against the evil army Ren Lucre has created."

"Aren't there others? More descendants of..."

"There is only one other. And he lies in Ren Lucre's dungeon. Yes, your father was searching for the Jerusalem Stones when he was captured. He believed he knew where they were and he knew how important they were. He risked everything."

"But...what about..."

Aquinas put a hand on my shoulder. "There are no others. You, my dear boy, are the last true Templar. This is why you must prepare. This is why you must train. Because, if you fail, the entire world may be lost."

Chapter Eight

I carefully slid back into my bed in the dorm, all too aware of the light creeping up in the eastern sky. Another night without sleep. Not only that, but a night where the weight of the world was placed squarely on my shoulders. I wondered if I would ever get a good night's sleep again.

Within minutes, the breakfast bell shattered the quiet of the morning and the young hunters all around me leapt out of bed.

Will appeared at my bedside. His eager expression quickly changed to concern. "Oh man, you don't look so good. Are you OK?"

Was I OK? The leader of the last monster hunting society on Earth just told me the fate of the world depended on whether I could find a weapon that had been missing for over seven hundred years.

Even better, there were no clues as to where it was or what it looked like. I was doing great.

"Yeah," I said, rolling my exhausted body out of bed. "Come on, I'll tell you all about it at breakfast."

As we walked out with the others to the breakfast area, pulling our cloaks tightly around us to ward off the freezing temperatures and softly falling snow, I spotted Eva standing to the side of the group. I remembered how uncool I had been to her the day before. With a deep breath, I walked over to her.

"Hey," I said lamely.

"Hey yourself," Eva said.

"Cold one today, huh?"

Eva looked at me. "Did you really just ask me about the weather?"

"Well, it's better than talking about what a jerk I was to you yesterday. Better than apologizing. And way better than asking you to forgive me."

"Wait," Eva said. "I missed that first part. Can you say it again?"

"You mean the part about what a jerk I was? Or about the weather?"

Eva didn't crack a smile. If anything, she looked angrier.

"Look, I am really sorry. You've been nothing but cool to me and I...I..."

"Was a total jerk?" Eva added helpfully.

"I think we already established that," I said. "I haven't adjusted well to being here. It's my fault. I just wasn't ready for, you know, all this."

I noticed her shoulders relax a little, which I took as a good sign. Or as a sign she was about to punch me. I couldn't be sure.

"I've been talking to Aquinas. I gave her my oath that I would stay here until I was at least a first degree hunter."

This got Eva's attention. "Really?"

"Really," I said. "You were right; I have a lot to learn by being here. So I'm going to give it my best. It'd be a lot easier if you weren't so mad at me."

Eva finally cracked a smile and gave me a nudge. I grinned.

"OK, you're off the hook," Eva said. "But forgiving people isn't my strong suit, so don't make me have to do it again."

"You got it," I said.

"Now get out of here," Eva said. "I don't want anyone seeing me talk to a newbie hunter, especially one who can't seem to stay in his own bed at night."

"Wait, so you knew about that?"

"I teach a class on tracking and camouflage. Maybe you should pay attention," she said. "Now go get some breakfast and try not to fall asleep in your scrambled eggs." She strolled toward the instructor table and I rejoined Will, who had picked up our plates of steaming food.

"What was that all about?" Will asked.

"Just giving a weather report," I said. Will looked confused but I didn't have the energy to explain. Besides, there were more important things I needed to tell him. "You're not going to believe the night I had," I said. I went through and told him everything.

When I was done, Will looked at me strangely. "What?" I asked.

"Dude, does this mean you're like a knight or something?" he asked. I quickly realized he was just having fun with me. "Do I need to call you Sir Jack?"

"I think that would be best," I said with a straight face. "Maybe bow down when I walk into the room. You know, just for appearances."

"And you should have a more knightly name."

"You're right. How about Jack the Brave?"

"More like Sir Farts-a-lot," said Will. I busted out laughing, unable to keep up the game. "Well, it fits you, doesn't it?"

The bell rang for classes to start. We carried our plates over to the Ratlings to save them the trouble of cleaning up after us. I noticed that one or two other hunters did the same this time. Bacho and T-Rex beamed from behind the tables when they saw this. He whispered to us as we passed, "If this keeps up, we'll 'ave the hunters doin' the dishes and the tidyin' up too."

Will and I jogged to our groups already assembled in the frozen training fields and began the day's classes. I glanced up at the Templar Tree and saw Aquinas standing on the balcony watching over us all. I fought down the urge to wave and simply acknowledged her with a nod of the head. As soon as I did, she turned and shuffled back into the house.

The rest of the morning was fairly uneventful. I felt better having patched things up a bit with both

Eva and Will, and I felt that, with the conversations with Aquinas, I was at least making progress toward understanding what my next steps might be. But as the morning wore on, the good feelings drifted away along with the morning mist on the practice field. The more I thought about it, the more worried I became that I was heading down a blind corner.

Finding the Jerusalem Stones, which were last seen over seven hundred years ago, and searched for by the Black Guard over those same centuries, seemed like a dead-end. I had a million more questions for Aquinas, especially about my father and how he had been captured, but she refused to tell me anything more, promising a complete explanation the next time we met.

As tired as I was, I couldn't wait until the evening when my lesson about the Black Guard could continue. Little could I have known then that it would be over a week until the next time I saw Master Aquinas, and under circumstances that still make me shudder to this day.

It was a good thing that the classes were fast-paced and coupled with aggressive physical challenges. This hardly gave me time to brood on my questions; instead, it forced me to pay attention. Besides the classes, Xavier attached himself to my side and spent the morning peppering me with questions at every turn about the wolves in the forest and about Tiberon in particular.

"How did they coordinate the attack?"

"Were they the same size, or were there young wolves in the pack?"

"Did Tiberon understand when you spoke to him? Or was it just body language?"

"Did any of them have armor on?"

I stopped him there. "Armor? Why would a wolf have armor on?"

Xavier stabbed the air with his finger. "Exactly my point."

Another hunter turned and hushed Xavier. The instructor paused and eyed us until we turned our attention to him. Under his breath, Xavier whispered, "As if this guy's lesson on harpy attack patterns is more important than understanding the wolves right outside our gates."

"Right, that's it," the instructor shouted at the two of us. "Two laps around the perimeter, the both of you."

We got to our feet, stamping off the snow from our boots and started our run. My cloaking medallion that Hester had given me rubbed oddly against my skin so I pulled it out to adjust its position. As I did, Xavier caught a glimpse of it.

"Is that what I think it is?" Xavier asked.

"That's kind of a tough question to answer," I said. "It sort of depends on what you think it is."

"A cloaking medallion. I'd heard that there was one in the Academy once, but that the hunter who owned it was out on assignment," Xavier said.

"Her name was Hester. She died helping me escape Ren Lucre," I said, fingering the intricate lines on the circle of metal. "I think this medallion has saved my life more than once."

"I'm sorry," Xavier said. We jogged along silently for a few moments but Xavier finally couldn't contain himself. "They're really rare, you know. Do you think I could see it?" he asked.

"I don't think it's a good idea for me to take it off," I said. "The most powerful Creach would be able to sense me." I shuddered remembering how it had felt when I had used my mind to go out looking for the Creach Lords. Their more powerful minds has smashed into mine and had almost destroyed me.

"Of course," Xavier said, embarrassed. "I was just thinking that if I could understand how it worked, I could replicate it. Just imagine if all the hunters had cloaking devices."

"It doesn't make you really invisible," I said. "It just shields you from a Creach sensing your presence. They can still hear you, see you and smell you. All the regular stuff."

"I know. I know," Xavier said, hardly able to contain himself. "But that would still make an enormous difference. If I could figure out how to do that, then I would have made a huge difference. When we have more time, can I examine it? With you wearing it still, of course."

"If you think it might help, then sure," I said. "But isn't it some kind of magic or something?"

"Bah, there is no such thing as magic," Xavier said. "Where science shines a light, the shadows of superstition shrink away. My Dad told me that."

We jogged around a group of hunters running around the perimeter of the wall in the opposite direction then joined back up.

"Sounds like a smart man," I said. "Just let me know when and I'm all yours."

"That's great," Xavier said. "Really great."

"I've appreciated your questions about Tiberon and the wolves too. You really seem like you want to understand them. Most people here only want to know how to kill them," I said.

"Look at me. With my size, I'm never going to have the strength to be a hunter like Daniel. Or like you. So I have to use this," he tapped his head. "Information is more important than anything. Without it, you can't make good decisions, you can't create strategy. Well, you can, but they will just likely be the wrong decisions and the wrong strategy."

"Like believing Tiberon is evil," I said.

"Exactly. Bad information leads to bad decisions leads to bad results. Can we slow down a little?" Xavier said, wheezing a little.

I pulled up and fell into a slower pace. "Asthma?" I asked.

"It's not bad. Don't tell anyone, OK?" Xavier said. "They'd make me a Ratling for sure then."

"Would that be so bad?" I asked, thinking of how happy T-Rex was in the role.

"No one becomes a Ratling on purpose," Xavier said. "Could be injury, a failure at the trials. Sometimes kids just can't hack it after they learn about all the scary things out there. They'd prefer to make oatmeal than chase zombies. Not me, though. I'll do anything to become a hunter."

On the far side of the training grounds, I saw Aquinas climb onto a horse, surrounded by three

149

armed hunters also on horseback. As a group, they trotted to the main gate that opened as they neared.

"Come on," I said, breaking into a hard run toward the horses. "Hey!" I called. "Master Aquinas. Where are you going?"

But she was either too far away to hear or she was ignoring me. As the horses reached the gates, all four riders broke into a gallop down the road and away from the Academy.

I ran all the way to the gate and went to the hunters standing guard there. I recognized Midge from the night when I had snuck into the Templar Tree.

"Where is she going?"

"An' 'ow am I s'pposed to know?" Midge asked. "An' if I knew, what's to say I'd tell you?"

"Do you know how long she'll be gone?" I asked.

"No idea. She comes. She goes. I'm not 'er keeper, now am I?" Midge said. I heard Xavier run up behind me. "Aint you two s'pposed to be on a run or somethin'?"

I heard Xavier's wheezing behind me. The sprint had made it much worse.

"Sounds like you needs the run, Xavier," Midge said. "You're not gonna pass out, are ya?"

I guided Xavier quickly away from the gate so Midge wouldn't realize the young hunter was more than just tired. Even though I wanted to pepper Xavier with questions about Aquinas leaving, I knew I had to get his breathing under control first. "No more talking. We need to get your air back before we rejoin the group." Xavier nodded and we plodded along in silence, our boots kicking through the thick snow on the ground.

As we neared the group, Xavier's wheezing was still loud and hoarse. "Just tell the instructor I went to the bathroom, OK?" Xavier asked between labored breaths. "You won't tell anyone about this, right?"

"Of course not. You can trust me."

Xavier nodded and turned to the building where the nearest bathrooms were located. I returned to the group and made his excuse for him. Ten minutes later, he returned, his breathing back to normal. "Thanks," he whispered.

I nodded, impressed by the little guy's backbone. I looked at the rest of the group. All young faces, not one over the age of sixteen, and hardly any real experience fighting monsters between them. A sinking pit formed in my stomach as it dawned on me that, if Aquinas was right, the lives of everyone here were in my hands.

"All right, losers, listen up!"

I groaned. It was the last voice in the world I wanted to hear right now. Daniel.

He walked in front of our group and our instructor stepped aside deferentially.

"I'm here to announce that we will have a trial tomorrow. There are no degree requirements so anyone can participate. Good luck to all of you," Daniel said.

"Do you know where Master Aquinas has gone? Or when she'll be back?" I shouted out.

Daniel smiled as he spotted me in the group. "Sure, Smith. She's out on business and she'll be back when she returns. You'll be happy to know she conferred leadership of the Academy to me in her absence. So for now, I'm in charge."

"I'm sure we'll all sleep better knowing that," I said.

The rest of the group was silent as Daniel and I faced one another. "Are you putting your name in for the trial, Smith?" Daniel asked. "It'd be one way to put all these rumors to rest. One way or the other."

"The name's Templar. And you can bet on it."

Daniel grinned. "Good luck to you, then."

I watched as Daniel stomped over to the next group to make the same announcement. As soon as he was out of earshot, I turned to Xavier. "So...what did I just agree to?"

The lunch bell rang. "Come on, I'll explain over lunch."

"A trial is a one-on-one competition between a student and an instructor," Xavier explained through a mouthful of food. Will perked up at this bit of information. "If you can defeat an instructor, you will graduate as a second degree hunter."

"It's like testing up a grade at school," Will said.

"Only this is a lot more painful," Xavier said. "Not to mention that's it's kind of impossible."

"Why's that?" I asked.

"They're instructors. Third degree and above. No novice has even come close to winning," Xavier explained.

"Then what's the point?" I asked.

"It's fun. I mean, fun to watch anyway. Sometimes it's just one-on-one combat, but other times the instructors create interesting contests. A few months ago, they put a marker on top of the mountain behind us and the contest was who could get to it first. No ropes."

"And the instructor won?" I asked.

"By like an hour. Like I said, not even close. It's not like these are fights to the death. Worse that happens is a bloody nose, maybe a broken bone or two. Even if you lose, it's considered an honor for the challenger."

"Takes courage," Will said.

"Or just a high pain tolerance," Xavier said. He pointed across the field. "Here it comes."

I looked over to see Daniel carrying a leather pouch. Behind him, Midge and Darter carried a handful of spears. Everyone in the lunch area stopped and watched as Daniel strode to the front and held out the pouch.

"We will have a trial tomorrow. If you possess the courage to try your hand, put your name in the pouch. Placing another's name in the pouch is the highest dishonor and will result in being removed from camp. Am I clear?"

Heads nodded among the group. Behind Daniel, Midge and Darter stabbed five spears into the ground at an angle so that they crossed together near the top, forming a natural bowl.

"Good; finish your lunch. This afternoon we train hard."

The lunch area erupted in excited babble as Daniel left.

I turned to Xavier. "Have you ever put your name in?" I asked.

"Are you nuts?" Xavier laughed. "I told you, I'm more of an intellectual. I'll leave the brute fighting to others."

"I'll do it," Will said. He looked me in the eye. "I'm going to do it."

"Easy tiger," I said. "It's not going to do you any good to walk around with a broken arm or leg."

Will turned to Xavier. "Which one will I go up against? Which instructor?"

"That's the thing, you won't know until you're chosen," Xavier explained. "But you should go into it thinking it's going to be whoever would be the worst person for you to face. Because once you're chosen, there's no going back."

"What does that mean?" I asked.

"It means what it means. You don't get to look all brave by putting your name in, only to back out if you're selected. If you do, you become a Ratling or you're kicked out of the Academy."

"I'm doing it," Will repeated.

"Come on, Will," I said. "We just got here. Better to sit this one out to see how it goes. Get the lay of the land."

"But it's a chance to stand out," Will said.

"It's a chance to get seriously hurt," I said. "We have more important things to think about. More important things to prepare for."

"But—"

"There's no time for games. This isn't about you."

"No, it's about you, right?" Will muttered. "Like always."

"Will, come on," I said.

"No, it's fine." He let out a heavy breath and nodded. "You're right. I get it. It was a stupid idea anyway. Hey, I've got to get to class. I'll see you guys later."

He stood up and left. I knew he was frustrated but it was the right decision. If he were seriously hurt, it would set back his training by weeks. Better to leave the games to others.

Seconds later, a massive cheer rose from the tables around us. We spun around and looked at the pouch held up by the spears. Will was there, a piece of paper in hand, grinning at the assembled hunters. He reached in, opened the pouch and slid his piece of paper inside.

The crowd erupted with excitement. Will pumped his fist in the air, causing an even louder uproar.

"Didn't he say it was a stupid idea?" Xavier asked.

I shook my head. "That's never stopped him before."

The bell rang and the hunters got up to go to class. Will didn't even make eye contact with me. He just left with the others and went to class.

The rest of the day passed slowly, every minute of it in the expectation that Aquinas would return so I could get the information I needed. There were still so many unanswered questions. What had my dad known about the location of the Jerusalem Stones? What lead had he been tracking down when he was captured? How much time did we have before Ren Lucre started his war against mankind? Every time the front gates opened to let someone in, my heart beat faster in my chest. But as the sun set, there was still no Aquinas.

Meanwhile, the trial loomed first in everyone's mind. The day and night were punctuated with cheers as more hunters put their name into contention. Will had given me a half-baked apology for the way he submitted his name into the contest. It was clear he wasn't apologizing for volunteering himself, just for the way he did it. I could never stay mad at Will for long and I understood his desire to prove to the others in the camp that he deserved to be here. Eva seemed more concerned. The next morning, she walked alongside of me at breakfast.

"There are twelve entries for the trial," she whispered. "Will has a one in twelve chance of being chosen. Is he ready for this?

"It's Will," I whispered back. "He's sure he'll be the first to ever beat an instructor. Do you know who he will go up against?"

Eva shook her head. "Either none of the instructors know or they aren't talking. It may not be revealed until after the challenger is selected."

"Any word about Aquinas?" I asked.

"None," Eva said. "But it's not unusual for her to leave a week or two at a time."

"A week or two!" I said.

Eva shrugged. "Got to go. Tell Will good luck for me."

I joined Will and Xavier at our table. T-Rex came over and sat down with us. The hunters around us glared at him, but didn't say anything. Will looked on edge and kept glancing over to the leather pouch.

"It's not going anywhere, Will," I said, trying to lighten the mood. "They're still doing the draw at lunch."

Will pushed away his uneaten food. "I think I'm gonna puke."

T-Rex covered his food with one hand. "Well, don't do it over here," he said.

I patted Will on the back. "You'll be fine."

"No, I'm serious. I think I'm gonna throw up," Will said, sliding out from his chair and running toward the bathroom.

T-Rex, Xavier and I watched him go. "Do you think he's OK?" T-Rex asked.

"Sure, just nerves is all."

"That he'll get picked?" Xavier asked.

157

"No, he's nervous that he won't be," I replied.

The morning classes might as well have been called off since no one paid any attention. Instead, everyone whispered about the upcoming trial, trying to piece together who had put their name in the pouch, and which instructor was likely to fight.

By lunchtime, the Academy was buzzing with excitement. As we went through the lunch line, more than a dozen people came up and wished Will luck.

Halfway through lunch, Daniel rose and walked to the front of the group. Everyone fell silent.

"Twelve hunters put their names forward for trial, but only one will be chosen. As is tradition, we will not read the names of those who have submitted. They know who they are and that is honor enough. I will now choose the name."

Daniel reached in and felt around inside the pouch, stringing out the tension for as long as possible. Finally, he ceremoniously pulled out a single piece of paper and opened it. He turned the paper to face out to the group.

I felt my stomach sink.

It wasn't Will's name.

It was mine.

Daniel turned to me and pointed "You have submitted your name and have been selected. Do you accept?"

I turned and saw Will glaring at me, his face burning red with anger. "You just couldn't let me have this, could you?" he whispered.

"I didn't put my name in, I swear," I whispered back. "Someone set this up."

"Why would anyone do that?" Will asked.

Daniel walked up to me. "Do you accept the trial?"

I stood up. The air was deathly quiet. Every eye was trained on me. "Uh...I...there's been a mistake. I didn't put my name in."

A rumble of conversation rolled through the hunters. I could hear snippets of conversation.

"Chickened out."

"Coward."

"Some nerve that guy has."

Daniel barely suppressed a grin. Suddenly, with perfect clarity, I realized Daniel had set this up. I remembered Midge talking to Darter under the Templar Tree. *First time Master 'quinas goes on one 'uv 'er trips, he's got a somethin' real good going for 'im,* he had said about Daniel. And here I was walking right into his trap.

"Wait...wait, everyone," Daniel said. "This is a serious accusation. Are you accusing another hunter of breaking the rules? Do you have proof?"

Heads swiveled my direction.

"No, I have no proof, other than to tell you I didn't put my name in there," I said. A chorus of catcalls came from the group. "Think about it. No one saw me do it so it's not like I was trying to look brave and hope I didn't get chosen. So, why would I possibly put my name in if I didn't want the attention? It makes no sense." I noticed this argument was reaching some in the crowd. The tenor of the conversation changed from outrage to debate.

I spotted Eva standing outside the group. I looked to her for help but she only gave me a discernible shake of the head. I was on my own with this one.

"I'm a fair person," Daniel said. "We will put it to a vote to your peers. Who here believes Jack should be allowed to withdraw from the trial?" Only Will and Xavier half-raised their hands. "And who believes he should be held accountable and forced to compete, or face the consequences any other hunter would have if he were to withdraw?" A roar of approval came from the group. Daniel smiled, no longer bothering to hide how much he was enjoying this public spectacle. "Well?"

I knew I should still decline. I knew that this entire circus was only a distraction from my goal to find my father. But reason was long gone. I was being called out by the school bully and how I handled it would mark me forever.

"Let me help you," Daniel said, producing a bag from his side. "This contains the names of every instructor here. Let's find out who you would face."

He wiggled his hands through the bag dramatically before pulling out a piece of paper and holding it up for the group. Scrawled on it was a single word.

Daniel.

He looked up at me but his grin disappeared when he saw the expression on my face. Suddenly he looked nervous. Really nervous. He could tell that his names was the one I was hoping for. Nothing could have made me happier than to have the chance to go one-on-one against him.

"In that case," I said flatly, "I accept. Let's do this."

"You shouldn't do this," Eva said. She had walked me off the field back into the dorm, Will and T-Rex right behind her. I pulled out my armor from my travel bag and started to put it on.

"I know," I said. "But your boyfriend didn't leave me much of choice, did he?"

"My boyfr...is that what you think?" Eva stammered. "Anyway, that's not the point here, is it?"

"What is the point then, Eva?" I asked. "Because if there is one, I'd like you to get to it because I'm about to get my butt kicked by the biggest jerk in this school. Even though I never put my name in, by the way," I said, directing the comment at Will. I struggled to tie the straps that held my armor in place down my side.

Will had hovered around the edge of the conversation until now. He stepped up and pulled the straps tight for me. "You mean you really didn't put your name in?"

"Of course not," I said. "For the same reasons I asked you not to do it."

"Then why are you going through with it?" Eva asked.

"Because I said I would," I answered. *And because I've wanted to take a swing at Daniel the moment I saw him put his arm around you,* I wanted to say but didn't.

Will pulled the last strap tight and handed me my helmet. "Sorry I doubted you like that," he said. "Won't happen again. I promise."

I clapped him on the shoulder. "Just make sure to pick up all the pieces of me when we're done." I turned to say something to Eva, but when I looked over at her, she was already gone. "I hate it when she does that," I said.

The entire Academy gathered around the front gate. Daniel arrived, flanked by Darter and Midge. He was dressed in a loose winter camouflage over black body armor and was equipped with an arsenal of weapons. A sword at his side, a bow and quiver of arrows on his back, and a heavy, barbed spear in his hands. I looked down at my solitary sword and suddenly felt naked.

Daniel walked up to me until he was so close I could feel his hot breath on my face. "Are you ready, Smith?"

"The name's Templar," I said. "Yeah, I'm ready. What are the rules?"

"The only rule you need to know is that the better man always wins," Daniel said only loud enough for me to hear. "Always."

"Do we fight here?" I asked.

Daniel laughed. Raising his voice, he played to the crowd. "No, out there," Daniel said, pointing beyond the walls. "This is a special trial of my own making. Are you ready for it?"

The assembled hunters yelled and cheered. Daniel basked in it.

"All right," he shouted. "Here it is. The first hunter to track and defeat the targeted monster and return to the Academy wins."

Eva stepped forward and spoke low enough so the younger hunters couldn't hear. I was close enough that I heard every word. "Aquinas would never agree to this if she were here. She doesn't want him in harm's way."

"But she's not here, is she?" Daniel growled. "And I'm in charge until she returns."

"Exactly, so you shouldn't leave the Academy unguarded," she said.

"I'm not," Daniel smiled. He turned to the assembled crowd. "Eva will be in charge while we are gone." He turned to me. "Unless you've had a change of heart?"

"Not a chance. What's the targeted monster?"

Daniel bellowed, "The targeted monster is Tiberon, King of the Black Wolves. Neither of us can return until he is eliminated as a threat."

The crowd roared in delight.

"No...that's not what..." I said.

"You can still withdraw, Smith," Daniel hissed. He leaned into me so no one else could hear. "You'll be branded a coward for the rest of your life. You can serve mashed potatoes with your Ratling friends and wash the dishes of real hunters. If you don't have the stomach to do what must be done, then you can just quit."

"You set this all up, didn't you? Ever since you found out I had contact with Tiberon."

Daniel leaned in closer. "Are you in or are you out?"

"Out. I'd rather be called a coward than be part of this."

"And how about Eva?" Daniel whispered. "She vouched for you. If you refuse the trial, she will be punished along with you. Are you willing to see her stripped of her ranking?"

"Why are you doing this?" I asked. "Why is this so important to you?"

"Last chance, Jack Smith!" Daniel shouted for everyone to hear. "Are you in or are you out?"

My mind whirled. I tried to see all the angles at one time, but every thread I pulled led to a terrible outcome. Withdraw and hurt Eva. Compete and lead Daniel to Tiberon. Even winning the trial meant killing Tiberon. There was no solution, so I chose the option that simply gave me more time to think. "I'm in," I said. "I'm in."

The crowd cheered as Daniel hefted one of two already packed backpacks onto his shoulders. I walked up to the other and hefted it onto my back. Whatever was in there was heavy. If it was food, it seemed as if we were expected to be gone for a while.

When I turned around, Will, Eva, and T-Rex were standing in front of me. By the looks on their faces, I decided I might be in more trouble than I originally thought.

Eva spoke first. "If you're doing this for me, don't. I'm asking you to withdraw. Do you think I care about my ranking?"

I shook my head. There was no way I could do that to her.

The crowd cheered louder as Darter led two horses out from the stables. A massive black Percheron, the same horse that I'd seen Daniel ride before. It looked majestic with its shiny coat and glistening silver armor. From behind it stepped a swaybacked pony that looked as old as the Academy itself. Apparently my horse for this quest.

"No, wait," Eva said. She ran from the group and returned leading a saddled Saladin by the reins. She handed them to me. "Make certain you bring him back," she said.

"I promise," I said.

"I was talking to him," Eva said, cocking her head toward Saladin.

"But I thought you were the only one who could ride him," I said.

"We had a little talk about that, didn't we, boy?" Eva purred. Saladin nodded his head up and down, his mane flying. "We agreed just this once it would be all right."

I nodded and patted Saladin on the nose. He snorted as if annoyed by the whole thing. The crowd cheered and the gates rolled open.

"Stay in the trees at night," Eva said, suddenly serious. "There are provisions in the pack for three days. Five if you stretch out the food."

"Judging by how many wolves chased us on the way in here, I don't think I'll need to worry about food lasting for five days," I said.

Eva looked like she wanted to say something, but decided against it. She put her hand to her chest, then extended her arm in the hunter's salute. "Hunt well, kill swiftly. Do your duty, come what may," she said.

Will walked up, hand outstretched. I shook it and he pulled me into a tight hug.

"Try not to die out there, OK?" Will asked.

"Yeah, that's the plan," I said, trying to sound braver than I felt.

"Then just stick to the plan," T-Rex chimed in, big tears running down his cheeks.

I gave him what I hoped was a reassuring look, then put my foot in the stirrup and hefted myself up on the saddle. Without asking him, Saladin reared up and whinnied like a warhorse before tearing out of the gate. At least he was ready for the adventure ahead of us, because I sure wasn't.

Chapter Nine

We made our way on horseback down the snow-covered trail through the woods. Neither of us said anything in the first few hours since we left camp. It had taken a mile or two before Saladin stopped tossing his mane and snorting because I made him walk behind Daniel's horse. He was accustomed to being in the lead, even if it was just walking down a trail.

I had no idea what was supposed to happen next. Since it was a competition, it made sense for me to break away from Daniel and head out on my own. But the thought of wandering through the forest by myself didn't seem like a good idea to me, so I stayed right behind Daniel.

All I could think about was how to get myself out of this mess.

"You never answered my question," I finally said. Daniel ignored me. "Why do you hate this wolf so much?"

Daniel adjusted the backpack on his shoulders and quickened his pace. I stopped in my tracks and Saladin and I stood in the middle of the road. Daniel was twenty yards away before he stopped and turned around to face me.

"What are you doing?" he asked.

"We don't need to stay together," I said. "I mean, that's the point, right? To do our own thing?"

Daniel walked back to me. "No, the point of this whole thing is for me to kill the werewolf. Whatever connection you have to that creature, I intend to use to my benefit."

"I'm the bait," I said.

"And Eva said you weren't very bright," Daniel said. Even though I knew he was just trying to get to me, the comment still stung. "Yes, you're the bait. Now come on. There's a good camp we should get to before sundown. Wolves aren't the only thing in this forest we have to worry about."

We marched on through the afternoon. I followed behind Daniel, walking in his footsteps in the snow. I kept an eye out in the woods on either side of us, waiting for the tell-tale flash of movement between the trees.

The forest was still. Snow hung on the towering pines around us. Periodically, a pile of snow would come loose from a bird landing on a branch, cascading down the tree in a waterfall of powder. Small tracks of deer, rabbits and squirrels crisscrossed the trail. At one point we came across a small waterfall that had frozen in place, the ice glowing a deep blue in the cold, winter sun. I found myself enjoying the ride through the forest and had to remind myself that serious business lay ahead.

Somehow, I had to find a way to end this challenge without Tiberon being killed in the process. The more I picked at the problem over the hours of riding silently through the forest, the more impossible it seemed. The answer, if there even was an answer, lay in getting Daniel to see that Tiberon, werewolf or not, wasn't the evil creature he thought him to be. But how to accomplish that feat? I had no idea.

We arrived at the camping spot near dusk. It was a deep draw with a decent elevation so we could see what was happening below us. We tied the horses and each of us cleared the snow away from a small area where we could sit.

"Are we going to start a fire?" I asked, hoping the answer was yes. Even with the additional cloak and gloves, it felt like the cold had seeped in through my skin and found its way into my bone marrow. I was too proud to admit it to Daniel, but I was freezing.

"Not a chance, Smith," Daniel said. He meant the name to be a slur, but I actually didn't mind it. After all, I had gone by Jack Smith for the first fourteen years of my life, so it felt pretty normal. But the fact that he thought it bothered me was enough for it to bug me.

169

I watched him pull a small shovel from his backpack and snap a second beam in place to lengthen the handle. I dug through my pack and found the same tool and put mine together as well. By the time I was done, Daniel was digging a long shallow hole in the dirt, about as long as he was tall. These were to be our beds for the night.

I cleared a larger area of snow and dug it. The top layers were frozen solid so it was hard going at first, but it became easier a bit further down. As we worked on our sleeping holes, Daniel and I inevitably eyed each other's progress, judging who was doing better. We worked faster and faster, trying to be the first to finish. Soon, we were both grunting from the exertion, sweat pouring off of us, clods of dirt flying through the air. Seconds before I judged my hole was large enough, Daniel, huffing for breath, threw down his shovel.

"Done," he said.

I put my shovel down. "Done. And you had a head start."

"Whatever," Daniel said. He set about gathering handfuls of pine needles from under the snow. Having no idea how to survive in the wild, I did the same. Soon there were two huge piles of needles stacked in front of us.

"Let's eat and then get some rest," Daniel said. "I'll take first watch."

"I can do first watch if you want," I offered.

"I said I'll do it," Daniel grumbled.

I shrugged and pulled out a sandwich with thick slices of cheese and ham. I remembered what

Eva had said about making the food stretch out over five days and decided to only eat half of it even though I was famished. Daniel ate quietly, standing at the edge of our little camp, lost in his own thoughts as he looked down at the forest below us.

"So, are you going to tell me why this wolf is so important to you?" I asked.

"No," Daniel said softly, his voice sounding hollow, like he was miles way. "I'm not going to tell you that."

"Why not?" I asked.

"Because it no longer matters," Daniel replied, an edge coming back to his tone. "All that matters is that he dies."

The night passed without incident. Following Daniel's lead, I lay in my shallow hole in the ground and covered myself with pine needles. At first I was freezing, but as the needles trapped my body heat and because I was below any breeze, over time I warmed up somewhat. It wasn't exactly like staying at a five-star hotel with room service, but it wasn't bad. The only time I was cold during the night was when it was my turn to keep watch over the dark forest. It didn't matter whether I sat curled up in my cloak, or if I paced back and forth across the camp—I just couldn't get warm. When the eastern sky finally lightened, I was more than ready for the meager warmth the winter's sun provided.

We ate breakfast without conversation and broke camp just as the sun broke the horizon.

171

"We have a long journey today to make it to our next camp," Daniel said. "It's in a cave so we can have a fire tonight."

As great as that news was, I didn't want Daniel to think I was overly cold, so I tried to play it cool. "If you say so," I said. But deep inside I was shouting for joy. The idea of rubbing my frozen hands together next to a fire was almost too much to bear. Turns out that disaster would strike us well before that ever happened.

The attack didn't come until nearly dusk on that second day. And it had nothing to do with wolves.

The screaming came first. Daniel had just turned to me and pointed to a rocky outcrop ahead of us. The cave. That meant a campfire and a chance to eat something hot. Just as Daniel turned, a black shadow streaked out of the treetops, emitting a deafening shriek that only stopped once it smashed right into Daniel's face.

In what seemed like slow motion, a splatter of blood arced through the air and landed in a pattern on the fresh snow.

Daniel spun around on his horse, and Saladin reared on his hind legs, nearly knocking me off his back. I looked over at Daniel and saw something attached to his face—a creature with pale grey flesh and wiry hair. About the size of a large rat, it was so emaciated that its skin looked like only a thin casing stretched tight against its skeleton. Adding to this bony appearance were thin, papery wings that were

172

wrapped around either side of Daniel's head, holding on while the creature's mouth gnawed on his face.

I put my hands to my ears as the forest erupted with the same maddening shriek, but now in a chorus. Judging from the ear-shattering volume, there had to be dozens of them. I knew exactly what these things were, remembering them from one of my classes. These were shriekers, members of the Lower Creach. Not overly dangerous by themselves, but deadly when they hunted as a group.

I caught movement out of the corner of my eye and looked up into the trees. At first I thought I was seeing things. The low light and the wind rocking the trees had created a bizarre dance of shadows, confusing my senses. But as I watched, I could discern dozens of dark forms gliding through the shadows.

Shriekers.

Everywhere.

Screeching and spitting.

Picking their way toward us with their stubby feet and their bat-like wings.

I could see their faces now. They were small, with pointed noses that reminded me of a ferret or a weasel. Only these guys had mouthfuls of pointy teeth that protruded out from elongated jaws.

The shriekers nearest me saw that I'd spotted them and they opened their mouths wide and hissed at me. They launched themselves off the trees, falling in an ungainly, barely controlled descent.

Saladin reared again and this time I couldn't keep my grip tight enough. I fell off the saddle and hit the ground hard. Instinctively, I rolled to one side.

Thump.

Thump.

Thump.

The creatures landed in the snow where I had been seconds before.

I climbed to my feet and drew my sword, struggling to block the shrieking from my ears as Saladin ran into the forest.

Daniel's horse reared, and seven or eight shriekers latched onto its back and sides. Daniel tumbled to the ground, still wrestling with the shrieker on his face. His screams became more urgent. As if attracted to the blood, the shriekers on the ground that had missed me clawed in the snow toward Daniel. Two of them reached the blood-covered snow near him and hungrily gulped it down.

I looked back up and saw three more of the creatures flying through the air toward me. I braced myself and swung my sword as they approached. I sliced through two of them, unleashing a spray of putrid black blood all over me. The rotten stench almost made me gag.

I looked down and saw a shrieker attached to my thigh. It burrowed through my armor trying to get to my skin.

I sliced downward and cut it in half. But the front half of the creature kept gnawing on my leg. With a yell, I hacked at it and peeled it off of me.

Without looking up, I lurched forward into a shoulder roll. Just as I did I heard more shriekers hit the ground.

Thump.

Thump.

Thump.

Even in the panic of the moment, I realized that if the creatures were able to fly, then both Daniel and I would likely be dead already.

But flyers or not, there were too many of them. It was only a matter of time before they overwhelmed us.

I looked to the outcropping Daniel had pointed out right before the attack. The way was clear. For now. I figured that if we were able to get to the cave, we would at least stand a chance.

But first, I had to help Daniel.

I rushed toward him, slicing through three shriekers on the way. I grabbed the creature on his face and pulled. His screams were terrible.

"Hold still!" I shouted. "I don't want to stab you by accident!"

But Daniel was in too much pain to listen. He continued to flail around, pawing at the creature eating his face.

The other creatures closed in around us. Hissing like snakes at the smell of blood in the air.

"If you want to live, then hold still!" I shouted.

This finally registered with him. Daniel froze in place for a few seconds, and it was all I needed. With one plunge of my sword, I skewered the creature and used the leverage of my sword to peel him off and throw him through the air.

Daniel held one hand to his bleeding face and used the other to pull his sword.

"I can't see!" he shouted.

I grabbed his hand and put it on my shoulder. "We have to make it to the cave. Hold on to me."

Swinging my sword wildly at the shriekers in our path, I led Daniel on a stumbling run toward the cave. I looked anxiously for any sign of Saladin and Daniel's horse, but they were gone. My gut twisted knowing that I was leaving them to fend for themselves against the shriekers, but there was nothing I could do. I focused all my effort on getting Daniel to the cave.

The creatures on the ground weren't so much my worry: it was the dozens in the trees above us. These moved quickly and threw themselves at us as we ran. Several landed on us and tried to latch onto our flesh, but they became quick work for our swords.

The forest gave way to a small clearing just before the cave opening. My heart pounded hard in my chest. Without the tree cover, the creatures would not be able to keep up with us. I gave myself a second to feel like we were going to be OK.

Then I saw the wolves on the other side of the clearing.

They stood within the first line of trees, spread out too evenly for it to be coincidental. This was a battle formation.

A trap.

The shriekers had pushed us straight to them.

Getting to the cave suddenly became more important than ever.

"Come on!" I yelled, pulling Daniel along.

As soon as we broke into a sprint, the wolves charged at us. We were far closer to the cave, but their speed gave them the advantage. It was going to be close.

The shrieking and hissing increased behind us as the last of the creatures launched themselves at us. They landed short, but scampered after us on the ground. The forest floor was coated with them like a rat infestation. The shriekers crawled over one another, biting and scratching their way forward.

Ahead of us, the wolves ran hard across the clearing.

"Push it, Daniel. Come on!" I yelled.

We were so close. The nearest wolves snarled and bared their teeth.

Just in time, we reached the cave entrance. It was low and narrow. I pushed Daniel in first, then backed in after him so that I could meet the first wolf who followed us head-on with my blade.

But no wolf came.

I saw shadows streak past the cave opening. The unmistakable growls of the wolves. Then a few seconds of eerie silence.

Suddenly the forest erupted once again with screams. Then I understood. The wolves were attacking the shriekers.

I turned to tell Daniel, but he was gone!

"Daniel!" I shouted in fear.

"Get back here," Daniel shouted back from deeper in the cave.

I sprinted toward his voice and quickly came to a metal door. I stepped through it and closed it behind me, effectively sealing us off from the outside world.

Daniel leaned against the cave wall, a flashlight illuminating half of the small cave. He held a cloth to his face. Even though his chest heaved from breathing hard, he was more in control now.

"The wolves saved us," I said.

Daniel shook his head. "Just because they killed the shriekers first, doesn't mean we weren't next on the menu."

I unslung my backpack and took out my own flashlight. I approached Daniel. "How bad is it?"

Daniel turned to me and I felt my stomach drop. No matter how much I tried, I couldn't help but look away.

There were scrape marks around his face, but they were all superficial.

But his nose.

His nose was completely gone.

Chewed off by the shrieker.

Daniel put the cloth back on his face. "Yeah," he said. "That's what I thought."

Outside the cave, a new sound arose. The howling of dozens of wolves in unison. They were right outside. We were trapped.

Daniel straightened at the sound, panic in his eyes. "See? They're back to finish the job." He shouted at the door, completely out of control. "Well, you won't get me, you mongrels! I can promise you that. You won't get me!"

Daniel slid to the ground as if he were suddenly exhausted, his back against the wall. His entire body trembled and tears welled in his eyes. Soon they had become long, flowing streams down his cheeks. He turned off his flashlight and I heard him sobbing in the cave. "You won't get me," he whispered.

I turned off my flashlight and the cave plunged into total darkness. From across the way I heard Daniel, his voice barely audible, mumble over and over, "You won't get me. You won't get me. You won't get me."

As another chorus of howls filtered in from the outside world, I seriously doubted that Daniel was correct.

After a few hours, it was clear the wolves weren't going anywhere, which meant that we weren't either. I found a bundle of wood in the back of the cave and started a small fire. Someone had ingeniously bored a flue through the rock roof that drew the smoke out. The wolves already knew where we were so there was no reason to worry about the smoke giving away our location.

Daniel had smeared a healing ointment on the scratches of his face. I had seen Eva use the same type of thing before; it could clear up cuts, gouges, even broken bones in a fraction of the time the human body could on its own. But given Eva's missing hand, I was pretty certain the ointment

179

would not regenerate Daniel's missing nose. At least the bleeding had stopped and he had been able to wrap a bandana around his head to keep pressure on the area.

"Does it hurt?" I asked.

Daniel shrugged. "I've been through worse."

With the injury to his nose, Daniel's voice came out stuffy and muted. Still, even with everything that had happened, Daniel was as cocky as ever.

"You're telling me that you've been through worse than having your nose chewed off by a ferret-faced bat-winged creature and then surrounded by wolves who you think want to eat you?" I asked.

Daniel poked the fire with a stick. "Yeah, that's what I'm telling you," he said.

I had just thought he was being his usual cocky self, but something about his voice struck me as sincere. I decided to leave it there and not stir up old memories. But without any prompting, Daniel began to tell me a story.

"I was thirteen years old. Still safe because of Quattuordecim, but my birthday was only four months way. My father was a great hunter and I wanted nothing more than to be like him. We lived out in the wilderness. Up away from the world in the Canadian Rockies. I trained non-stop. He was hard on me. Never cruel, just hard. He knew the life I had in front of me and he made sure I was ready for it."

I looked over and saw that Daniel's eyes were locked on the flames in front of him, staring into some far off day that only he could see.

"The camping trip was supposed to be just another training run. Up in the mountains. Basic survival skills, you know? Just my father and my two little nine-year-old twin brothers, Andre and Felix. They were good kids. Into everything, always with a million questions, could never sit still. It was their first time coming with us. My dad didn't think they were ready, but they begged so much that it was hard to say no. He asked me whether I thought we should let them come. That it was my decision.

"It felt good, you know? Like I was an equal. The twins looked at me with their blue eyes, wide and hopeful. No, they weren't ready, but how could I say no? I nodded and said they could come. The twins went crazy, but when I looked up at my father, he was staring at me with an expression I couldn't read. It wasn't amusement. Certainly not pride. Was it disappointment? Sadness? Or was he thinking about something else entirely and I was reading into it? All these years I've tried to figure that out. What that one look meant that lasted for only three seconds. That look that won't stop haunting me."

A lone wolf howled outside, but even this didn't break Daniel's focus on the fire and the scene replaying in his mind.

"The twins hung in there for the first two days. We kept our usual pace, my father intent in giving them the full experience. We tracked caribou, made and set traps to catch our dinner, caught fish in the clear running streams. At night, the sky was on fire with the Northern Lights, bands of shimmering light that danced in the darkness. We were all together. Those were the best two days of my life."

Daniel fell silent, lost in the embers of the fire. He swayed gently back and forth, absently poking at the ground in front of him with a stick. For a long time, he said nothing. I knew this story wasn't going to end well. Part of me didn't want to know how it ended. Part of me hoped it would stop right there. A father and his three sons camping under the clear night skies.

"If you don't want—" I offered.

"We heard the first wolf at dawn on the third day," Daniel continued. "It wasn't rare to hear them in the mountains. And it didn't concern us. This was the summer. A time of plenty for all living things in the mountains. In the lean, hungry days of the winter, we would have paid it more notice. We should have known better."

"At noon we spotted the first of the pack. Three massive beasts on a ridgeline ahead of us. Silhouetted against a bright blue sky, they stood stock still, watching us. My father, always with the hunter's eye, saw them first. He pointed them out to the twins like we were on a visit to the zoo, telling them details about the species. Then, as we stood there, one of the silhouettes raised its front paws in the air, balancing on its rear legs, clawing the air. Slowly, the shadow transformed into the shape of a man. I looked to my father and my chest tightened in panic. For the first and only time in my life, I saw fear on my father's face.

'Run! Run, boys!' my father shouted. 'Run!'

182

"In a beat, we were in a full sprint to the tree line. I heard my father's blade slip from its scabbard and I reached down and did the same. From the trees in front of us came five more of the pack. Snarling, teeth bared. My father pushed us to the right, toward a ravine. The twins were moving too slowly, so my father scooped them up in his massive arms and carried them. Even with the extra weight, he was faster than me. He was ten yards ahead when the ground gave way and they disappeared.

"It was a trap. The wolves had pushed us to this spot. Only by luck was I not in the hole with them. I ran to the edge and saw them curled in a heap at least fifteen feet below. *Come on. Give me your hand. Father! I'm here! I can save you!*"

Daniel held his hand out over the fire, as if still reaching out to his father and little brothers. He seemed not to notice the heat and soon the sleeve of his cloak smoked from the flames. I reached out and pulled his hand back. Still, his eyes remained fixed on the fire, thousands of miles away.

"My father looked up from that hole in the ground, blood coating his teeth, clutching the twins to him. I knew instantly what he wanted me to do. I shook my head. I won't leave you. I can't. Then he said the words that have stayed with me every day of my life since then. *Avenge us, Daniel. Survive and avenge your family. Now, run!*

"A lifetime of following orders saved my life. I turned and ran down the ravine, tears blocking my vision. I heard the yelps and growls of the wolves behind me. I almost stopped when those snarls were joined by the screams of my father and brothers being torn to pieces.

"In front of me, a man dressed in a black cloak stepped from the tree line into my path. I recognized his shape as the creature that had transformed from the wolf. Behind him was a fast moving river. An escape. The figure drew a sword from his side and waited for me. I had my own sword in hand and I clutched it hard as I ran. This was my vengeance.

"I flew at him with all the anger and pain I had in me. But even in my fury, I was no match for the all-powerful Ren Lucre."

I drew in a sharp breath at the sound of the name, reliving my own face-to-face encounters with the Lord of the Creach. Daniel, for the first time since starting his story, looked up at me and nodded.

"Yes, I too have faced Ren Lucre. But unlike you, I didn't last more than a few exchanges before he batted my sword away and held the point of his blade to my throat. He grabbed me by the front of my cloak and drew me close. Then he stared at me with those black, soulless eyes. I could feel him in my head, like he was scraping the inside of my skull, searching for something."

I shivered at the description. I knew exactly the feeling.

"But whatever it was, he didn't find it there. *You're not the One*, he said. *You're no Templar.*"

With a growing feeling of dread, I realized what this meant. "He was looking for me," I whispered. "Ren Lucre and the wolves only attacked you because they were looking for me."

Daniel ignored the comment and continued, less telling me the story than reliving it himself. I wondered whether he could stop now even if he wanted to or whether he was somehow locked into it and had to see it through.

"Ren Lucre threw me to the ground and let out a cry. The wolves, dozens of them, howled in unison in response, a mournful cry that filled the mountains. I took the one chance I had and crawled on my hands and knees to the edge of the ravine and launched myself off the edge. How I missed the rocks below, I don't know, but the icy waters alone almost killed me. But they didn't. I escaped. Then, through friends of my father, I made my way to the Academy. I did as I was told. I survived so that I could avenge my family."

The wolves howled outside.

"That's why you hate the wolves," I said.

"No," Daniel whispered, his eyes welling with tears. "That's why I hate. The wolves, Ren Lucre, my father for giving me the decision to bring the twins, myself for running away..." He stared at me hard and added, "And the last true Templar, for not being caught before Ren Lucre came looking for us that day."

My stomach turned over on itself. He was right. Ren Lucre had been searching for me. I felt the weight of his family's deaths fall on me. A weight that already included Aunt Sophie, Hester and possibly my own father. I wondered how much more weight would be added before all was said and done.

And I still didn't even know if I was the One. Or, even if I was, what that meant.

I just knew that too many people were being hurt because of me.

"I'm sorry," I said. The words sounded too meager, too inconsequential. But I had to say them. "I'm so sorry."

Daniel laid down on the ground next to the fire, curling up as if to sleep, but still staring into the flames. "Yeah, me too," he said.

There was nothing more to say. We laid down on the hard cave floor as the fire burned down, both of us finally drifting off to an uneasy sleep, the howls of wolves continuing through the night.

Chapter Ten

I woke with a start. A scratching noise came from somewhere in the cave. It was soft, just a distant, but constant, twitch of sound. I got up and crossed over to Daniel. Even in the faded light of the fire I could tell he was worse off now. He was pale and sweaty, his hair pasted to his forehead. He mumbled and whimpered as his trembling hands carved shapes in the air above his chest. Whatever dream world he was in, it was filled with nothing but terror.

The scratching sound came again, louder this time. I reached down and shook Daniel to wake him, but it had no effect. His skin was hot to the touch with fever. That wasn't good. I pulled a stick from the fire, its end now a bright red ember, and carried it toward the sound.

My heart pounded as my mind imagined all the creepy-crawly things that could be making such a sound in a dark cave. My first thought was that it was a lone shrieker that had somehow survived the onslaught of the wolves and managed to squirm its way down the chimney flue. But a quick survey of the cave showed no movement.

My makeshift torch lit up the metal door. The sound came faintly from the other side.

I put my hand against the cold metal, expecting to feel the vibrations of whatever was trying to claw through. But there were none. I pressed my ear up against the door and held my breath to hear better.

Scratch.

Scratch.

Scratch.

Coming from outside the cave.

Daniel let out a stifled cry from the middle of the cave and rolled to his side in his troubled, fevered sleep. I had to get him back to the Academy to get some real medicine.

I considered the possibility that a search party from the Academy was out there. We weren't expected back for at least two more days, so it didn't make sense, but desperation can do strange things to your mind.

I decided I had to take a risk. Carefully, trying not to make any noise, I unlocked the door and slid it back so only a crack appeared. I was surprised that a beam of sunlight burst in. After so many hours in the confines of the cave I had lost all track of time.

I squinted, relieved that nothing had thrown itself at the door the second I opened it, and sought out the source of the scratching sound. It was louder now, clearly coming from the mouth of the short tunnel. I kept my hand on the door, ready to slam it shut again if something charged from outside.

A long black shadow crossed the beam of light. Then a second one. I almost panicked and closed the door. Then I heard the most beautiful sound I'd ever heard. The low, throaty rumble of a horse. The long shadows were legs. I opened the door wider. The scratching sound was a hoof pawing the snow away from the ground, followed by a massive head lowering to munch on the soft grass.

Saladin.

I couldn't believe it. I had already mourned the horse's death at the hands of either the shriekers or the wolves, but there he was, peacefully eating without a care in the world.

I gave a low whistle and his nearest ear rotated toward me. He quickly stood, stamped the ground and whinnied as if saying it was about time I'd gotten my lazy behind out of bed. I opened the door wider and carefully walked through the tunnel, my eyes slowly adjusting to the bright light.

Saladin stood in front of the mouth of the cave, his head bobbing up and down, shaking the hair of his mane. Seconds later, I understood what he was trying to tell me.

Arrayed in a semi-circle in the clearing around the cave was the entire pack of wolves.

I froze.

It was exactly how I imagined Daniel's descriptions on that deadly day when he had lost his family. I doubted I had time to make it back inside the cave before the nearest wolf could reach me. Saladin whinnied softly, but I noticed there was no panic in the sound. Certainly, the wolves had been there while Saladin munched on the grass. I moved toward him cautiously and put my hand on his muscled neck. He felt relaxed and calm, even ducking his head for another quick bite of food. I wished I could say I was as calm as he was but my heart was pounding like it might explode from my chest.

From behind the wolves, at the apex of the semi-circle, walked Tiberon. Even next to the other wolves, he looked massive. His jet-black coat seemed unnatural in the pale, winter sun; the white cross on his chest was too perfectly formed, almost as if it had been stitched onto him.

It took everything I had not to turn and run back into the cave, but I stood my ground as the massive wolf crossed the distance between us. Saladin shifted his weight nervously at the new arrival, but I gripped his mane and he became still.

The wolves around us lifted their heads to the sky and howled into the winter air. Tiberon approached me, his head nearly level with my own. His dark brown eyes never left mine. He stopped only a few feet from me, so close that the white plumes of his hot breath in the cold air rolled up into my chest and face.

"My friend is injured," I said, my voice cracking. "I need to get him help or he will die."

Tiberon looked past me into the tunnel and then back to my eyes. He raised a massive paw and I couldn't help but notice each claw was nearly the length of my hand. Slowly, almost as if he too were afraid he might injure me, Tiberon laid a paw on my shoulder.

A flood of images entered my mind. Fractured and disjointed, like seeing snippets of a newsreel. A wolf caught in a steel trap. A wolf shot with an arrow. A hunter chasing wolves on horseback through the woods. Daniel.

I realized that these images were somehow coming from Tiberon.

I nodded. "Yes, my friend has hunted you in the past. But haven't you hunted him as well?"

Tiberon growled and the pack around the perimeter answered with a chorus of snarls.

I closed my eyes and recalled the story Daniel had shared with me the night before, filling in as much detail as I could from my imagination. I hoped my guess was right and that Tiberon could somehow see these same images. When I opened my eyes, Tiberon was staring into the cave behind me. I could tell he understood.

"So, there has been death on both sides," I said. "And too much fear and hate. We can continue to kill one another if you want. Or we can find another way."

I swallowed hard, knowing full well one swipe of his giant paw could send me reeling, probably killing me before I even realized anything had happened. This was the moment of truth. Even if

191

Tiberon didn't kill me on the spot, I still needed to convince him to let us go. With Daniel getting worse, he needed medical help soon if he was to survive his injuries.

Tiberon stared at me, sizing me up. I clutched my hands to my sides so he wouldn't see them trembling. He huffed out a burst of air and I felt my hair blow backward. But I forced myself to meet him eye-to-eye.

You look like your father, said a deep rumbling voice in my head. *Perhaps you have his strength too.*

It took me a second, but finally I stammered, "Th...that's you, isn't it? In my head? You knew my father?"

I did, Tiberon said. *A good man. Different than the rest.*

I tried to keep my wits about me. I had so many questions to ask, starting with how this wolf could possibly have known my father. But Daniel's health had to come first.

"My friend, he's injured. I need to get him back to the Academy."

Tiberon emitted a low growl. *You may go if you choose, but the wolf-killer will not leave this forest alive.*

"Please," I begged. "He'll die if I don't get him help."

Then the deaths of many of our brothers will be avenged, Tiberon said. The wolves around him howled eerily, as if calling to the memories of their fallen comrades.

"You saw what happened to him," I said. "You saw what made him the way he is."

Tiberon snarled and one of his claws dug into my shoulder. *Does the world afford me leniency because of how I turned into this monster you see before you? No. Not even from the people who most ought give it to me.*

"What happened to you?" I asked. "Maybe I can help."

Your father once promised the same thing years ago. And then broke that promise when he left these woods, never to return.

"Don't you know?" I exclaimed. "He was captured by the Dark Lord Ren Lucre! He's being held in his dungeon right now!"

Tiberon growled and looked away into the distance. His shoulders sagged as if a weight had been placed on him. *I know those dungeons well. Once you enter, you never leave. Even if you escape, that place stays with you forever.*

Something odd was happening. As Tiberon spoke, I felt strange emotions rise and fall inside of me, competing with my own. I not only heard his voice but sensed his emotions as well. Pangs of terrible fear coursed through me. I heard screams in the distance, the sound of fire. "You were a prisoner in those dungeons, weren't you?" I asked. "You know where it is."

Tiberon nodded.

"Tell me," I said, my head spinning from the possibility that I was about to find out where my father was.

Tiberon paused, as if considering his options. Finally, his voice rumbled in my head. *If I tell you where he is, do you intend to go there?*

"Yes."

Then, I might as well just kill you myself and save you the trouble.

I felt the excitement drain away. The giant wolf's tone left no doubt he had no intention of telling me. Still, I had to try. "Let me be the judge of that," I declared. "I faced Ren Lucre in battle once before and bested him. There's more to me than you might think."

I see a fire inside you, young one, Tiberon said. *But that fire will not be enough to survive the dungeons of Ren Lucre. There are terrors there beyond reckoning, beyond what you can imagine.*

"That's why I can't wait. I have to save my father before it's too late," I said.

The minute he was put in the dungeon, it was already too late, Tiberon rumbled. *I should never have told him where the Jerusalem Stones were hidden. He wasn't ready to go after them, but he wouldn't listen. He had many virtues, your father did, but patience was not one of them. And before you ask where the Stones are hidden, the answer is no. I will not make that mistake again.*

The Jerusalem Stones. The location of the dungeons. Everything I had come to the Academy to discover was suddenly in front of me. But it felt like seeing the destination on the other side of an impossibly wide canyon with no way across. Tiberon gave no indication he had any intention of telling me anything. I racked my brain for some clever way to get him to tell me, but I had nothing. Besides, I had a feeling that he would sense any trickery. I decided just to speak my mind.

"How can giving a son the chance to free his father be a mistake?" I asked.

This is no longer my concern, Tiberon said.

"How can you say that? You said it yourself, you told him where the Stones were." I felt a surge of remorse come from Tiberon, so I kept at it. "He wouldn't have been placed in harm's way if it wasn't for you. And you know it," I said. "In a way, he's only in those dungeons because of you. Don't you feel any responsibility at all?"

Tiberon roared at me, his open jaws wide enough to take off my head in one bite. I felt a bolt of anger from Tiberon stab through me, so intense that it took my breath away. The word 'responsibility' had hit a nerve and that nerve very well may have signed my death warrant.

I held my ground in the face of his fury, knowing there was nothing I could do if he decided to kill me, so I figured I might as well go out looking him in the eye. Even so, my legs turned wobbly as Tiberon raged.

Don't lecture me about responsibility, boy. You know nothing about it. You want to know what responsibility looks like? I'll show you.

The flood of images washed over me once again, too fast at first for me to make any sense of what I was seeing. I felt dizzy and had a sense of vertigo, as if I might fall into the pictures as I saw them. It was like watching a movie being rewound. Tiberon's memories were on full display for me to see.

Suddenly, the images stuttered to a halt and then the image played forward in real time. I felt disoriented as I was seeing everything from Tiberon's point of view, as if I were actually looking through his eyes. Finally, the movement slowed as Tiberon, in whatever time and place the event occurred, focused on a man in armor who approached him holding a torch.

The man was older, with lines around his eyes and flecks of grey in the heavy beard that hung down below his neck. Where blood and mud didn't cover it, the man's armor shone in a deep, gold luster as it reflected the torch's fire. He carried a shield with a red Templar Cross on his left hand and I saw the insignia of the Templar Order, the emblem of two knights on one horse, stamped into his chest plate.

"Tiberon," the man called as he rushed forward. "Thank God we found you. How did you escape?" Screams erupted from somewhere nearby. "Tell me, do you know where he is? The Dark Lord?"

The man pulled at Tiberon's hand and the world shifted as he stood up. My focus trained on Tiberon's hands. Human hands.

"Master de Molay, you should not have come. Ren Lucre has used me as bait to get you to leave the Citadel." It was Tiberon's voice, weak and thin, but similar enough to the voice in my head for me to identify it. I also recognized the name. Aquinas had told me about Jacques de Molay, the last Grand

Master of the Knights Templar, my namesake and ancestor who was burned at the stake on Friday the thirteenth. But that was over seven hundred years ago. How could Tiberon have been there?

De Molay clutched Tiberon's forearm. "Where is he? Even without the Jerusalem Stones, I must face him."

As I shared Tiberon's memory, I could feel an echo of his emotions as well. Hot shame washed over me as Tiberon felt it.

"I told him," Tiberon whispered. "I...I...I'm so sorry. So sorry."

"Told him what?" de Molay asked.

"Where the Stones were hidden," Tiberon cried. "And with you here, they are not protected. I couldn't take the pain. It was too much...too much..." De Molay's face registered horror at the words. But it was more than just what Tiberon was saying. Something else was happening.

"My God, what have you done?" de Molay asked, terrified.

My view went down to Tiberon's body, only it was no longer fully human. Hairless flesh bulged out from the clothes, ripping them apart at the seams. The legs stretched out long and sinewy as claws tore through his boots. Black hair grew from the skin, like thousands of black threads being pulled through by invisible needles. The hands were in my line of vision now and I watched as they transformed into the claws of a wolf.

"I'm sorry, my Lord. I tried to resist. I swear I tried." I heard the words in my head, but they came out from Tiberon as a guttural snarl. I realized that Tiberon had tried to say the words, but that his ability to speak was gone. De Molay had his sword in front of him and was backing away.

"Are you still there, Tiberon?" de Molay asked. "Or just this beast? If you can hear me, show me a sign or so help me, I'll run you through. I swear I will."

My point of view shifted to the clothes and armor scattered on the ground that Tiberon had been wearing before his transformation. A massive paw stabbed at a piece of cloth and pierced it with a single claw. Tiberon held it up. It was the part of his tunic with the red Templar Cross embroidered on it.

De Molay lowered his sword. "You are still there. We will deal with your treason later. Until then, there may be a use for you. Come, Tiberon, and pray we are not too late."

The scene spun forward. I had the sense of vertigo again as images flashed past me. When it stopped, I was outside, standing in front of a stone wall next to a gate. I recognized it immediately. The Citadel. Nearby there was a sapling oak, barely as tall as a man, its trunk no thicker than my wrist. I marveled at it, knowing that over time it would become the great Templar Tree.

De Molay was there, dressed now in a heavy fur-lined cloak, not too different from the ones worn by the instructors at the Academy today. He walked along the wall, followed by a group of six other men. I could tell I was looking through the eyes of Tiberon the wolf now. The world was sharp and crisp through his eyes. Even the colors appeared more brightly, as if every sense had been enhanced. I heard the low huffing of his breathing as he walked behind de Molay and saw the look of fear on the faces of the soldiers in the camp they passed.

They walked under the gate with the jagged metal teeth and entered the darkness of the cave. They came to stop next to a bronze door embedded in the rock. The door to the Cave of Trials. De Molay turned and addressed Tiberon and the six hunters. "The end is near, my friends. Without the Jerusalem Stones, Ren Lucre grows bolder each day. He uses the greed of men to turn the Courts of Europe against us. Soon, they will come for us, and the Knights Templar will be no more."

Tiberon gave a low, lonely howl, full of grief and remorse. The six hunters glared at him, hatred in their eyes. Only de Molay showed him any kindness.

"I know the burden of your guilt lies heavy on you, my old friend." De Molay motioned for Tiberon to come close. "I cannot absolve you of it, but I can give you an opportunity to earn back your honor." De Molay motioned to the door to the Cave of Trials and addressed the other hunters. "Today, we hide the Templar Ring from both Man and Monster. It is the last thing of magic we have from the Temple Mount in Jerusalem. The enemy must not be allowed to unite it with the Jerusalem Stones, for then he will become all-powerful and the Creach will rise again. Only this time, they will be unstoppable."

De Molay pulled out his sword and grasped the blade with his hand, holding it with the point to the ground. He lifted the hilt over his head. "One day, after years of darkness for our Order, a hunter of the Black Guard shall return to this place, pass the Trial of the Cave and be worthy of bearing the Templar Ring. He will take back the Jerusalem Stones, destroy Ren Lucre and avenge us all. This I pledge."

De Molay lowered his sword to his lips and kissed it. "May he be pure of heart and ready for the task. Only a true Templar will pass this test." He turned to Tiberon. "The enemy has turned you into this terrible creature and perhaps the punishment is fitting for your betrayal. There are others here who would see you slain."

As the other hunters stared at Tiberon, it wasn't hard to gather that they all wanted him dead.

"But I cannot forget our many years of friendship nor the countless times you have saved me in battle," de Molay continued. "So I give you a chance to earn your honor back and serve the Black Guard one last time. You will be bound to this place, sworn to protect it, until one who bears the ring releases you of your oath. You will make this oath not only on the Templar Ring, but to the brothers who you betrayed. Do you accept this duty?"

Tiberon bowed low and de Molay reached out and touched the ring to the wolf's forehead. There was a bright light and I felt an electric energy pass through me. When Tiberon raised his head, the other hunters pointed at him and whispered among themselves.

"The mark of the white cross on his chest."

"It wasn't there before."

"What does it mean?"

The voices faded away as the images spun forward. When it stopped, I was in the middle of a battle. Or what seemed like a battle at first. Then I realized there was no enemy, only members of the Black Guard who had Tiberon surrounded, thrusting spears at him, brandishing swords. Hatred on their faces.

"Kill the beast!" one cried.

"He's responsible for de Molay's death!" shouted another.

I recognized some of the faces as the men who had been in the cave with de Molay when he honored Tiberon with his new duty. But these men led the charge against him.

"Kill him! Kill the traitor!"

Tiberon turned and ran. He plowed through a wall of soldiers, bounded up the stairs to the top of the wall and sailed over the edge with a graceful leap. I felt my stomach sink as Tiberon fell through the air and landed with a thump on the hard, frozen ground. He looked back and I felt a complicated mix of emotions run through him. Anger. Shame. Fear. Sadness. Betrayal. And, of all these, betrayal strongest of all.

Archers appeared on the wall and arrows rained down on him. Tiberon roared at the men, his brothers no longer, and ran into the woods.

As he did, the images spun, faster than ever, and in an explosion of light, the connection to the past was broken and the bright light of present day nearly blinded me. I staggered back, trying to get my bearings. I would have fallen over except for Saladin who moved his head behind me for support.

"But that was so long ago," I said. "How is it possible...?"

How is it possible that I have lived for these seven centuries? Tiberon's voice once again rumbled inside my head. *It is a mystery, even to me. I can only say that the Templar Ring and the Jerusalem Stones were part of a strange and mysterious power that none of us, not even Jacques de Molay, truly understood. Perhaps the ring wanted to ensure my penance matched my crime. One mere lifetime was not enough suffering.*

"But if you're supposed to protect the Citadel, why did you attack us?"

Tiberon growled and the wolves around us did the same.

I long ago decided that I had served my penance. For two hundred years after the Black Guard cast me out, I honored my oath and kept these forests clear of both Creach and adventurous men seeking Templar treasure. Until, over time, this place faded from the minds of regular men. I held out hope that de Molay's pledge would still come true, that the "One" would come back to the Citadel. But when I discovered what Ren Lucre had done to hide the Jerusalem Stones, I knew they would never be reunited. De Molay's prophecy of a hunter who would reclaim the Ring from the Cave of Trials and gather the Jerusalem Stones was nothing but a fantasy. I turned my back on my oath and formed a new brotherhood.

He looked at the wolves that lined the clearing.

This is my family now.

"But you said you met my father and that you told him where the Jerusalem Stones were."

Yes, I did meet your father. I was foolish enough to let him convince me to have hope once again. He promised that he would find the Templar Ring to free me from my bondage. So, I swore him to secrecy and I told him the fate of the Jerusalem Stones. But it was for nothing. He broke his promise and disappeared soon after.

"He didn't break his promise," I said. "I told you, he was captured by Ren Lucre trying to find the Jerusalem Stones."

What does it matter? Tiberon asked, his voice suddenly tired and resigned. *The result is the same. I remain trapped in this body, perhaps for eternity.* Tiberon stretched his neck and looked up to the sky. He removed his paw from me, but surprisingly, I could still hear him in my head. *The day grows long and I tire of these bitter memories. As I said, you can take your horse and leave this place. The wolf-killer must remain. He belongs to us now.* Tiberon turned and walked away. The wolves nearest me licked their chops as if ready for a meal. I felt the opportunity slipping through my hands.

"I will keep my father's promise," I blurted out. "I will free you."

Saladin snorted and whinnied behind me. Tiberon spun around and his eyes burned into me.

Careful, boy. Oaths are more than just words in our world.

Aquinas had said the same thing to me. I knew I couldn't leave the Academy without becoming a full hunter first, but I was desperate. "Tell me where the Jerusalem Stones are and I will find them. I swear it. And when I do, I will unite them with the Templar Ring, defeat Ren Lucre, save my father and break the curse that binds you. On my father's life, I swear it."

All of the wolves howled in unison. It was a haunting sound, mournful and terrible at the same time. Once they quieted down, I took a confident step toward Tiberon.

"But I get to take my friend with me," I said. "That's my offer."

Tiberon walked a slow circle around me, his lips pulled back in a snarl.

You're no more than a boy, Tiberon said. *You have no idea what you are getting yourself into.*

"But you lose nothing. If I fail, you're no worse off," I said.

But the wolf-killer will live. That is the price.

"That is the price," I agreed. "But I will also promise he will never hunt your kind again."

Tiberon finished his slow circuit around me and faced me head-on. For several, long drawn out seconds, we stared at one another. Finally, his voice filled my head.

No, he said simply. *I do not agree to your terms.*

My stomach fell. I didn't know what else to do. There was no way I could sacrifice Daniel, even if it meant I lost everything I came to the Academy to achieve. I felt it all slipping away.

But there are terms I can agree to, Tiberon said. *One where we both get what we want and the wolf-killer goes free.*

"OK, what is it?" I asked.

I listened as he explained his conditions and his reasons for them.

I was left with no choice but to agree.

Tiberon and I touched claw to fist and the pact was made. Without another word, Tiberon turned and broke into a run. The rest of the pack followed their leader into the forest and disappeared.

I blew out the breath I'd been holding in and wrapped my arms around Saladin's neck. My legs wobbled beneath me. Saladin nuzzled me as if both approving of my actions but also reminding me that we had work to do.

I ran back into the cave and found Daniel where I had left him. His clothes were soaked through with sweat and I could feel the heat from his fever without even touching him. The bite marks from the shriekers had black rings around them, with dark streaks branching out into the still-healthy flesh. It didn't look good.

I managed to half carry, half drag him from the cave. He woke up just long enough to help me get him up onto Saladin, but nearly fell off once he was there. I had to resort to laying him on his stomach behind the saddle and tying him on with a rope. I climbed up onto Saladin and took the reins in hand.

"You know better than me where we're going," I said to Saladin. "Swift but careful. Let's go."

Saladin set off at a gallop through the snow-covered forest; all the while I could feel Tiberon's eyes follow our progress. I knew he was going to hold me to the promise I had just made to him with my life. As we rode, I worked out in my head how to keep my oath to Aquinas at the same time.

Daniel groaned behind me and I put those thoughts out of my mind. He was growing steadily worse and there was no guarantee he would survive the journey back. I clung tight to Saladin's mane and urged him to run even faster as we tore through the forest on the path back to the Academy, where both our fates were to be decided.

Chapter Eleven

Saladin chose his path carefully over the uneven ground, going as quickly as he dared. Daniel sat behind me on the saddle, his arms wrapped around my waist, tied at the wrist so he wouldn't fall off. He hovered in and out of consciousness, his head resting against my back. Even through my clothes I could feel the heat of his fever on my skin. I knew I had to get him to the Academy as quickly as possible if he was to survive.

As we rode, Daniel muttered strange things, often in languages I didn't understand. Sometimes it was a low, mumbling conversation, as if he were having a long argument with someone in his dreams. Every so often he erupted in shouts and screams where he kicked at me and tried to pull me off the horse. All I could do was hold on tight to the reins until he lost his strength and sagged against my back, fading into the darkness of whatever bizarre dreams haunted him.

Finally, a cry sounded from up ahead of us. We'd been spotted by the guard on duty at the Academy. I clutched Daniel close to me.

"We're here," I said. "We made it."

I felt him lift his head and lean to the side to look at the road ahead of us. But he leaned too far and his body began to slide off the saddle. I gripped his arms and heaved him back into position.

"Easy, there," I said. "Only a little further now."

Saladin snorted and took the uphill approach to the Academy wall in long, powerful strides. The gate opened and people poured out to greet us. As Saladin came to a stop, the crowd stilled, broken only by hushed whispers as the young hunters stood in front of us. It seemed like their curious reaction was more than just from seeing Daniel hunched forward against me. They all kept their distance, looking as if they had seen a ghost.

"Jack! Are you all right?" Eva pushed her way through the crowd, followed quickly behind by Will and T-Rex. They encircled Saladin.

"Daniel needs help. He's hurt badly." I untied Daniel's hand and slowly lowered him off Saladin's back. I jumped down and grasped Daniel's hand as a stretcher was brought out. His eyes opened suddenly and he sat bolt upright, staring at me right in the eye. "Don't trust him, Jack. Whatever you do...don't trust him...not the wolf." His eyes rolled in the back of his head and he collapsed back into the stretcher.

"Bring him inside," a voice boomed from the bulwark above the gate. I looked up and was surprised to see that Aquinas had returned. "Hurry, now. We may not have much time."

Eva, Will, T-Rex and I each took a corner of the stretcher and carried him inside the Academy walls.

"What happened?" Eva asked.

"We were attacked by shriekers," I said. "Dozens of them."

"That's not good," Eva said. "Their bite is poisonous. How many hours has it been?"

"Yesterday at sundown," I said.

Suddenly Aquinas was by our side. "There may still be hope then," she said. She produced a vial of blue liquid from a pouch on her side and poured it into Daniel's mouth. He sputtered and coughed the liquid back up. "A thin hope. Take him up into the Templar Tree. Hurry now. Every second matters."

We did as she told us and carried him as quickly as we could to the tree and up the stairs. Aquinas sped ahead of us and was busy in her laboratory when we arrived. Daniel clawed at the air in front of him, swatting away imaginary enemies.

"No...leave me...get them off me..." he shouted.

"Help him!" T-Rex called out to Aquinas.

Eva put a hand on T-Rex's shoulder to calm him. I turned to Aquinas. "What do you want us to do?"

Aquinas walked over, mixing a glass jar of glowing green fluid. "Hold him. The poison inside his body wants to turn him into a Creach. It does not want to be cured and will try to reject this medicine."

Eva and I each grabbed an arm and Will and T-Rex took hold of a leg. Daniel moaned softly, teetering on the edge of consciousness. Aquinas leaned in with the medicine. "Easy, now. Easy does it," she said.

Just as the jar touched his lips, Daniel's eyes opened. He glanced at each of us holding him down, the look in his eyes full of pure hatred. "No!" he shouted. He kicked his leg and T-Rex went flying across the room. With a savage growl, Daniel kicked across at Will and tagged him with a brutal uppercut.

"Hold him!" Aquinas shouted.

Will jumped onto Daniel's legs, wrapping his arm around them in a bear hug. Daniel bucked and kicked his body, trying his best to wrench his hands free, clawing at us like a wild animal. Aquinas tried unsuccessfully to pour the medicine into his mouth.

"Daniel!" she cried, her voice booming in the small room. "I command you to be still!"

It seemed like she had gotten through to him. The convulsions stopped and he looked at her as if recognizing her for the first time. I weakened my grip slightly. Big mistake.

A split second later, Daniel tore his hand away and shoved Aquinas. He punched at Eva who, unwilling to let go of Daniel's other hand, took the blows to her forearm and shoulder. Daniel snarled, his mouth foaming.

"Let go of me," he roared. "You'll never be

210

able to—"

SMACK.

A potted plant smashed into Daniel's head, dirt and leaves flying wildly into the air. His eyes rolled back in his head and he fell back onto the cot.

We all looked back behind us where the potted plant had come from. T-Rex stood there, probably even more surprised than the rest of us over what he had just done. "I didn't kill him, did I?" T-Rex asked sheepishly.

Aquinas put her hand behind Daniel's neck and lifted his head. She poured the green glowing medicine down his throat and then carefully laid him back down.

"No," Aquinas said. "You may have just saved his life."

"And given him one heck of a bump on the head," Will added.

"Will he be OK?" I asked.

"Time will tell," Aquinas said. "But there's nothing more for you to do here. Leave us. Get some rest. Later you can explain why the two of you were outside the Academy walls."

"It was—" I started, but Aquinas held up her hand.

"Not now," she said. "There will be time later."

I nodded and turned to the stairs. The other three were already a few steps ahead of me.

"Eva," Aquinas said, "if I'm not mistaken, young Daniel here has certain feelings for you. Am I correct in this?"

I felt a sudden knot tighten in my stomach. I looked to Eva.

"I don't...I guess you..." Eva stammered.

"This is not a time for games, child," Aquinas said sternly. "Does he have feelings for you?"

"Yes. Yes, he does," Eva said.

"Good," Aquinas said. "That will be helpful in pulling him back from the darkness. Come sit here and take his hand. The rest of you leave us. I'll send word if anything changes. You have my word."

I watched as Eva took a seat next to the stretcher and cupped Daniel's hand in her own. Will tugged on my shoulder.

"C'mon, Jack," he said. "Let's give them some space."

I nodded, and, with one last look at Eva, followed Will and T-Rex down the stairs.

As we descended, my legs turned weak and began to shake. Will noticed and grabbed hold of my arm to support me. After the constant adrenaline rush of facing down death at every turn, it was as if my body finally recognized it was safe and decided to give in to the fatigue. The rest of the hunters were gathered below the tree in the courtyard and they looked at me curiously. I knew they wanted answers to their questions. That they wanted to hear what had happened outside the Academy gates. But now was not the time.

"Just get me to the dorms, Will," I whispered.

"You got it. Come on, T-Rex. Clear a way," Will said.

T-Rex walked in front of us, asking the hunters to step aside. They parted easily, creating a long path for us through the crowd. Will continued to hold me up as we walked and I was thankful he was there. Without him, I was sure I would have fallen to the ground. I expected the hunters to bark out questions as we passed, but they didn't. They were as quiet as if we were in church. I mostly kept my eyes to the ground, trying to focus on keeping my balance, but when I glanced up I was taken by the looks on the faces around me. Rather than the suspicious stares I'd been given since I'd arrived at the Academy, the other hunters looked at me with a mix of curiosity and respect. Admiration, even. Some of them even reached out and patted me softly on the shoulder as I passed.

I nodded, thankful they weren't asking questions. I made my way into the dorms, intending to take a shower to scrub the shrieker blood off of me. But the second I saw my bed, I knew a shower would have to wait. I fell into my bunk, not even bothering to kick off my muddy boots, and curled up in a ball. Will and T-Rex were saying something but it sounded distant... hazy, like they were deep underwater. I closed my eyes and felt the world begin to melt away. As sleep washed over me, I saw the black, hulking form of Tiberon pacing back and forth impatiently on a snow-covered field. He turned in my direction as if he had seen me, his eyes piercing into mine.

Tiberon then lowered his head to the ground and ran straight at me. Faster and faster he came, until he was right on top of me. At the last second, he jumped and seemed to dissolve as he passed through me. It was the last thing I remembered before dropping off into a deep, black, dreamless sleep.

I had no sense of how much time had passed when I opened my eyes. I was under the bedcovers and my clothes had been replaced with sweatpants and a t-shirt. Sunlight filled the room and the rest of the bunk beds in the dorm were still made and empty. I swung my legs over the edge of the bed and waited for my head to clear. I stretched my arms, surprised to find that I wasn't that sore. The bruises on my legs were gone too, even if smudges of the shrieker blood still remained. Shrieker blood. The attack. The wolves.

Daniel.

I stood up and ran to the door.

Outside, lessons were in progress in the snow-covered courtyard. A brilliant winter's sun reflected off the snow, nearly blinding me. A young hunter doing a disciplinary lap around the Academy walls approached me. He smiled wide when he saw me.

"You're awake," he buzzed. "Everyone will be so excited."

"Daniel. How is Daniel?" I asked. "Did he…"

"Are you going to tell us what happened?" the young hunter asked. "Some people thought the wolves got the two of you. I smelled the stench on you, though. That's not wolf's blood, I told them. That's something else."

214

I grabbed the young hunter by the arm and pulled him to me. "What's your name?" I asked.

"Hector," he said, the fun disappearing from his eyes. "M...my...name's Hector."

"OK, Hector," I said patiently. "I really want to know how Daniel is doing. Do you know anything?"

"Daniel? He's fine. I mean, not fine like walking around and stuff yet, but he's going to make it," Hector said.

I took a heavy breath and felt a weight lift from my shoulders. Daniel was alive. Good. Now my thoughts turned to what I needed to do next. I patted Hector on the back. "That's great news. Thanks." I turned and walked back into the dorms. I felt Hector's curious eyes on me so I looked over my shoulder and said, "Shriekers. It was shrieker blood, not wolf. You can tell your friends you were right."

Hector grinned. "Thanks, Jack. Hope you feel better."

I smiled and walked back inside. I did feel better, but I also knew I had a big decision ahead of me and a conversation I didn't think was going to go very well.

I made my way to the showers and turned two of the heads to the hottest setting. A hot shower had never felt so good. I used a heavy brush and scrubbed at the shrieker blood until my skin felt raw. Then I washed my hair three times trying to get the stench out. Finally, I just stood there, letting the torrents of water pound on my muscles.

"Jack? Are you in there?"

I almost slipped and fell onto the floor. It was Eva.

"Yeah," I called. "Don't come in here." I searched the room. The towels were way on the other side.

"Are you all right?" Eva called, closer now.

"I'm fine. I said don't come in here. You heard me, right?"

"What?" she called out. "You need a hand?"

I saw movement near the doorway. "No!" I shouted, just as Eva turned the corner. "I'm naked!"

Just in time, Eva whirled around, keeping her back to me. "Whoa, why didn't you say so?" Eva asked.

I ran across the room to the shelf of towels and wrapped one around my waist. "What did you expect I'd be doing in the shower?" I asked.

"Are you decent?"

"Yeah, I guess," I said.

She turned around and studied me. "How are you feeling?"

"I'm fine. I heard Daniel's better."

"His fever broke. He's eating food now so the danger has passed. The poison has worked its way out. He should be back to full strength in a day or two."

"That quick?" I asked. "That's fantastic. I thought he was in real trouble."

"He was. You saved his life by getting him back here the way you did," Eva said.

"It was nothing," I said, a little embarrassed by the attention.

"It was the kind of nothing that took a lot out of you. Do you realize you slept for over twenty-four hours?" Eva asked.

"Really?"

My body must have needed it. And I could feel the difference. Ever since my Change the night before my fourteenth birthday, my body had been freakishly stronger. Now it seemed like it repaired itself faster, too. I stretched my neck to look at my back in one of the mirrors on the wall. The deep scratches from scraping against the trees in our escape from the shriekers were just faint red lines. It was exciting, but it scared me a little at the same time. My body wasn't done changing...and I wasn't entirely sure what it was changing into.

"Hello?" Eva said. "Anyone there? You just went a million miles away."

"Sorry, just a lot to process. There's something I need to tell you but I think I should tell Aquinas at the same time. Will you come with me?"

Eva could see I was serious. She nodded. "Of course. Can I make a suggestion, though?"

"Sure."

"Maybe put some pants on first," she said, nodding to the towel around my waist.

Minutes later, fully dressed, Eva and I walked across the training field toward the Templar Tree. The hunter trainees glanced over at us as we passed despite the instructors shouting at them to maintain their focus on the exercise they were doing. I spotted Will on the opposite side of the field, locked in a mock knife fight with one of the older boys. I headed in that direction, Eva keeping up beside me.

As we walked up, Will executed a brilliant move, sliding on the snowy ground through the legs of his sparring partner, jumping up and jamming the blunt wooden practice knife between the older boy's shoulder blades.

The other boys cheered for him. Will beamed and waved off the applause, but I could tell he loved it. He saw me and the smile disappeared, replaced with a concerned look. He patted his sparring partner on the back and walked over to us.

"Look who's risen from the dead," he said. "I thought you were going to sleep until Christmas."

"Nice move," I said.

"A little showy for my taste," Eva muttered.

"Got the job done," Will said.

"Can you come with us? I have to tell Aquinas something and I'd like you to hear it too," I said.

Will glanced over to the instructor hovering nearby who nodded his head. "Sounds exciting," Will said. "Let's go."

The three of us walked back through the training field. Eva turned toward the tree but I stopped her. "Not yet. We're still missing one."

We found T-Rex in the kitchen scrubbing pots. He looked up and rushed to me, giving me a huge, wet, soapy hug.

"C'mon," I said. "There's something you need to be a part of."

As we walked out of the kitchen I heard T-Rex whisper to Will. "Any idea what this is all about?"

"No idea. Better than washing dishes though, right?" Will said.

One final time, the four of us strode across the training field. Now, even the instructors stopped what they were doing to watch us make our way through the snow. All activity stopped on the yard as we neared the tree.

None of us spoke. Even without telling them what I was about to do, my friends could sense something serious was about to happen. I felt stronger with them next to me. I just didn't know how they were going to react when I told them I had decided to embark on the most dangerous journey possible.

And that I would be doing it on my own.

We sat in the deep cushioned couches in the far corner, away from where Daniel was still recovering. I described to Aqunias in detail everything that had happened in the woods. How the challenge from Daniel had come about, the attack by the shriekers, the appearance of the wolves and how we had hidden in the cave. I didn't recount the story that Daniel had told me about the day Ren Lucre killed his family. I was sure Aquinas already knew and it was Daniel's story to tell the others if he chose.

It was when I came to the part of the story about Tiberon that Aquinas rose from her chair and paced the room as I spoke. I shared the visions of the past that Tiberon had shown me and how he had become the creature he was today. I told them everything, except the terms of the pact I had made with him.

"He said that he told my father the location of the five Jerusalem Stones," I said.

"Impossible; he would have told me," Aquinas said.

"He was sworn to secrecy," I explained. "And when he went for the Stones, he was captured."

"And you trust Tiberon?" Eva chimed in, with one eye trained on Aquinas. "You said so yourself—he betrayed the Order. He's a traitor."

"My father trusted him. That's good enough for me. Besides, he saved us from the shriekers. If he wanted to kill me, he could have just done it while we were out there," I said.

"Maybe it was just payback," T-Rex said.

"What do you mean?" I asked.

"Yeah, T-Rex might be onto something," Will said. "You saved his bacon that first night, right? That whole thing with the arrow. So he owed you one."

"A blood debt," Eva said.

"Yeah, a blood debt," Will agreed. "He paid you back out in the woods and now you're even. What's to say he's not just trying to get you out there one more time so he bites your head off?"

"Ewww…" T-Rex groaned. "I just pictured Jack's head getting bitten off. Can we use a different figure of speech?"

"I don't think it's a figure of speech. The wolf is big enough to take Jack's head clear off in one bite. You're lucky you survived," Eva marveled.

The three of them turned to me and waited. I glanced up at Aquinas who seemed deep in thought.

"You weren't there," I said. "I was able to communicate with him. Like I was inside his mind. I think I would have felt it if he meant to hurt me."

Aquinas tapped the floor with her walking staff. The rest of us fell silent. "As you know, I recently traveled from the Academy," Aquinas said. "Although I perhaps could have stopped all this from happening if I stayed, the trip was not without merit. Certain allies of the Black Guard were able to share with me that Ren Lucre's preparations have reached new heights. They speak of a goblin army being raised and Creach infiltrators worming their way into the halls of power of the great nations."

"All the more reason we need not only the Jerusalem Stones, but the Templar Ring as well," I said.

Aquinas shook her head. "It's too early. You're not yet ready."

"There is no time!" I exclaimed, raising my voice. "I have to do this. I wanted your understanding; I'm not here to ask your permission."

"Enough!" Aquinas bellowed, her eyes flashing anger. "You gave me your oath that you would stay at the Academy until you became a full hunter. I expect you to honor that pledge, young Templar." She walked up to me and stared me in the eye. "Or will you prove yourself not worthy of that name and go back on your word?"

"I think he intends to keep his pledge to you, Master Aquinas," Eva whispered. "Jack, I know what you're thinking. You can't."

"I'm sorry," I said. "But I have no choice." I turned and strode toward the stairs. Aquinas seemed to realize too late what I had planned.

"Wait, Jack," Aquinas called out. "Have patience."

"Sorry," I called over my shoulder. "Turns out that patience doesn't run in the family."

I ran down the staircase, ignoring Eva, Will and T-Rex's calls behind me. The training field fell quiet at the spectacle of the three of them chasing me down the stairs and across the field.

I made a straight line to the rock in the center of the training area and climbed up to the bell. I grabbed the hammer and held it in my hand as the hunter trainees and instructors gathered around.

"Jack, let's talk about this," Eva called out. "Once you strike the bell, there's no turning back."

"I know," I said. With all my might, I struck the bell on the side three times.

CLANG

CLANG

CLANG

Three bells to drop out.

Five bells to accept the Trial of the Cave.

If I passed the trial, I would be a full monster hunter and fulfill my oath to Aquinas. With the Templar Ring in my possession, I could free Tiberon as payment for the rest of the information about the Jerusalem Stones.

It was the only way.

I gripped the hammer and swung hard twice.

CLANG

CLANG

It was done.

That night I was going to enter the caves and either emerge as a hunter or not emerge at all. By the look of horror on Eva's face when I had climbed down off the rock, I could tell which result she thought most likely. To tell the truth, if I had seen that look before I had rung the bell, I might have second-guessed my decision.

"What?" I said to her. "It can't be that bad, can it?"

"Whatever you're thinking, it's like..." Eva started, "...it's way worse."

A few of the younger hunters began to clap. It caught on and soon the entire group was cheering wildly. I pumped my fist in the air, trying to act more confident than I felt. I looked up to the tree and saw Aquinas watching from the balcony. She shook her head, turned and disappeared back inside.

I swallowed hard and steeled myself for the challenge ahead. For better or worse, I was committed. One thing was certain. It was bound to be an adventure.

I just hoped it was one I would survive.

Chapter Twelve

With Will's help, I pulled the chainmail over my long-sleeve shirt. T-Rex stood nearby, fumbling with the leather straps on the armor breastplate. This was the same troll armor I had used in my fight against Ren Lucre. It not only fit surprisingly well, but had proven effective against the Dark Lord of all the Creach. So I figured it could handle whatever battles waited for me in the caves.

"Are you sure you know what you're doing?" Will asked, snatching the armor from T-Rex and lowering it over my head.

"No more than you do," said Eva, coming into the room. "You're putting that armor on backwards."

"I thought that looked weird," T-Rex said.

"Who are you kidding? You had no idea," Will said.

She put her hand on Will's shoulder. "Here, let me."

Will stepped aside and Eva lifted the armor up over my head, rotated it and lowered it back down. She and I then stood face-to-face.

"You don't have a sensible bone in your body, do you, Jack Templar?" she said softly.

I grinned. "Oh, I don't know. My kneecap is pretty sensible. Stays right where it's supposed to pretty much all the time." I felt pressure on my knee and looked down to see her boot pressed up against it.

"This kneecap right here?" she asked. "You know, I could break it in one move. Put you in the infirmary for a month. Probably save your life if I did."

"Only one thing you're forgetting," I said.

"That you'd still go through with it with a broken knee?"

"You got it."

"So maybe I'd need to take out an arm. Maybe bust open that head of yours. You wouldn't miss it much, right? It's not like you're accustomed to using it for anything like actual thought."

T-Rex whispered to Will, "Is Eva going to beat Jack up?"

"Maybe," Will whispered back. "That would be totally awesome, wouldn't it?"

"I'm right here, guys. I can hear you," I said. "Make yourselves useful and hand me those boots, will you?" I turned back to Eva. "I've actually thought this through more than you think. This was the only way out I could see."

"Finish your training. Become a hunter first so you have a chance of surviving past the first fifteen minutes," she said.

"And how long would that take to even reach first degree hunter? Five months? Six, if I pushed it? You heard Aquinas, Ren Lucre is getting ready." I pulled on the leg armor that covered my knees. "I can't let my father waste away in that dungeon. Not if I have a clear path on how to get the information I need to find him. No. There's no time. I have to do this now."

"Aquinas was right," Eva said. "Your impatience will get you killed."

I picked up my sword and gripped it with both hands. Even though I was trying to project confidence, my insides churned from the nerves. "She might be right. Let's just hope she's not right today."

Eva looked at me hard and I thought for a second that I saw tears well in her eyes. And then, just as fast, the expression was gone, replaced by the aloofness of a professional doing a job. "All right, let's see if we can't give you a fighting chance." She turned to the door and gave a low whistle. "Xavier, you can come in now."

Xavier walked in carrying a backpack with him. He gave us all a sheepish grin and a wave. "Hi everyone. Sorry for lurking around out there. Eva told me to wait until she called for me."

"Xavier is a bit of an expert at...well...everything," Eva said. "I asked him to bring some of his toys with him today."

Xavier rushed up to me, tripped over my helmet on the floor and nearly bit it in front of us. He gathered himself up and grabbed my hand, shaking it vigorously. "I just want to say how excited we all are for this, Jack. Everyone's rooting for you."

"How's the betting pool going out there?" Will asked.

"Ahh...we kind of gave up on it. You're the only one willing to bet Jack's going to make it back alive," Xavier said.

I looked over at T-Rex.

"What? I didn't have any money," T-Rex explained quickly.

"I'm glad everyone has so much faith," I said.

Xavier unloaded items from his backpack and stacked them on the table next to us. "It's just that no one's attempted the trial in over a hundred years and the last three hunters who tried it were never seen again. They haven't even opened the door since then. There's no telling what's back there nowadays."

"Maybe whatever monsters were in there have all died off," T-Rex suggested. "Maybe you'll just walk right in, grab the ring, and walk right back out."

I liked the sound of that. I found myself grasping onto that idea. A dead, empty cave. A short, pleasant hike. I'd grab the ring and be back at the Academy an hour later for a hot meal and a shower. Could it really end up being so easy?

"Oh, I doubt that," Xavier said. "That cave goes on for miles and miles. No one really knows how far. More likely it's overrun with bizarre species we haven't seen for decades. It really should be quite fascinating. Scientifically speaking."

Eva cleared her throat and nodded to the assembled items Xavier had emptied from his backpack. "We don't have much time. Maybe you could give Jack a quick run-through on the items you brought him."

"Of course," Xavier said. "On such short notice, I just grabbed a few things I've been working on that I thought might be helpful." He held up a bulkier version of the winching device I'd seen him use on the obstacle course. This one looked like a heavy gauge fishing reel, the kind used on deep-sea charters.

"You think Jack might be going up against a giant tuna in there?" Will asked.

Xavier clipped the reel to a belt around his waist. He pressed a button and a tiny spear exploded from the reel, trailing a silvery line behind it. The spear sunk into the wooden roof in the dorm. A whirring sound came from the reel and Xavier was lifted off the floor, dangling by his belt.

"That's so cool," T-Rex said.

"Did you fix that little glitch it had before?" I asked.

Xavier pressed another button and the reel spooled out the other direction and lowered him to the ground. "Absolutely. I think so, anyway." Xavier then began digging through his items again.

228

"Check this out. This is an ultra-strong line I've developed. As strong as a rope an inch thick but only a fraction of the weight. There are four ejectable fasteners so don't use them all at once."

He handed me the belt and the reel and I stuffed it into my backpack.

"This is just like James Bond," Will said. "What else to do have?"

"Sorry, no fancy guns or tracking devices, although that would have been a good idea now that I think about it." Xavier pulled out a notebook and, suddenly lost in thought, scribbled a note to himself. "I could have combined a GPS transponder with an echo-location sensor. And that could have generated—"

"Xavier!" Eva cried. "Do you think you could do that later? Little short on time."

Xavier looked up as if just remembering we were all there. "Right, sorry. Of course." He put away his notebook and handed me a small bag filled with golf balls.

"I'm guessing these aren't really golf balls," I said. Will reached in and grabbed one, tossing it up in the air.

"They're grenades. Small ones, anyway," Xavier said. "More flash than bang, I'm afraid. They're loud and produce a bright light, but it's not going to blow anything up." He glanced at Will, still tossing it in the air and catching it. "Well, maybe a few fingers if it goes off in your hand." Will stopped playing with it and put it back in the bag. "I made them as a distraction device. They might help."

"Thanks, Xavier. These are great," I said.

"Oh, one more thing," he said. He opened a can of paint. We all looked carefully inside.

"What is it?" T-Rex asked.

"An explosive?" Eva guessed.

"Liquid armor?" Will suggested.

"Some kind of sticky glue-trap?" I asked.

Xavier looked at us like we were all crazy. "It's paint. Didn't any of you play with paints when you were little?"

We all stepped back, amused at Xavier's quirky ways. "OK, I'll bite. What am I going to use the paint for?" I asked.

This paint has the highest luminescence possible. Flashlights can run out of batteries. A torch can be blown out. Whatever you paint with this will light up like it was plugged into a wall socket," Xavier said proudly.

"What if he's being stalked by a monster and needs to hide?" Eva said. "He could turn a flashlight off."

"Ahh...I thought of that," Xavier said. "Your sword. Paint the blade of your sword and hold it in front of you. If you need to hide, just slide it into your scabbard and, *voila*, no more light."

"Brilliant, Xavier," I said, handing over my sword. He brushed the paint along the blade and handed it back to me. It was already dry to the touch. "It doesn't seem very bright. Are you sure it will be enough light?"

"It's just too light in here. It will be plenty bright in the cave. And if you need more light, there's a spray can of the stuff in the backpack. Just spray it on any surface to light it up." Xavier handed me the backpack. "That's everything, I'm afraid."

I grabbed Xavier's hand and shook it. "Thank you. These could make all the difference."

A bell sounded outside. At the sound of it, my stomach turned over on itself. I'd been too busy getting ready that I hadn't had the time to be nervous yet. I knew the bell was the signal for me to go to the cave. The time had arrived and a tidal wave of nervousness had arrived with it.

Who was I kidding? A few weeks ago I was just Jack Smith, a middle school kid who worried about bullies, making the football team, my grades and whether any girl would ever notice I was alive. Now I was supposed to be Jack Templar, some kind of hero who laughed at danger and who always managed to find victory, regardless of how impossible the odds seemed. As I stood there with my friends, armed with a sword, body armor and a backpack full of tricks, I didn't feel like a hero. I just felt scared.

"Do you know why all the young hunters stopped and stared at you when you arrived at the gate with Daniel?" Eva asked, interrupting my thoughts of self-doubt.

"No, I never found out," I admitted. "I noticed it though. The way they stared."

"Think of the insignia of the Templar Knights," Eva said.

"Two knights sharing one horse," said Will.

"Right," said Eva. "It's been said that the One would arrive at our gates as a true Templar. Hard to look more like a Templar than showing up the way you did."

"It doesn't mean anything, though," I said. "It doesn't mean I'm the One."

"Maybe not," Eva said. "But the hunters out there have started to believe in you. The people in this room believe in you too. All that's left is for you to believe in yourself."

The bell rang again.

With one last look at my friends, I slid my sword into my scabbard and took a deep breath. "Okay, let's do this," I said.

The entire Academy was waiting outside the dorm and a cheer went up when I appeared. Eager to get to the cave before I lost my nerve, I trudged across the training field, the crowd parting in front of me as if pushed away by an invisible force. Will and T-Rex flanked me on either side. I glanced back and saw that Eva and Xavier followed directly behind us.

I looked up at the mountain looming over me. As I did, the last of the sun dipped behind the cold, craggy rock face, casting a shadow over the Academy. A breeze swept across the clearing and I shivered despite the layers of armor and clothes I had on me. It had suddenly occurred to me that I might never see the sun again.

The Templar Tree in the center of the field was dark; it appeared that the balcony lanterns were unlit. I knew Aquinas was angry with me, but I thought she would at least watch the proceedings. Maybe even wish me luck. I guess I misjudged just how much I had upset her.

We reached the old battlements and the main gate. I stopped ten feet out and took another breath to steel my shaky nerves. From inside the dark gate approached Aquinas's hunched figure. The crowd fell quiet as she shuffled toward me, leaning heavily on her walking stick. She looked me up and down, then raised her stick and thumped me in the chest with it as if testing my armor.

"Are you ready?" she asked.

"No," I replied. "But I don't think I ever will be."

"Hmmm..." she said, studying me. "The bravado is gone. That's a hopeful sign. I just hope the courage remains." She took my hand and held it up in the air, spinning me toward the crowd. "The Trial of the Cave begins now. Cheer on your champion!"

The crowd exploded into the loudest cheer yet. Will and T-Rex, filled with tension, screamed their heads off right in front of me. Only Eva remained silent, looking past me into the dark shadows of the cave.

Aquinas walked me forward in through the gates. The cheering hunters stayed behind except for Will, Eva and T-Rex, who followed us into the darkness of the mountain.

I pulled out my sword and the space around us was suddenly awash in light. Xavier's luminescent paint worked better than I could have ever imagined.

It was as if my sword had been transformed into a giant lantern.

It caught Aquinas off-guard, but only for a second. "I see young Xavier shared some of his treasures with you," she said. "Just beware. The place you go has been a world of great darkness for thousands of years. The creatures that live there may not thank you for bringing light into their domain."

"I'll keep that in mind," I said.

Eva spoke up, her bearing serious. "I found an old book once that described the ring being in a great room across a river, protected from any who would try to possess it," Eva said.

"Yes, yes," Aquinas mumbled. "A great room. But where? And protected how? These are the real questions. If the book is even accurate, that is."

We came to a stop at the wide set of metal doors, crisscrossed by heavy chains and padlocks. Aquinas produced a set of old keys from her pocket and set to work unlocking each of them. Finally, the chains lay in a heap in the ground and Aquinas's hand hovered over the last lock.

"Are you ready?" she asked. "Once you enter, the gate cannot be opened unless you have the Templar Ring. Do you understand me? No matter what, the gate will not be opened."

I looked to Will, T-Rex and Eva. They watched me with a mixture of nervous excitement and fear. "No goodbyes, all right?" I said. "I'll be back in no time."

"You bet, Jack. Go get 'em," Will said.

"Just be careful," T-Rex croaked, his voice trembling.

I looked at Eva, who stood with her arms across her chest. I nodded toward Will and T-Rex. "You've got these two, right? You know, if anything happens."

Eva nodded. It was clear she wasn't going to say anything, so I gave her a smile and turned back to Aquinas. As I did, I heard Eva say softly, "Do your duty."

"Come what may," I replied without turning. "All right, let's see what's behind door number one."

"Good luck, Jack," Aquinas said. "Remember what I told you when you first came here. You must find what you stand for. Not what you stand against, but what you stand *for*. Do you understand?"

I nodded, even though I truthfully wasn't sure that I did.

"When you discover what it is, you keep it in here," she said, putting her hand on my chest. "It's only for you. For your power. A hunter with a strong enough *why* can endure any *how*. Remember that."

"Thank you, Master Aquinas," I said. "Just be ready to open the door back up when I get back."

She smiled. "May you be pure of heart and ready for the task. Only a true Templar will pass the test."

Jacques de Molay had said those same words the day he hid the Templar Ring. I prayed that the challenge of those words would not prove too great a task.

I nodded in acknowledgement to Aquinas, took a deep breath and readied myself as Aquinas inserted the key into the final lock, turned it and unlocked the gate.

Chapter Thirteen

A great grinding noise filled the air as a series of gears and levers moved inside the door, unraveling a complicated locking mechanism that groaned from centuries of disuse. Some final bolt pulled out of place and the door bulged outward with a whoosh of air like a bottle that had been sealed under pressure.

I stood in front of the door, my glowing sword in hand, praying that Will's hypothesis had been right and that nothing alive remained in the cave.

Only seconds later, that idea was blown away by a great, angry howl coming from deep within the darkness.

"Hurry," Aquinas said. "You must get as far from the door as you can before the creatures find you. If you are to have a chance, you must hurry!"

Without giving myself time to think, I ran forward into the cave. Behind me, the gate slammed shut and the locks slid back into place. My heart sank at the sound. I was on my own.

I held my glowing sword over my head, running through a narrow opening roughly cut through the black granite mountain. Xavier's paint gave me enough light to see, but not more than ten or fifteen feet in any direction. After that, it as pitch-black. The passageway was covered in veils of spider webs that clung to me as I ran past. Suddenly, the floor crumbled underneath my feet and I was falling. In a flash, I wondered if this were already the end. Could it really be that I was going to fall to my death only feet away from the door? Weirdly enough, I mostly felt embarrassment at the idea that I'd been so careless.

Fortunately, a moment later my backside hit a steep, rocky slope. My relief was short-lived as I started to slide down the gravelly surface. I dug my feet in, but succeeded in only kicking more rocks loose. I reached out with my hands, trying to grab onto anything solid. Nothing. I looked down below, the panic rising up in me. At first I thought it was just the light playing tricks on me, but, sitting up a little as I slid, I could see what was ahead of me: a drop-off into a black void.

I scrambled even harder, desperate now to cling to anything that could slow me down. But now I was surrounded by an avalanche of loose rocks and dirt. There was no stopping. It was starting to look like I had celebrated too early. I really was about to plunge to my death.

But I wasn't about to give up that easily. I flipped over so that I was still sliding feet first, but now on my stomach instead of on my back. Dragging my hands out on either side of me for balance, I raised myself up on my knees, as if I were surfing. With a quick look behind me, I saw the avalanche of rocks beneath me pouring off the cliff. I was going to get one chance at this.

I gripped my sword with both hands and held it over my head, blade pointed to the ground. With a loud cry I plunged my sword as hard as I could into the ground, just as I felt my feet slide over the cliff.

By luck, it hit something soft and sunk in. I held on tight. With a violent jerk, my body stopped, my legs dangling over the edge of the chasm. One of my hands slid off the sword and I spun around, my whole body hanging in midair.

With a cry, I swung my legs around and reached back for the sword. I missed. I felt my grip weakening; any minute now, I was going to be an eternal addition to the darkness below. I reached again and missed again. Worse, I felt the sword move. Whatever I had dug the blade into was loosening. I watched in horror as the blade slid out an inch. Then another.

Summoning all my strength, I reached for the sword with my free hand.

Got it.

I pulled myself up just as the sword slipped out of the ground, reaching safety only seconds before the earth around the blade crumbled away.

I sagged on the side of the cliff, panting from the exertion.

The avalanche of rocks and debris continued to smash its way down the chasm, sending resounding echoes throughout the cave.

"So much for the element of surprise," I mumbled.

As if in answer, a rustling, screeching sound erupted below me. Carefully, I leaned over the edge and held my sword in front of me. At first I thought it was a cloud of dust rising up from the chasm, but as the sound grew louder and my eyes adjusted to the gloom, I realized I was wrong. It wasn't a dust cloud. It was a swarm of thousands of bats!

I scrambled to my feet and worked my way back up the cliff. Seconds later the bats tore up from below in a wild, screeching mass. They were so thick that it looked like a waterfall in reverse as they flew up higher and higher into the cave. A few of them separated from the main group and buzzed around my head. I waved my arms to shoo them away, but it was no use. The few turned into dozens, and soon I was surrounded by a buzzing cloud of the little creatures. After my battle with the shriekers a few days before, these bats seemed more of a nuisance than a real threat. That is, until they started biting.

I felt the first little bite on my leg. Then another on my arm. On my elbow. Then the entire swarm dive-bombed me, clinging to my body. They clawed at the joints in my armor. Tried to wriggle their ways into my helmet. I felt one trying to climb up my pant leg. Every time I swatted a bunch of them away with the back of my hand, twice the amount flew in to replace them.

I was in real trouble.

I stumbled forward, my hands in front of my helmet to keep the little devils away from my face and eyes. It was like I was the first food these bats had seen in years and they weren't about to let it walk away. I racked my brain for a way out of this mess. Desperate, I reached into my backpack and pulled out one of Xavier's grenades. Holding my forearm across my face, I threw the flash grenade at the ground next to my feet.

BOOM!

It exploded with a blinding white light and enough of a concussive blast to spray me with dirt and shards of rock. Most importantly, the bats shrieked and lifted off into the air, flying back into the gloom of the cave. I felt a little bite on my calf and reached up my own pant leg to pull out the one that had crawled up there. I held it, a pinched finger holding each webbed wing, and studied it. Its little face was dominated with massive black eyes, an adaptation from living in the dark. It screamed at me and bared a row of sharp teeth, freakishly oversized for the creature's tiny head.

"Sorry, you'll have to find something else to eat today," I said, and tossed it up into the air. With a scream, it flapped its wings and flew off to join the swirling column of its still-hungry friends.

I spotted a path worn into the side of the sloped rock face a few yards below where I stood. Quickly, I crawled to it and headed deeper into the cave, leaving the screeching bats behind me.

The light from the glowing paint on my sword was only half as bright as when I had started. The tumble down the rock slope had scraped it completely off in several places and the rest of it was dull from small scratches. I was having a tough time picking my way over the rough cave floor with the limited light so I stopped and dug through my backpack for the spray bottle Xavier had given me. I wiped off what dirt I could from the blade and then reapplied the glowing paint from the spray can. The paint recovered my sword and the glow returned in full force, but it was the spray that missed the blade that surprised me. Little particles of glowing paint drifted in the still air, making a tiny glowing cloud of light. I sliced my sword through the middle of it and it swirled around in cool little light tornados. Under different circumstances, I would have hung out and played with the spray, but the sound of rocks rattling in the chasm beneath me reminded me that I wasn't alone and that I had to keep moving. I put the spray bottle back in my backpack and restarted my hike. As I had absolutely no idea where I was going, forward seemed like the best direction.

For the next hour I kept to the rough path carved into the cave floor. Sometimes it looked like a well-worn track beat down by years of heavy use, but occasionally it would turn into no more than a narrow path within a field of giant boulders. I wondered what type of feet had worn away the stone over the years to create the trail. I had a bad feeling that they weren't necessarily human. Still, the only other option to following the trail was to strike off down one of the many side tunnels that branched off into the darkness. While some of them had rough trails of their own, I decided to stay on the clearest path possible.

I remembered Eva's voice telling me that the ring was in a large room somewhere below. I reasoned that it made sense that the most well used path would lead me there. Or lead me right into whatever traps had been set over the years to protect the ring from discovery. Still, I reminded myself that finding the ring was only half of the battle. It wouldn't do anyone any good if I were to find the ring, only to get hopelessly lost in the cave system. I shuddered at the thought of wandering aimlessly around the cave for days or weeks on end.

Even worse, I imagined what it must be like for my father as a prisoner in Ren Lucre's dungeons, not only in the dark, but chained to the wall, living without hope. And that was one thing I still had. Hope. But with every step deeper into the cave, I felt the oppressive darkness press in on me, trying to stifle the idea that I had any chance of success.

In fact, the longer I walked without running into another creature, the more time my mind had to second-guess what I was doing. The underground system was enormous. If the room wasn't on the main trail, it would take months to explore even just a small fraction of the system. And a ring could be hidden anywhere. I could have passed right by it over an hour earlier and I would never know. Just as my hopes were bottoming out, I heard a sound up ahead.

I gently crouched down to the ground and slid my sword into its scabbard to hide my light. I strained my ears to pick up the sound again. Without the noise of my walking, the sound came to me clearly. A soft, constant roar. There was a river ahead of me.

My heart leapt. Eva had said I had to cross a river to get to the ring. I was about to pull my sword back out when I heard another noise.

This time it came from just behind me.

First, I heard a rock tumble across the ground as if it had been kicked.

Then the soft wheeze of a creature breathing. Something big.

I froze in place, my hand already on the handle of my sword.

The breathing turned heavier—from a wheeze into a series of small grunts. Then I realized that the creature was sniffing the air.

I thought back to Eva's lesson about trolls and how the Creach who live underground develop a stronger sense of smell in order to hunt. After sweating in my armor for the last couple of hours, I figured whatever creature was tracking me wouldn't need any special skills to find me in the dark. Even with my cloaking medallion, hiding wasn't going to work. I had two options. Fight or flight. I huddled against the rock, not sure which to choose. And then the creature caught my scent.

A roar erupted behind me. The ground literally shook as the creature stampeded in my direction. With only seconds to react, I stood, pulled my sword and raised it toward the beast. Shocked by the light, it stopped in place, temporarily confused.

I nearly dropped my sword from seeing what stalked me.

Chapter Fourteen

It was a Creach unlike I'd seen before—hairless, with pale, wrinkly skin criss-crossed with scar tissue from hundreds of old injuries. It walked on all fours, but its front legs were twice as long as its back, giving it a tall, ungainly look. Each foot looked almost human, except for long black talons that stretched out and *click-clacked* against the rock floor.

The Creach's head was an outlandish size, two or three times larger than what appeared possible for its body. It was boxy and dominated by a single enormous black eye that reminded me of the bats I'd seen earlier. A wide nose stretched out, engulfing nearly half its face. Below that was an even wider mouth with a lower jaw that jutted out, making room for giant teeth that stuck upward sharply past its upper lip.

Adding to its odd appearance was a mane of thick spines that looked like the quills of a giant porcupine. Even as I stood there shaking in my boots, one of the lessons from the week before came to me and I remembered a description of a similar Creach. This was a cave ogre, and it was one nasty looking monster.

Beyond its horrifying and grotesque appearance was the sheer size of the creature. By the sound of it, I had expected it to be big. But when I pulled out my sword, I found myself looking at the lower part of its chest. I had to lean back and crane my neck upward to see all of it. The cave ogres described in class were supposed to be no bigger than a small horse. This one was every bit as big as an elephant, and scarier than anything I'd ever seen.

Unfortunately, it seemed to have the memory of an elephant too, and it quickly got over the initial shock of the light and remembered that it was stalking its dinner. It reared up on its hind legs and then slammed its claws into the ground. The violence of the action caused a half-dozen or more of the spines from its mane to fly at me through the air like arrows. I dove to the side behind a rock and heard them smash into the ground around me. The Creach roared and stomped its feet.

I quickly decided fighting wasn't the best plan. It was time to run.

I grabbed one of my flash grenades and flung it at the ogre as hard as I could. I covered my eyes as it exploded on its thick skin, the flash lighting up the cave. The Creach screamed, but I knew the grenade didn't have enough power to actually hurt the beast; I hoped that it would at least stun it for a few seconds. I took the opportunity and ran as hard as I could down the trail, in the direction of the water.

It was only a few seconds later that I heard the heavy footsteps behind me. A look over my shoulder confirmed the cave ogre was smashing its way along the path, knocking rocks out of the way with its arms and shoulders. I grabbed two more of the grenades and chucked them blindly behind me. They exploded in rapid succession and the ogre roared. I'd bought myself another few seconds. I felt inside my backpack. I only had two grenades left. Not good.

I spun out on the gravel floor as I turned a corner in the path, barely catching myself from crashing. When I looked up, I realized the air was filled with the roar of running water. Using the light from my sword, I ran toward it, thinking the river might be a way to escape the four-footed death machine chasing me. It had worked once before when I had escaped Ren Lucre, although I had died as a result and only came back to life after T-Rex gave me CPR. There was no T-Rex in these caves to save me this time. But the cave ogre smashing through the rocks behind me left no doubt that I had to do something creative to escape.

But as I ran toward the water, my heart sank. The path ended at the edge of another crevasse, a deep cut in the rock about twenty feet wide and at least twice that deep. Through this narrow funnel raged a torrent of white water that looked like it was jetting out of a massive fire hose. A wooden bridge extended from the path across the river. Thick ropes formed handholds on both sides and planks of wood were tied together to make the bridge itself.

While I was excited at the prospect of having a way across, it looked like the thing was built hundreds of years ago and probably hadn't been used since. On closer inspection, many of the boards were rotted away and the ropes were hopelessly frayed. I looked down through a hole in the bridge at the river below. Jagged rocks poked up from the wild, frothy water. Falling in would mean certain death.

A snarl behind me reminded me that certain death was also chasing me from behind. Desperate, I looked up and down the length of the cliff edge. There were no other options.

"Here goes nothing," I said.

With a cry, I ran onto the bridge.

The rope on the right side immediately snapped and I tipped right over the edge. I grabbed the rope on the left and regained my balance. Moving slower, I worked my way across the bridge, trying to avoid the boards that looked the most rotten.

The ogre reached the bridge and screamed at me in frustration. I turned and, feeling a little cocky, gave him a little wave.

"Sorry, buddy. Maybe next time," I said.

I doubt the cave ogre spoke English, but it apparently knew when someone was making fun of him. It roared and then followed that with a high-pitched scream. It backed up down the path, clawing at the floor. With horror, I realized it was preparing itself for a running start. I moved as fast as I dared on the rocking bridge and reached the other side of the cliff just as the ogre bolted toward the ravine.

It launched itself off the cliff edge, reaching out with its overly long front legs for the opposite side.

It fell short and smashed into the wooden bridge, obliterating it in a tangle of rope and splinters. The ogre tried to grab onto the sheer face of the cliff, but its talons slid right off the slick rock. Screaming, it tumbled down into the river below.

I fell backward and rested on a rock, trying to catch my breath and slow down my pounding heart. Slowly, the euphoria I felt from escaping the cave ogre was replaced by a scary realization. I had no way of getting back over the river. Once I found the ring—if I found it—then I was going to have to find an entirely new exit.

"Find the ring first," I said to myself. "Then worry about getting out of here. One thing at a time."

I knew it was good advice, but it didn't make me feel any better. Knowing the way back home was the one small comfort I had carried with me from the beginning of the quest. Now that that was gone, I felt like my chances of survival, slim to begin with, were steadily migrating toward being non-existent.

I took a drink from the water bottle in my backpack, then forced myself to stand up. I had never solved a problem by feeling sorry for myself and I didn't figure this time was going to be any different.

The only solution was to keep pushing forward, no matter the odds, no matter the obstacles.

Out of nowhere, I pictured Eva's face and heard the last words she had said to me. *Do your duty.* I suddenly wished I had said something more to her. Something more significant. I thought back to the kiss she gave me before I faced Ren Lucre. Just the memory of it somehow made me feel a little stronger.

Surveying the area, I noticed the path on this side of the bridge was even harder to find. Rockslides from the steep walls had littered the ground with piles of loose stone. Still, even without being able to see the path, I knew where I had to go. I picked my way over the rock field toward three tunnels cut into the mountain just ahead of me.

Unlike the caves I'd been hiking through for the last several hours, these were obviously man-made. They were large, arched openings, twice my height and just about as wide. They also each had identical wrought iron gates bolted straight into the solid rock. At least, I assumed they had once been gates. They lay twisted and broken on the ground, only jagged fragments still attached to ancient hinges. Whatever had busted through the gates had done a number on them.

I held my sword up to each tunnel, trying to penetrate into the inky gloominess. I had a bad feeling that the choice I made here was going to spell the difference between success and failure, life and death, so I looked for any clues that would guide me on the right path. Nagging me in the back of my mind was the knowledge that I didn't know if any of the tunnels were the right choice. I didn't even know whether I was anywhere near the right section of the cave.

I realized just how much I had invested in Eva's information that I had to cross a river and that the ring was in a manmade room. Even Aquinas had said she didn't know if the book was accurate, but it was all I had. And I was learning that sometimes that's what it takes to keep hope alive: just some small glimmering chance that things are going to work out.

I figured if she was right, then manmade tunnels had a good chance of leading to manmade rooms. But which one?

I waved my sword over the archway, looking for clues. The stone around the edge was shiny and smooth, as if something had repeatedly rubbed against it. Still, faint and barely visible, I felt etchings in the rock, but they were too worn away to tell what they had said.

I stepped back in frustration and looked at all three openings, considering my next move.

I rummaged through my backpack and dug out my water bottle, trying to think the problem through. When I slid the water bottle back in, my hand nudged against the spray bottle of glow paint. I pulled it out and weighed it in my hand, letting an idea take form.

I stepped up to the first tunnel and sprayed the glow paint all around the edge. The paint highlighted even the most faint marks in the stone, even those invisible to the naked eye. Everywhere I sprayed, carvings seemed to pop out from the rock in perfect detail. While I was pleased my idea worked, what I saw didn't exactly fill me with all kinds of warm fuzzy feelings.

The archway was covered with rows and rows of skulls.

All with enormous empty sockets and mouths open as if locked in eternal, silent screams.

I sprayed the second tunnel and the exact same carvings popped out at me. I wasn't sure what I was hoping to find on the third tunnel—maybe smiley faces, indicating that it was the right choice? Not a chance. Identical screaming skulls covered the entrance to the last tunnel as well. I stepped back and looked at my handiwork; three glowing archways of super-creepy skulls stared out at me, mocking my frustration.

"Well, I wouldn't call that an improvement," I said out loud, half wondering how long it would take for me to have longer conversations with myself, ultimately devolving into Golem, the character from *The Lord of the Rings* books, and decided that I would draw the line when I started repeating, "*My Precious...*"

I was about to put the paint away when I noticed I had missed a spot on the last arch. Since everything else had repeated the pattern over and over, I had stopped spraying the paint about a foot before hitting the ground, a spot about the size of one more skull.

Shaking the can, I kneeled down on the

ground and ran my hand over the area. I barely felt anything. Even though the paint was my one precious light source, I sprayed the last little section of rock.

A Templar Cross burst out from the wall as if I had set it on fire. I rocked back and stared. This was it. This was my tunnel. I slid the paint in my backpack, got to my feet and hustled into the opening...running straight into a pile of skeletons.

I heard them first. A brittle crack, crack, crack as bones snapped underfoot. I pointed my sword down and saw my foot was stuck in the middle of a human ribcage. Grossed out, I shook my foot to get it free. This had the unfortunate effect of making the entire skeleton shake and gyrate like it was coming back to life. I finally pulled my foot free and stumbled backward, stomping into another pile of old bones. An ancient human skull, looking just like the ones carved into the rock outside, rolled to the side so that its face stared up at me. I kicked at it with my boot and it soared through the air like a soccer ball, clattering into the dark.

As I listened to the skull rattle around and finally come to a rest, I felt a pang of guilt. As the initial shock wore off, it occurred to me that these skeletons were likely hunters from the past who had been on the same quest as me. And there I was, stomping through their remains, basically desecrating their graves. And not only monster hunter graves, but the graves of other creatures too. As I looked closer at the piles of bones littering the floors, I saw that only a few of them appeared human. There were long serpentine skeletons with rib cages that looked like they were made of fish bones. Massive skulls with horns. Squat bodies with boney armor plating. Creatures with two or three heads. Small bodies the size of dogs. And, spread throughout, piles of hundreds, if not thousands, of skeletons of small rodents.

I swallowed hard, wondering where the creature was that had done all this killing. Either this was its lair and I was on the wrong track, or the creature that had done all this was the protector of the ring and I was getting close.

I didn't know which it was, but I liked the idea that there was at least a logical chance I might be closing in on my goal. It looked like the bones were ancient, so I held out hope that the creature had long since died or moved on to look for food elsewhere. As I picked my way over the field of bones, I had a sneaking suspicion that this was wishful thinking and that it wasn't going to be that easy.

A few minutes later, the tunnel curved to the right and then opened up into a dark, cavernous space. I couldn't see how large the room was because the light from my sword didn't penetrate that far into the gloom. There was a swirling breeze so I sensed the room was either huge or there were other exits to it. I was running low on glow paint, but I wanted to know what was in front of me. I took it out again and sprayed a little in the air. Just as I guessed, the breeze took the particles for a twisting ride up in to the air and toward the middle of the cave. I kept spraying and soon the air toward the top of the room was filled with swirling light. Just that sight alone would have been enough for me to marvel at, but what the light revealed captured all my attention.

The space had been carved out of solid rock. On each side was a series of wide pillars with arches between them, looking like pictures I'd seen before of old European cathedrals. In the center of each archway was a flat platform with a suit of armor laying on it, a sword clasped to its chest. I guessed these were graves of knights from long ago. I looked up and saw that the ceiling was covered with hundreds of Templar Crosses, all of different sizes, fitting in together like a massive, stone jigsaw puzzle. I wondered if this was the burial chamber for the Grand Masters, the ones who had secretly run the Black Guard, the monster hunters, within the Knights Templar.

But my curiosity was going to have to wait. At the far end of the room was a throne of rough-hewn stone on which sat another suit of armor. Only this one had its visor open and gauntlets off, showing the skeletal remains inside. On the skeleton's right hand, there was a gold ring, encrusted with brilliant diamonds. Even from across the room, it glinted from the swirling light, as if beckoning me forward.

It was the ring. It had to be.

I fought the urge to run straight for it. Something felt wrong. There was no way this was going to be so easy. The pile of bones in the tunnel behind me testified to that. But what was the catch? I studied the floor and saw nothing out of the ordinary. No trip wires or booby traps as far as I could tell. There were cracks in the walls and ceiling, little areas where the stone had crumbled over time, but overall it looked sturdy enough. The only thing that made me nervous, besides all the dead guys in suits of armor, that is, were two large tunnel openings on either side of the throne. But as I stood there for a full minute, the only sound was my heart pounding in my chest; nothing moved from those dark shadows.

I gripped my sword and took a deep breath. "OK, here goes nothing," I said.

Gingerly, I picked my way over the floor, still on the lookout for some kind of trap. I made it halfway across the room before everything went wrong.

Chapter Fifteen

The first thing I noticed was that the breeze had simply died. The glowing paint particles stopped swirling above me and fell to the floor. It wasn't just a lull either; the air had turned dead still. I felt an iceball churn in my stomach as I realized what it meant. Something was coming down the tunnel. And it was so big that it blocked the passage of air completely.

I saw its legs first. Impossibly long and hairy, four of them poked out of the tunnel, feeling the air like black, wiry antennas. The legs curled around and braced against the wall as the rest of the creature's body slid out from the tunnel along with its other four legs.

Stretching out to full height after being cramped in the tunnel, now standing between me and the ring, was the largest spider I'd ever seen.

It looked just like the tarantulas I'd seen on TV—brown and hairy, with wicked pincers near its mouth that opened and shut with audible clicks. Only it was fifteen feet tall.

The tunnel filled with bones was apparently this spider's lair. And if I didn't think of something quick, I was going to be the newest skeleton added to that pile.

The spider seemed to have the same idea because it reared back, its front two legs clawing the air. Then, with its pincers snapping, it charged.

I sprinted to my left, reaching the pillar of the first archway just as the spider reached me. I ducked behind it as one of its grotesque legs smashed into the stone right over my head in an explosion of rock. I rolled forward, feeling a second leg scrape across my backpack as I scampered toward the next pillar.

I thought I was clear of it when I felt a violent tug on my backpack and I was suddenly flying backward through the air.

The spider lifted me like I was a ragdoll and hung me upside-down, thrashing me back and forth.

I still had my sword and I twisted midair to reach the leg that had a hold of me. But I was being tossed around so hard I couldn't get the right angle.

Finally, the spider paused, maybe to see if it had shaken me to death yet. I seized the moment and stabbed it as hard as I could into the leg nearest me, sinking my blade in its flesh nearly to the hilt.

The spider freaked out. Its whole body broke out in spasms from the pain, and with a flick of its leg, it sent me literally flying across the room, smashing me into a wall. The impact knocked the wind out of me and I slumped to the floor.

The spider thrashed wildly across the room. I hadn't really hurt it; I had just made it really mad. I only had a few more seconds until it attacked again.

Quickly, I oriented myself within the room. I was no longer separated from the ring. In fact, I had a clear shot to it if I made a run for it.

The clack-clack of the spider's pincers got my attention. I turned back toward it, my hand already closing around the next to last grenade in my bag. As the spider charged at me, I chucked it at the creature's head.

It exploded in a satisfying boom and bright flash. The spider staggered back, slamming into the far wall. I knew it was just stunned, probably for only a few seconds. Still, I had come this far to get that ring and, even if I didn't really have a plan to escape, I wanted to at least hold it in my hand.

I sprinted the last half of the room and reached the throne. I was about to grab the ring when something stopped me. I remembered what Aquinas had told me of the Knights Templar. Even though they ended up being one of the wealthiest orders in Europe, it was because the knights themselves had taken vows of poverty. That's what the Templar symbol of two knights sharing a horse was all about. So what was a Templar Grand Master doing with a diamond-encrusted gold ring?

I looked at the gaping black eyes of the skeleton on the throne.

"That's the test, isn't it?" I whispered. "Jacques de Molay said only a true Templar would pass the test. It's the vow of poverty. It has to be."

I looked at the skeleton's other hand. There it was. A ring carved from stone with a simple Templar Cross etched into it. That was the ring of a true Templar.

I reached over and respectfully slid it off the skeleton's hand. I felt like I should say something profound, but a sudden noise behind me let me know I was out of time. I pocketed the ring and jumped to the side just as the spider's leg smashed into the throne, destroying the skeleton in one swipe.

I had only one grenade left. I was sure running for it wasn't an option since this creature was both faster than me and knew the caves better than I ever would. I clutched my sword and decided I had to make a stand.

The spider must have sensed the fight in me, because it paused and stared at me as if determining whether I represented any danger. Quickly, it decided against it and launched its attack.

I fended it off as best I could, but the ends of its legs weren't like the soft part I had stabbed earlier. They were hard as steel and flew at me in a flurry of blows. It was like sword fighting against eight top-notch adversaries who were bigger, stronger and more talented. It wasn't looking good.

Then I had an idea: a crazy one, but I was ready for crazy.

I pulled Xavier's turbo-charged reel from my backpack and attached it to my belt. There were four projectile arrows left to shoot and a full reel of super-strong wire. What better way to capture a spider than with a web?

I shot the first projectile and embedded it in the ceiling above the spider, the wire trailing behind it still attached to my belt. With a cry I charged forward, blade pointed out. I ran right at the spider, stripping out more wire as I did. My little charge took the spider by surprise and I was actually able to run underneath the spider and come out the opposite side.

As it turned to face me, I ran around it in the opposite direction, still spooling out the wire as I did it. Two of the spider's legs got caught up in the wire, throwing the monster off for a moment. As it tried to shake off the wire with its free legs, it only got more tangled up. I tied the wire off to a stone pillar and then quickly fired a second projectile into the ceiling, where it dug into the rock. I ran around the now-struggling spider, looping the wire over and under its legs. Finally, I braced myself behind the throne and pressed the button on the reel to winch in my web. Instead of it pulling me, I just wanted to pull the wire tight. Really tight.

It worked. As the wire cinched, it bound the spider's legs closer together until finally, trembling from exertion, it fell over on its side, hopelessly enmeshed.

I tied it off and cut the wire with my sword. The spider struggled on the ground, but the more it struggled, the tighter the wire became. As it realized this, it stopped moving, its beady eyes turning toward me.

I walked to its head to finish the creature off, my sword up in case one of the legs popped free. Then the unexpected happened. The spider let out a high-pitched scream in an octave that seemed to pierce right into my brain. I held my hands to my ears to block it out but even then it still hurt. It stopped and I carefully lowered my hands, but the second I did, it screamed again. I didn't know spiders could even make sounds, let alone use them as a weapon. Then again, I'd never run into a spider the size of a bus before either.

I had to make it stop. With my hands still covering my ears, I made my way closer and closer to the spider's head, meaning to strike it the next time it paused. When it finally did, I was in position. I raised my sword over my head, but stopped when I heard a new sound.

A dull roar grew exponentially louder, as if a subway train was hurtling toward us from the tunnel next to the throne. A second later, I didn't have to guess anymore about what had caused the sound.

A wave of millions of tiny spiders, stacked up so that they filled the tunnel completely, came pouring into the room like a geyser. Above me and through every tiny crack in the rock walls, there streamed thousands more.

I looked down at the giant spider. This wasn't some horrendous monster. It was a mother protecting her babies. And trying to feed them. I lowered my sword because I knew she didn't deserve to die. Even so, I wasn't about to be lunch for her kids either. It was time to run.

I turned and ran to the skeleton-filled tunnel I'd used to come into the room. As I reached the entrance, I risked a look backward and saw the tidal wave of baby spiders swarming over their mother. In a matter of seconds they had sprung her loose. She rolled off her back and spun toward me. I could tell immediately I wasn't going to get any mercy for having spared her life. As if on cue, the flood of tiny spiders, now at least eight feet deep, flowed toward me as the mama spider charged.

I grabbed my last grenade and threw it at the advancing swarm. Even before it went off, I was hauling down the tunnel, crunching skeleton bones beneath my feet.

I ran as fast as I could but I had no idea what I intended to do once I reached the cliff. There were the other two tunnels out there, but something told me they would be filled with spiders too.

The bridge was gone. And the river was way too violent for me to survive jumping into.

I checked the reel on my belt. There were two projectile arrows left. It was the only choice I had.

I saw the mouth of the tunnel glowing from the paint I had sprayed around the arches. I looked behind me and saw the mama spider right on my heels, pushing a pile of her babies in front of her.

I sprinted out of the tunnel, and, without breaking stride, fired the projectile across the river.

Just as I did, the cave ogre rose up from the chasm in front of me with a roar, pieces of the old bridge still tangled around his body.

The projectile nailed him in the shoulder.

He grabbed at it, yanking on the wire before I had a chance to cut it. I fell to the ground as the ogre dragged me to him.

Just then, the spider burst from the cave. The ogre turned his attention on this new foe just as the spider launched itself onto the ogre, sinking its pincers into the ogre's chest.

The ogre grappled with the giant spider, holding it in a bear hug and trying to keep its pincers away from biting it a second time. Meanwhile, I was still getting dragged around mercilessly by the wire attached to the reel on my belt.

The only thing that saved me was the ogre slowing down, its eyes suddenly heavy like it was ready to fall asleep. The spider's venom from the first bite was doing its work.

But even as the ogre staggered, trying to keep its balance, it didn't let go of the spider. Finally, in what seemed like a slow-motion pirouette, the ogre spun around and tipped over the edge of the chasm, taking the spider with him.

The split second of excitement was replaced by sheer terror when I realized I was still connected to the ogre by the wire.

In the blink of an eye, I was dragged across the ground and down off the cliff.

Midair, I swung my sword and cut the wire, twisted upward and fired the last projectile.

Up, up, up it flew.

Thwack.

It stuck solid into the top of the cave.

With a yank, I hung suspended just over the raging river. Below me, the ogre and spider continued their epic battle as they were swept away down the river and into the dark reaches of the mountain.

I clicked the button, and I don't think I've appreciated any sound more in my life than the soft whirr of the reel pulling me upward. Once I was even with the cliff top, I swung the wire until I could make the jump easily to the far side.

After I was back on solid land, I looked across the ravine and saw that it was still covered with millions of spiders. I shivered at the thought of the other hunters and how they must have been devoured by those tiny things. There really weren't any good ways to die, but being eaten alive by a swarm of spiders certainly qualified as a bad way to go.

I reached into my pocket and took out the ring. I'd done it.

"Don't get cocky. You've got to make it back first," I reminded myself. I slid the ring back into my pocket and set off for the exit to the Academy.

Thankfully, the way back was uneventful. Good thing too because I was out of glowing paint and the light from my sword was steadily dimming as I walked. I spotted a few dark shadows crawling on the walls, but they appeared to have no interest in me. Even the bats had moved to another part of the cave. The hike up the steep face where I slid down was a challenge because it was so slippery and I knew I could easily start another avalanche if I wasn't careful. But I took my time and made it up safely.

As I got closer to the door, my pace quickened. I was eager to get out of the cave and see the light of day. Although I wasn't even sure how long I had been underground to know if it was day or night outside, I had honored my pledge to both Aquinas and Tiberon. Not only would I have full monster hunter status and be free to leave the Academy, but Tiberon would have to tell me the location of both the Jerusalem Stones and the dungeons where Ren Lucre held my father. I was one step closer to saving my father.

But besides all this, there was one other reason that I was eager to get out.

Eva.

She had been the voice and the face I had carried with me through the entire ordeal. I found myself thinking about her more with each step closer to the door.

Besides, it was steadily getting darker as the paint faded. I wasn't eager to try to finish the journey without light.

When I finally spotted the iron door at the end of the final tunnel, I broke into a run. I had heard the locks engage when they had shut the door behind me, so I wasn't surprised when it didn't open when I pushed against it.

I knocked on the door, but it still didn't open. I grabbed a rock and pounded on the door, thinking perhaps it was just hard to hear on the other side.

Still nothing.

"Hey!" I shouted. "It's Jack. Jack Templar. Open up!"

Silence.

Over and over, I pounded on the door. With my hands, my sword, rocks. Anything I could use to make sound.

Still nothing.

For over an hour, I hammered and banged on the door until my hands nearly bled from the effort.

Over time, the light on my sword faded, allowing the staggering darkness around me to crowd in. But there was no reply behind the gate. Not a sound of any kind from the other side of the door.

I sagged to the ground as the last of the light disappeared from my sword, tears welling up in my eyes from exhaustion and frustration. I couldn't understand what was happening. Why weren't they opening the door? I had made it back. I had the ring. I had...

And that's when it hit me. What if I had been wrong about which ring to take? What if it had been the diamond ring all along? Maybe Aquinas was on the other side of the door with the others, refusing to let it open because I hadn't completed my quest.

I pulled the ring out of my pocket and rolled it over in my hand in the pitch black. Doubts flooded my mind. I tried to imagine finding my way back to the old tomb in the dark, crawling through the caves, not knowing what creatures could be lurking around me. I shuddered at the thought. It was impossible. Even if I did make it back there, how was I supposed to cross the chasm again? How was I supposed to survive the millions of spiders?

No, I had trusted my instinct and I had chosen the wrong ring. Unless Aquinas took pity on me and opened the door, there was no getting out. I had enough food for a day or two, but after that I was going to have to hunt if I wanted to stay alive. Maybe if I was lucky I would find another way out of the cave. But if I wasn't, I knew I was already standing in my grave.

As I mulled over my fate, I slid the stone ring onto my finger.

With a burst of light, the cold stone blazed red with fire. I nearly clawed it back off my finger for fear of being burned, but there was no heat and no pain. I heard the bolts and gears of the door clank around in front of me; then, with a whoosh of air, the seal broke and the door opened.

As I stepped through the thick iron gateway, the ring on my finger turned back into a simple, black stone. But I didn't have a chance to marvel at what had just happened because I immediately heard shouts and screams coming from the training fields.

I ran toward it as fast as I could but stopped when I cleared the gates that led from the caves. All the buildings were on fire. Hunters were running in every direction, brandishing their weapons. In the center of the training grounds, the Templar Tree was ablaze like a giant torch.

The Monster Hunter Academy was under attack.

Chapter Sixteen

Instructors barked orders at the younger hunters, organizing them into fire brigades in long lines from the wells to the worst of the blazes. Those not fighting the fires were caring for the injured. And there were a lot of them. I saw hunters with blood soaked bandages, others limping toward the protection of the Citadel.

Anything not made of stone was on fire. I looked to the main gates and saw they were intact and shut. Whatever had done this hadn't broken through the defenses yet. I grabbed a hunter running past me. I recognized him from one of my classes. His name was Ben, one of the younger boys. He had a fluffy mop of reddish brown hair, sharp, twinkling eyes, and spent most of his classes cracking jokes.

There was no humor in him now. His eyes looked me over like I was a wild creature.

"Ben, it's me, Jack! What happened?" I asked. I felt his body trembling in my hands.

"Th...th...they came from the sk...sk...sky," Ben stuttered. "L...l...looking for...looking for..."

"What were they looking for, Ben? What was it?" I asked.

He pointed toward the mountain face above us. There, burning right on the rock face, were four enormous letters, each as tall as a building.

J...A...C...K.

A piercing scream erupted overhead and a black shadow soared over the field. A burst of flame geysered from its mouth and hit the ground like a bomb. A deluge of dirt and snow blew into the air with a loud rumble. Ben tore himself from me and ran away from the streaking form. The terrifying figure flew past the raging fires and I was able to see it more clearly. A dragon.

Every bit as terrifying and awesome as Hollywood made them out to be. It was long and serpentine, with an elongated neck and a waving, supple tail that twitched behind it during flight. Its body glistened with the reflection of the fiery destruction beneath it but was covered with thousands of small scales, giving it the look of a snake. It had tall horns next to long pointed ears that lay flat against its head like an angry cat. A long snout and beady, black eyes swung back and forth across the field, as if searching the faces of the hunters who ran scattered beneath it. I watched in horror as it grabbed a hunter about my height and with my color of hair. The kid screamed as the dragon's talons wrapped around his midsection and he was lifted into the air. The dragon held the hunter up to one of his eyes, then tossed the kid aside like he was a piece of unwanted trash. The hunter hit the ground hard and lay there, writhing in pain, as the dragon banked hard and came back across the field for another pass.

I felt that someone had taken a sledgehammer to my stomach. I looked at the devastation all around me. This was all my fault. I should never have come to the Academy. I'd put everyone at risk. Especially Will and T-Rex, who, without me, would still be safe in Sunnyvale.

A cry went up behind me. I spun around and saw a second dragon, this one even larger than the first. It ejected a searing stream of flame across the camp and ended its pass across the field by kicking down the burning mess hall. The structure crumbled into itself with a burst of flame and sparks. As I watched it fall, I felt my fear and guilt transform into anger. I gripped my sword in my right hand and decided there was time to feel bad later. Right now, I had some dragons to take care of. It was time for this hunter to fight back.

I sprinted across the field toward the main wall. I needed height in order to reach the dragons. Halfway across, I suddenly felt a stiff wind behind me. Without turning, I threw myself to the ground just as one of the dragons streaked over me, its powerful wings kicking up clods of dirt. As I scrambled back to my feet, I spotted Eva running toward the Templar Tree.

"Eva! Wait!" I yelled.

But there was no way she was going to hear me over the noise of the battle. She reached the tree, now just a raging fire, and climbed up onto one of its lower branches, picking her way through the fire to get higher. Even as I worried about her, I couldn't help but smile at her audacity. That was one crazy girl.

Another blast of fire on the far side of the training ground erupted over by the stables. Seconds later, I saw Bacho's unmistakable silhouette framed against the raging fire. He swung open a pasture gate and dozens of horses ran free into the training grounds. Leading from the front, I spotted Saladin. At almost the same time, the great white horse must have seen me as he banked hard and ran straight in my direction. I readied myself as he galloped closer. I reached up for his neck as he ran by and swung up onto his back.

"Good boy!" I yelled. "To the walls!"

A shriek split the air over my head. A dragon arced low over the field and came up behind us.

"Run, Saladin!" I cried.

But Saladin needed no urging. He ran hard, dodging the running hunters as he did. Still, the dragon bore down and I heard a great inhalation of breath. It was about to spit fire.

Sensing the same, Saladin planted his hooves in the snow, sliding for a second before changing course ninety degrees to the right.

The change was so sudden that I lurched to the left and only stopped myself from falling off by grabbing handfuls of Saladin's mane.

Behind us, I felt the wall of fire blaze, incinerating the ground where we had been seconds before. The dragon flew past us and circled up in the sky, looking for other targets.

I patted Saladin's neck. "Good boy," I said. "Now, to the wall. Hurry!"

Saladin ran to the wall. The buildings that lined its base and served as bulwarks were all ablaze. I jumped off Saladin and was about to climb the stone stairs that led up to the watchtower next to the gate itself, when I heard a familiar voice behind me.

"C'mon you dirty lizards, I'll run you through!" Will yelled at the flying dragons, a crossbow in his hands.

"Will!" I called out, running to him.

He spun toward me, his eyes wild. It took him a second to process what he was seeing, then he grabbed me in a bear hug. "You made it!" he cried.

"Looks like things really fell apart while I was gone," I said, trying to sound braver than I felt. "Where's T-Rex?"

Something smashed into me from behind, nearly knocking me over. I thought one of the dragons had me for sure. Then I felt arms squeezing me on both sides and T-Rex's voice. "Oh man, oh man, I can't believe it," he stammered.

Once he let me go, the three of us had a split second where we stood in a small circle, grinning at one another. No one said anything. No one had to. We were just happy to be together again.

A blast of fire right over our heads ended our little moment and put us into action.

"Will, you and T-Rex go to the armory and see if you can still get in. Hand out as many crossbows as you can."

"Who should I give 'em to?" he asked.

"Everybody," I said.

"What about them?" Will asked, pointing at a group of Ratlings just behind T-Rex.

It was a motley collection, some rail thin and scrawny, others pudgy and soft. Half of them had some kind of permanent injury, like a missing limb, or a patch over a missing eye. All of them looked terrified, but I could tell by their faces that they weren't about to run away. They stood bravely and awaited instructions.

"Where's Bacho?" I asked.

"Freeing the horses and livestock," T-Rex said. "He left me in charge of these guys." He grabbed my arm, determined. "We Ratlings can fight, Jack. It's our Academy too."

I grinned at T-Rex, welling up with pride at his courage. It seemed the nose-picking young boy was long gone. "Right you are," I agreed, turning to the Ratlings. "And glad to have you. We need everyone's help. All of you, go with Will and get the weapons. Hurry!"

"What are you going to do?" T-Rex asked.

I nodded to the watchtower behind us. "I'm going up there."

"And then what?"

"I don't know," I admitted. "I haven't gotten that far."

Will grinned. "Then you better get going so you can figure it out. Come on, you guys. Let's go."

I watched them disappear into the smoke-filled field. For the second time in as many days, I was left wondering if I would ever see my friends again.

I mounted the stairs and bounded up them two at a time. When I reached the top I had a view of the entire Academy. For the first time, I saw a band of hunters putting up a defense. In the center of them was a familiar figure, Daniel. Recovered from his poisoning, he stood his ground with a bandage wrapped around his head covering his nose. He fired a crossbow repeatedly at the dragon swooping over the field. Despite our differences, I couldn't have been happier to see him.

In between firing crossbow shots, he barked instructions at those around him, organizing a retreat through the Citadel gates. Most of the instructors fought by him even as they corralled as many hunters as possible toward the caves. I spotted Aquinas among them, helping two injured hunters off the battlefield.

I turned my back to the fighting and looked out into the calm of the dark forest beyond the main walls. It seemed like a different world from the chaos behind me. I didn't know if what I was going to do would work, but I had to try.

I shouted as loud as I could, "Tiberon! If you can hear me, we need your help!" I listened and, even with the screaming and crackle of fire behind me, I heard my voice echo through the forest. I raised my hand with the ring over my head. "Tiberon, brother of the Black Guard! The bearer of the Templar Ring asks that you come to the aid of your Order." My voice drifted through the valley, lost among the snow-covered pines. Then silence. I shouted again. "TIBERON! In the name of your sworn oath, it is time for you to do your duty!"

An explosion from behind spun me around. Overheated sap must have finally blown out one of the main branches in the tree because with the explosion the fire blazed even brighter. I searched the few areas where the fire hadn't reached yet, desperately looking for Eva.

Just when I had about given up hope that she had survived, I saw her climb out on a limb nearly thirty feet off the ground. She had a sword in one hand and what looked like a grappling hook screwed into her other arm.

One of the dragons swerved down for a pass over the field, fire pouring from its mouth. Everything moved in slow motion as the dragon banked side-to-side, searching the faces of the fleeing hunters. With a beat of its wings, it veered to its left, cutting close to the tree. Taking a running start, Eva jumped from her perch and fired the grappling hook from her hand The hook shot out over the dragon's neck, wrapping Xavier's super-strong wire around it. With a jolt, the slack in the wire was taken up and Eva soared through the air, swinging under the dragon.

Using the momentum from one of the dragon's turns, Eva managed to reach the leading edge of a wing. In a blink of an eye, she had crawled along the wing and onto the dragon's back. By now the beast had realized it had a passenger. It started rolling and thrashing in the air, reaching back to bite at Eva. But she was just out of reach. She plunged her sword into the dragon's back, no more than a splinter for a monster that size. Still, nobody likes splinters. Roaring in anger, the dragon beat its wings and soared up higher into the night sky.

"Eva!" I cried out as the dragon disappeared up over the mountain.

But it was no use. She was gone.

A noise rose from the forest behind me. I spun around and looked outside the Academy walls, hoping with all my strength that it was Tiberon and his army of wolves.

Instead, emerging from the tree line along the entire length of the wall was an army of goblins.

Chapter Seventeen

The dragon swept above the goblin army, ejecting fire along the treetops. Suddenly, the wall was bathed in light. My knees nearly gave way at the sight of it.

There were hundreds of them—snarling, drooling monsters, with hooked noses and protruding mouthfuls of decaying teeth. All were in heavy armor covered with nasty barbs and spikes. They carried long spears and matching heavy shields.

This was no rag-tag group. Someone had organized and outfitted them and prepared them for battle. And now they had arrived at just the right time to overrun the battlements. Spaced every few yards was a detail of goblins holding sturdy ladders.

I suspected they would be exactly long enough to crest the walls.

I ran to the bell on the watchtower and pulled the cord as hard as I could. The peal of the alarm bell rang out over the Academy, louder than I expected. I pulled it again and again, trying to invest the sound with every bit of urgency I could.

Heads all around the field turned toward my direction. The dragon was far overhead, circling for another pass, so I had an opening where my voice could be heard.

"To the walls!" I cried. "We are under attack!"

No one moved. Hunters looked to each other, not sure what to think of this pronouncement of the obvious.

"There is an army of goblins at our walls! Hunters, defend the Academy!" I yelled.

A few hunters started to jog my direction. Back by the Citadel, I saw Aquinas and Daniel step forward from their defensive position as if straining to hear what I was saying. A few of the instructors jogged a bit closer to hear. I could see people pointing in my direction and I realized they still might not be able to hear me. I tore off my helmet.

"I am Jack Templar, Monster Hunter, Keeper of the Templar Ring of Jacques de Molay, Member of the Black Guard, and the Sworn Enemy of the Dark Lord, Ren Lucre. Brothers and sisters! It is time to do our duty, come what may! It is time for us to hunt!"

Every hunter within the sound of my voice yelled as one and broke out in a sprint toward the wall. Even the injured pushed themselves from the ground and hobbled toward the fight. I saw Aquinas and Daniel leading the charge of instructors.

Will and T-Rex appeared below me with a group of hunters carrying armloads of crossbows and swords. Xavier was with them carrying his own stack of weapons.

"Will, hand them out!" I yelled. "As fast as you can!"

Hunters grabbed weapons and streamed onto the walls just as the first ladders slammed into the battlements.

I ran to the nearest one and heaved it backward with all my might. I looked down and saw it was filled with goblins who screeched as they fell away from the wall.

"Push the ladders!" I cried. "Don't let them up."

Up and down the line, hunters pushed back against ladders as soon as they thumped against the stone wall. The cries from the goblins filled the air. A heavy ladder made from rough-cut wood slammed onto the wall beside me. I leaned into it and pushed it backward, but it was too heavy. Suddenly, there were two old, gnarled hands next to mine. It was Aquinas.

"Well, come on," she said. "We have a battle to win."

We pushed together. The old woman was stronger than she looked and before long we had the ladder tipping backward until it fell away from the wall, sending four goblins crashing to the ground.

Aquinas and I shared a grin from our small victory together, but it didn't last long. A roar went up from the horde below. We looked down and saw dozens of ladder-carrying goblins march out of the forest.

"There are so many," Aquinas said. "I should have seen this coming."

"Can we hold them?" I asked.

"I don't know, but we have to if we're to survive," Aquinas said. "If we retreat to the Citadel now the goblins will breach the walls before we get there and run us down. Over half of us will be killed for certain."

"Then we must defend the wall," I said.

"In retreat, half would die, but half would live," Aquinas said. "If we fail here at the wall, everyone will be killed. These are the decisions that leaders must make."

I heard a call further down the wall and saw Daniel not too far away from me. He was high-fiving Bacho and a group of Ratlings that had just sent a handful of goblins flying through the air on their ladder. Daniel looked up and we made eye contact. He saluted me with his sword and I returned the gesture.

I was about to ask Aquinas how it would ever be possible to decide who would live and who would die when a black cloud rose from outside the walls and hovered above us. Aquinas realized what was happening before I did.

"Shields!" Aquinas called. "Everyone, shields!"

Instinctively, the hunters raised their shields or crouched under any cover they could find. Aquinas grabbed a shield from the floor and threw it to me. I grabbed it and held it over my head. A split second later, black arrows rained down on us in a deadly barrage. Three arrows slammed into my shield, sticking out like porcupine quills. I ran to Aquinas to try to cover her, but I was too late. A long, wicked-looking arrow struck her in the upper chest and dropped her to the ground.

"Master Aquinas!" I shouted.

I reached her quickly and held her up. She groaned from being moved. When I pulled back my hand it was covered with her blood. I heard cries of pain all around me as hunters were hit in whatever small part of their body was left exposed. A foot here. A shoulder there. Screams of the injured rang out up and down the wall.

"Somebody help!" I yelled.

"You see?" Aquinas said, her voice trembling. "Sacrifices must sometimes be made. I suspect it will prove to be worthwhile."

Then Bacho was next to me, lifting Aquinas into his arms.

"Now look what they've done to you," he muttered, tears in his eyes. "Get you off this wall, that's what we've got to do."

Aquinas grabbed me. "You must decide," she whispered, fighting to remain conscious. "You must...decide."

Bacho couldn't wait any longer. He stomped off and carried Aquinas down the stairs to safety.

I felt the weight of responsibility fall onto my shoulders as they left. But I didn't have long to reflect on what I should do next. While we had taken cover, the goblins had used the opportunity to raise their ladders back in place and climb up.

"The walls!" I cried when I saw the goblin jump over the battlement. I ran to it and engaged the creature. I'd fought goblins before and hadn't found them very hard to defeat, but it was immediately clear these guys were different. The goblin crouched down in a defensive posture, using its large shield for cover and poking at me with its spear. With its longer reach, it was able to keep me away. I realized it was trying to hold me off long enough so the goblins behind it could hurry up the ladder. This was good training and even better discipline. Neither of those two things were good news. Someone had trained this army well. We were in trouble.

"Jack!" Xavier called out. "Try this!"

I looked up just in time to see a spear flying through the air at me. I had to dodge it to avoid being impaled.

"Oops, sorry," called Xavier.

I grabbed the spear and felt a button on the handle. Another one of Xavier's inventions. I pressed the button and the spear extended to twice its length. Using the full length of spear to get inside the goblin's defenses, I quickly had him on the run.

Tiring of the goblin, I rushed straight at him, sliding on the ground at the last second with my shield lying on top of me. I slid under him and got him with my spear in the side. With a cry, I kicked him in the midsection and sent him flying over the edge.

"Show-off," Daniel said with a smile. The bandage wrapped around his face was flecked with blood and it gave him a wild look. He had two goblins trapped in a headlock. He ran forward and smashed both of their heads into the wall. They sank to the floor in a heap.

"Not too bad yourself," I said.

Further down the line I saw Will and T-Rex fighting side-by-side, firing crossbows into the goblins. We were holding our own. Even outnumbered, we held the defensive high ground. We actually had a chance of stopping them.

I turned my attention back to the goblins coming over the wall and charged at the nearest one, swinging my sword right next to Daniel.

I don't know how long we battled, but dead goblins piled up around our feet. Soon, my arms ached and I cried out with every swing of my sword. All the hunters fought valiantly, chopping down the enemy by the dozens. But still they kept coming. After dispatching a particularly ugly-looking goblin, there was a lull in the action. We all remained in our fighting stance, waiting for the next wave, but none came.

I allowed myself to hope that we had turned them away, that we had won somehow. I stole a look over the wall and my heart sank. The army below had doubled, maybe even tripled, in size. We hadn't won. The goblins were simply organizing themselves for a final push to finish us off.

I felt a hand on my back. It was Daniel. He glanced over the wall and by the look in his eyes I knew we both had reached the same conclusion. There were too many of them. There was no way we were going to survive this fight. I stood up on a rock so that the hunters on the wall could see me.

"We have to get as many of you as we can back to the Citadel," I shouted. "I'll stay here with anyone willing to make a stand to cover the retreat."

The hunters turned to face me. Many had ripped clothing stained with blood, both goblin and their own. Their eyes were alive and on fire, ready for action. T-Rex and Will made their way to the front and Xavier slid over and joined them. A group of Ratlings stood with T-Rex and stared me down with grim determination.

"You've got to hurry," I said. "I don't know how long we can hold them."

No one moved.

"Don't you understand?" I said. "We have to retreat now."

Still, they are stared at me.

"Why isn't anyone moving," I shouted. "What's wrong?"

Daniel walked up to me, a grin on his face. "There's nothing wrong, Jack. Only, I don't think anyone is in the mood to retreat."

"It's pretty comfortable up on this wall," Will said loudly, milking it to the crowd. "I kind of like it up here."

"Yeah," T-Rex chimed in, "and it's a long walk to the Citadel."

The hunters and Ratlings laughed softly, the quiet camaraderie of soldiers about to face their fate.

"See?" Daniel said. "They'll fight with you until the end. As will I. And I'll be proud to do it as your friend, Jack Templar."

It was the first time Daniel had called me Templar instead of Smith. I nodded in acknowledgement. I looked over the assembled group, blinking back tears as their show of courage overwhelmed me. "The honor has been mine," was all I could manage.

Heads nodded in agreement and the hunters and Ratlings murmured the words to one another over and over again.

A hunter turned to his injured friend.
The honor had been mine.

Two young hunters, barely ten years old, solemnly shook hands.
The honor has been mine.

A hunter instructor bowed to a Ratling.
The honor has been mine.

All right," I managed to say after clearing my throat. "Man your stations and get ready for the attack. This is our Academy and we're not going to let one goblin step foot in it!"

The hunters and Ratlings cheered and went back to their positions on the wall. Daniel, T-Rex, Will and Xavier walked up. They stood quietly together, no one sure what to say. Finally, Daniel broke the silence.

"I never thanked you for saving my life," Daniel said.

"Too bad I can't do it this time," I replied.

Daniel reached out his hand and I shook it. "There are worse ways to die than fighting next to a fellow hunter."

Will and T-Rex were both covered in goblin blood. T-Rex looked on the edge of tears and Will grinned like he had just won something.

"Fellas," I said. "I'm sorry I got you into this."

"Are you kidding me?" Will exclaimed. "Best vacation, ever."

But T-Rex patted me on the shoulder and looked at me seriously. "It's not your fault, Jack. We chose to come, remember?"

I looked up and down the wall lined with hunters, some as young as eight years old. There were a few tears, but even those crying stood facing the wall, ready for the final battle. I was disappointed that I was unable to lead them to victory, but I couldn't have been more proud.

"Xavier, if you had an invention in your bag of tricks to help us out of this mess, now would be a good time to get it out," I said.

"Sorry, Jack," Xavier said. "I don't have anything."

"I figured you didn't. But it never hurts to ask," I replied.

Suddenly, a dragon reappeared at the far end of the wall and I looked to see if it was the one Eva had ridden away on. There was no sign of her. The dragon blew fire once again at the treetops to illuminate the attack.

As the dragon neared the end of its pass, Daniel shouted, "Get ready!"

The goblin horde stamped its feet on the ground, ready to rush forward. There were so many of them that I could feel the vibration in the walls.

"Ready..." Daniel said.

Then, in the middle of the tension rose the most beautiful sound I'd ever heard in my life.

The howl of a single wolf.

The goblins froze, looking around to see what direction it had come from.

Another howl erupted from deeper in the forest.

And then another.

More and more until the forest was filled with the sound.

Then, as if someone had flipped a switch, it was gone. The night was silent except for the crackling fires burning behind us.

"Tiberon," I whispered. "About bloody time."

A horn blew and the entire goblin horde erupted in a guttural battle cry as they charged the wall. Immediately, screams ripped through the air. Flashes of black and grey darted in and out of the tree line, grabbing goblins by whatever body part was most convenient and dragging them back into the trees.

The goblins on the front lines heard the screams behind them and their charge lost momentum. When they turned around, over a hundred giant wolves slowly walked out from the forest in a line, with Tiberon at their center.

The goblins froze and for a second it seemed as if the entire world had fallen silent. Clouds of white breath swirled in front of each of the wolves with each huff of air. Many of them crouched low, teeth barred, eagerly clawing the ground in anticipation of the destruction to come.

With a snarl, Tiberon leapt forward and attacked the goblin army. In unison, the other wolves followed his lead with a deafening roar. .

The carnage was almost too devastating to watch. The wolves reached the goblins in only a few strides and then slammed into the front line of defense. The goblins raised their spears to ward them off, but it was no use. Tiberon's army was an unstoppable wave of death, all claws and teeth, ripping through the goblin ranks with furious energy. Goblin bodies flew through the air as wolves crunched their teeth through their necks and then tossed their limp bodies aside like they were ragdolls.

Tiberon stood in the center of it all, a monstrous, snarling figure that fought as if he were waging his own personal war. As I watched, he took out three of the enemy with one great sweep of his paw, knocking them end over end. He kicked backward and sent a fourth goblin flying through the air. A group of five or six, mercilessly whipped from behind by one of their leaders, charged at Tiberon. He rose up on his hind legs then jumped straight into their line, biting through their armor with his massive jaws. Within seconds, he had worked his way through them and turned with a bloody mouth and wild eyes to find new targets.

Elsewhere on the field of battle, the leaders of the goblin army tried to organize a defense, but their soldiers had no interest in listening. Even as they used their whips to get them into line, the goblins quickly realized they were no match for the brute strength of the wolves. Some of them ran back up the ladders toward us, now trying to get away from the sure death that waited them below, only to run into our swords and spears above.

Soon the ground ran red with goblin blood. After a few minutes of the wolves' merciless attack, the goblins broke rank and ran for their lives into the forest. The wolves looked to Tiberon for instruction. He made a motion with his head and the wolves ran into the woods after the fleeing goblins. Soon screams once again filled the valley. There were to be no prisoners.

The hunters cheered from the walls. We had won. I removed my helmet and bowed to Tiberon down below. The great wolf stretched his neck upward and returned the gesture by bowing low to the ground.

Daniel was standing a little down the wall from me. I wondered how he would react to all this. He shifted his eyes from Tiberon to me. "Looks like you and your friend saved my life a second time," Daniel said. "I guess I owe both of you."

I knew how hard this had to be for Daniel. I wanted to talk to him more about it, but a dark shadow caught the corner of my eye. "Daniel, look out!" I yelled.

But it was too late. In one swift motion, the dragon grabbed Daniel's body in its talons and ripped him off the ground.

"No!" I cried, running along the rampart, keeping pace with the dragon flying low alongside the interior wall. Daniel struggled in the monster's grasp, kicking and punching the claws holding him. There was no way he was getting out.

I launched myself from the edge of the wall, arms windmilling as I flew through the air.

I landed on the dragon's back with so much force that I felt like I'd just run into a moving car. I bounced off the hard, smooth scales and slid across the beast's back. I was about to roll right off when the dragon veered to the right and I rolled in the opposite direction. Remembering what I'd seen Eva do, as I rolled, I got my sword into position, then plunged it into the dragon's flesh.

The sword sunk in deep and its scales quivered. I heard Daniel cry out but I couldn't see him from where I was. I held on for dear life as the dragon twisted and contorted, trying to shake me off its back. As we spun around, I caught a glance of the ground not far below and saw Daniel there. The cry I'd heard was the dragon dropping him. OK, I thought, he's safe. Now what?

The dragon had plans of its own. It took me on a wild ride across the Academy grounds, smashing through burning buildings, scraping its back across the mountain, trying to reach me with its mouth and claws. I tried to find the best time to let go, but the dragon was flying too fast. Jumping off would have been like jumping out of a car going sixty miles an hour. If it was a fire-breathing flying car with a bad attitude, that is.

So I rode it as best I could; like riding a wild bull, half the time my body flailed in the wind from the sheer momentum, but I held tight to my sword's hilt. I tried to plan my next move but it took all my energy just to stay on.

Suddenly, the dragon stopped bucking and smoothed out its flight. It craned its neck and, while it couldn't reach me with its teeth, its large yellow eye looked me over. With an ear-shattering screech, the dragon turned and with a few beats of its massive wings, we soared high up over the Academy and turned east toward the rising sun.

With a sinking feeling, I realized what had just happened. The dragon had realized that it was carrying the one hunter it had been sent to collect. I was being whisked away from the Academy and taken directly to Ren Lucre. I'd played right into his hands. And now I was hundreds of feet up in the air, trapped.

In the distance ahead, I saw a dark shape coming at us, silhouetted against the rising sun. It was the other dragon, the one that had taken Eva. I felt a pang of dread, worried that this meant she hadn't made it. Now seeing the dragon return, I figured there was no way she could have survived. Just like there was little chance I was going to survive, either. I lowered my head against the dragon and held back tears. So many sacrifices, so many people hurt, the Academy destroyed, all for nothing. All just to end in failure. I'd never felt so hopeless in my life.

But then a sound reached my ears, floating on the early morning breeze, so distant that at first I thought I'd imagined it. A beautiful sound I'd convinced myself I'd never hear again. I looked up and the sound grew stronger.

It was Eva's battle cry.

Chapter Eighteen

Eva was on the back of the dragon's neck, the wire from her grappling hook wrapped around the creature's snout in a makeshift harness and reins, her sword used as a bit in its mouth.

My dragon realized too late what was happening, as Eva steered her captive dragon right into us. The impact nearly knocked me off but somehow I managed to hold on. The two dragons clawed and chewed at each other, their leathery wings wrapping around one another as we fell from the sky.

"Hold on, Jack!" Eva cried. She pulled back on her reins and her dragon's head jerked backward as her sword cut into the corners of its mouth. The dragons disengaged with only twenty or thirty feet left before we all crashed into the ground. My dragon snarled and I could feel its chest expand beneath me as it drew in a huge breath.

"Fire!" I yelled. "It's going to breathe fire!"

Just as I said it, my dragon spewed a column of fire. Eva's dragon reacted by bringing both wings together in front of its body. The fire billowed against the shield harmlessly. My dragon turned and retreated, Eva's dragon in pursuit.

She zigzagged behind us and I soon realized she was pushing my dragon back toward the Academy grounds. Soon, we soared over the training field, the hunters and wolves below.

"Get ready!" Eva cried.

She steered her dragon ahead of mine and forced it to reverse direction. As we entered into the walls of the Academy again, I saw a double line of hunters and Ratlings in the center of the field, all holding crossbows. Will and T-Rex each commanded a group.

My dragon didn't see it. At the last second, I twisted my sword in the dragon's back and shoved it as deeply as I could. This distracted it just enough for it to fly right into the line of fire of the hunters below. Two dozen crossbow bolts whizzed up and struck the dragon in the neck. It wasn't enough to injure the beast, but just enough to make it mad. It stopped midair, hovering with great flaps of its wings, searching the ground for something to kill. I felt the dragon fill its lungs again, taking aim at the line of hunters below us.

Eva's battle cry erupted behind me. I didn't even take the time to look. I just jumped from my dragon, hoping I was judging the distance to the ground right at twenty feet. As I jumped, Eva's dragon collided with mine in a violent mix of talons, scales and wings. The stream of fire arched over the group of hunters and fell harmlessly in the training field.

I hit the ground, rolled and ended back up on my feet, near a group of hunters hurling bolts into the sky. As the two dragons fought, I saw Eva's dragon break through the harness and spit out the sword in its mouth. Eva leapt from its back and landed safely on the school grounds. Even with the harness gone, the dragons continued to fight, locked in a death match.

I ran over to where I saw Eva jump. After the swing of emotions in the last few hours, I just wanted to see her.

I gave the fighting dragons a wide berth and finally reached her. Just in time to see her hugging Daniel. I stopped in my tracks, suddenly wishing I was back on the dragon. Eva saw me and she and Daniel both ran over to me. She locked me up in a hug and this time it was Daniel's turn to feel out of place. Even with everything going on around us, I admit that the hug felt really good. But only seconds later, she pushed me away and punched me in the arm. Hard.

"You jerk. I thought you were dead," she said.

"Me? You're the one who went off flying with a dragon," I said.

"Hey guys," Daniel interjected. "I think we have a problem."

The two dragons had parted, snarling at each other, but remembering their task. As we watched, they rose back into the air and hovered over the battlefield.

"We're not out of it, yet," Eva said. "Any ideas?"

"You're the dragon-whisperer," I said. "You tell us."

"I don't think it's going to offer me another ride," Eva said.

"And we're no match for them with the weapons we have," Daniel said.

The dragons simultaneously spewed streams of fire across the field. Hunters scattered everywhere, looking for cover. Daniel was right—we didn't have anything that could match the dragons' might. If we couldn't beat them, at least I could save the others from getting killed.

I waited until the barrage of fire stopped, then huddled close to Eva and Daniel. "Get the hunters to safety. Hide in the forest if you have to. Tiberon will keep you safe."

"What are you going to do?" Eva asked.

"Don't worry about me," I said with a grin. "I'll think of something."

I turned and ran as hard as I could into the center of the field as far away from the other hunters as possible. I waved my sword over my head. "Hey, you two! Over here! Come on, you ugly lizards!" The dragons turned in my direction. "Yeah, that's right. You know you're ugly!" I yelled. I jogged backward as I taunted them, making my way toward the

Citadel gates. Behind the dragons, I saw Will and Eva directing the other hunters toward the outer wall gates. Both dragons stopped beating their wings and landed with a heavy thump that shook the ground.

One of the dragons turned and hissed at the sight of the escaping hunters. Its buddy followed suit and turned to look at the main gate.

"Hey, I'm the one you came looking for, right?" I yelled. "Right here. I'm Jack Templar!" Both of them snapped their heads in my direction. "Yeah, that got your attention, didn't it?"

The dragons walked slowly toward me, hissing and spitting drips of fire from their mouths.

"Come on," I whispered. "That's it, both of you." I glanced at the Citadel gate, judging the distance. It was now or never. I pumped my sword at the dragons and shouted with everything I had. "What are you waiting for? Come and get me! I dare you!"

With a roar, the dragons stampeded toward me, staying side-by-side as if they were joined at the hip.

I turned and sprinted as hard as I could toward the gates, praying I had judged both the distance and the dragon's speed accurately. More importantly, if I made it to the gate, I hoped my crazy idea worked.

I ran, my legs burning, my ears ringing from the roars behind me. I was twenty yards from the gate. Fifteen yards. But I could feel the hot breath of the dragons on my neck. Ten yards. I didn't dare look back. It would just slow me down. At this point, I was either going to make it or not. All I could do was run. Five yards. I felt a blast of breath and something tug on my armor. I jerked to the side and the sensation went away. Whichever dragon had nearly gotten me roared in frustration. That roar slowed them down just a little, and a little was all I needed.

I reached the Citadel entrance, looking up at the row of jagged teeth at the bottom of the massively heavy gate that hung suspended over the opening. I remembered shuddering the first time I had crossed the threshold, thinking about that gate coming loose and slamming down on top of me. Now, the gate was my only hope.

I ran to the heavy chain that held the gate in place and struck it as hard as I could with my sword. Nothing. I didn't even leave a mark.

Both dragons stuck their heads into the gate, their long necks making them look like two giant serpents, writhing back and forth as they looked for me.

I struck the chain again. Nothing.

As if sensing my desperation, the dragons pushed further into the gate. They were so big that they wedged together, neither willing to let the other go first. They snapped and bit at each other, fighting for dominance. I knew as soon as they sorted it out, I was a goner. With me gone, my friends would be abandoned, my father would die alone in a dungeon cell and Ren Lucre would be free to launch his war against the human world.

Only once you know what you stand for will your true power be known.

It was Aquinas's voice.

I heard it as clearly as if she stood next to me.

What do you stand for?

I closed my eyes and pictured everything that was important to me. My friends. My family. The Templar insignia. They were interwoven with one another. They were all interwoven with who I was. I wasn't fighting against Ren Lucre or against the Creach who wanted to kill me. I was fighting for something. Something greater than myself. Sure, I fought for the people I loved, but it was somehow bigger than that. It had to be. If I failed, millions of strangers would suffer at the hands of Ren Lucre, not just the people I knew.

And that's when I knew. To make this journey, to have the strength to win, it couldn't be about me, or about my friends, or about saving my father, or even about stopping Ren Lucre. The *why* behind everything I did had to be bigger. In the middle of all the madness, I had to stand for something greater than myself.

Only once you know what you stand for will your true power be known.

What do you stand for?

I finally understood what Aquinas had meant. I whispered the word out loud, only for me to hear, only for me to know.

I opened my eyes.

The world zoomed into a sudden, perfect clarity. I felt the hot breath of the dragons behind me. Tasted the saltiness of my own sweat and blood in my mouth. Heard the leather of my gloves creak as my hand tightened on the hilt of my sword.

With a cry, I swung down with everything I had.

My sword struck with a burst of sparks and cut straight through the chain.

The chain above the cut whipped upward as the gears holding the gate in place spun loose.

The dragons sensed the danger and tried to back out, but they got in each other's way and couldn't move fast enough. Both of their necks still poked through the opening. They screamed and hissed at one another as the gate started to descend with a loud, shrieking grate.

With a final thunderous BOOM! the giant gate crashed down on the shrieking dragons. The weight smashed them into the ground, followed by a vicious crunch as the jagged teeth buried into their flesh and severed both of their heads.

I stumbled back on my heels, still not ready to believe it had actually worked. The two dragons stared at me blankly with their dead, yellow eyes.

It was over.

We had won the day.

Even so, I knew in my heart that this was only the first of many battles, and that what today had really shown us was that Ren Lucre would go to any lengths to fight us. He was not going to go easily. Finding the Jerusalem Stones was more important than ever.

The adrenaline rush of the battle slowly wore off and a wave of fatigue hit me so hard I dropped to one knee. After going non-stop for nearly two days, between the Trial of the Cave and the battle for the Academy, everything hurt. I felt like I could lay down right where I was and sleep for a week.

But voices outside were calling my name. Only a few at first. And then more. The howls of wolves added to the sound. Fighting through the pain, I stood up. There—a small metal door in the bottom corner of the gate, large enough to allow a single man to enter at a time without having to raise the entire gate.

I walked up to it and threw back the heavy bolts that sealed it.

When I opened the door, morning sunlight poured in, nearly blinding me after the darkness inside the Citadel. But it was the wave of sound that caught me most off-guard. All of the hunters and all of the wolves had gathered outside the gates and when I walked out they erupted in the loudest cheer I'd ever heard. Will and T-Rex ran up and hugged me. They were talking but I couldn't hear anything they were saying.

Daniel limped up, favoring one of his legs and with his bandage falling off exposing the open wound that was once his nose. But he was otherwise unharmed. He grinned and held out his hand. I shook it and he pulled me into a tight embrace. He held my hand up in victory and the sound of the cheering swelled. Some of the hunters parted and Bacho carried Aquinas forward, her shoulder now bandaged where the arrow had struck her. I ran to her.

"I thought you were dead," I said.

"Takes more that a little goblin arrow to kill me," Aquinas said.

"Should be in bed restin' is what I say," Bacho grumbled.

She smiled at me kindly and I nodded my head toward her in respect. I could tell she knew something important had happened to me. That something had changed.

"So you found what you stand for," she whispered. "Good. Now keep that inside where it will have the most power. You will need all the strength you can get before this is finished."

"I still have so many questions," I said. "About my mother. About Ren Lucre's plans."

"All in good time, young hunter," Aquinas said. "All in good time. For now, enjoy the moment and share it with your comrades and friends."

Eva broke through the crowd, then hesitated when she finally saw me. We walked slowly toward one another until we were face-to-face. I don't know if it was because I was so tired that I could barely stand up, or because I had faced certain death more times than I could count, or because I thought I had lost her, but I decided to ignore the fact that everyone we knew was watching us and just kiss her right there and then.

But just as I reached out for her, Will and T-Rex circled around us and locked us in a group hug. Eva and I made eye contact and grinned. Whatever moment there might have been had passed and I couldn't help wonder if it would ever come back again.

I left those thoughts behind and gave into the pure joy of sharing this moment with my best friends. Will, T-Rex, Eva and I laughed together, relishing the fact that for the second time we had overcome impossible odds to live to fight another day.

Some of the instructors pulled me away, hefted me up on their shoulders and paraded me through the crowd. I looked back over my shoulder and saw Eva smiling at me.

This might have only been the first battle, and there might have been a long war ahead, but at that moment I'd never felt more alive.

I was Jack Templar, Monster Hunter.

And I was ready to hunt.

Chapter Nineteen

I waited for Tiberon as he slowly walked among his pack of wolves one last time. Eva, Will and T-Rex stood next to me while the rest of the hunters stayed inside as I had asked them. We grimly looked at the piles of goblin carcasses spread out across the battlefield. There would be time to clear them away later. Right now, it was time to both fulfill a debt and to have a promise fulfilled.

Tiberon gave one last deep bow to the wolves gathered around us before walking up the hill. I fingered the Templar Ring nervously, not quite sure what was supposed to happen next.

You fought bravely, young Templar, Tiberon's voice echoed in my head.

"You didn't do too bad yourself," I replied. "For a seven-hundred-year-old hunter, that is."

A deep, chugging sound filled my head. It took me a second to realize Tiberon was laughing. Finally, the sound faded away and Tiberon turned serious.

As I promised, I will tell you the locations of the Jerusalem Stones and where your father is being held. But before I do, I must warn you that pursuing either will likely lead to your death. He looked over my shoulder at Eva, Will and T-Rex. *Or the deaths of those you love.*

I nodded. There had been so much death and destruction already because of me, but I knew my enemy. I knew that unless we fought him, he would be merciless. "I understand," I said.

Tiberon placed a paw on my shoulder.

I'm afraid you will not like what I have to show you.

A flurry of images flashed in front of me. They happened in quick sequence, one short scene after another. It didn't take long for me to obtain everything I needed to know. Then the images ended and I staggered backward, gasping for breath. My heart sank. The difficulty of the task ahead of me was worse than I ever could have imagined. In fact, it seemed impossible.

I warned you that you would not like what you saw. What you do with this information is now up to you, Tiberon said.

I steadied myself and stood in front of the great wolf. "You have kept your word and I will keep mine," I said. "Are you ready?"

Tiberon glanced over his shoulder at the wolves standing in the tree line. It was a long, lingering look, and for a moment I thought he might change his mind. But he turned back to me and nodded. *I am ready.*

"Tiberon of the Black Guard, trusted friend, comrade-in-arms," I said, trying to match what I had seen Jacques de Molay do all those years ago. "You have served your penance and restored your honor. As bearer of the Templar Ring, I release you from your oath. Go in peace and find the rest you deserve."

On impulse, I reached out and touched the ring to Tiberon's chest, right in the center of the white cross. There was a loud *crack* and flash of light where the ring touched him. Tiberon closed his eyes. The air around him vibrated and buzzed with energy. Slowly, he transformed out of his wolf body, his hair pulling back into his skin, his limbs shortening, his face growing smaller as his features became defined.

The vibration in the air intensified, obscuring him from view. But I was able to catch a glimpse of him for just a second, fully returned to his human form. We made eye contact. He smiled, placed his fist to his chest, then stretched it out in front of him with the hunter's salute.

I returned the gesture as the entire energy field lifted off the ground, swirled like a small tornado, then dissipated into the wind as if it had never existed.

Tiberon was gone.

The wolves let out a single, unified howl to say farewell to their friend and protector, and then retreated slowly back into the forest.

I turned back to my friends, each of them speechless from what they had just witnessed. It was Eva who finally spoke.

"Did he tell you what you needed to know?" she asked.

I nodded. "It's not good news."

"Tell us," Will said.

I let out a long sigh and described as best I could what I had seen.

"Ren Lucre gave a Jerusalem Stone to each of the Creach Lords for safe-keeping," I said. "To get them back, we need to find each of the Lords, figure out where they have hidden their Stone, then somehow get it away from them."

"The Creach Lords?" T-Rex asked, looking puzzled.

"The vampires, zombies, demons, werewolves and the Lesser Creach all have their own Lord," Will said.

We all looked at him strangely.

"Just because it looks like I'm sleeping in class, doesn't mean I'm actually asleep," he said.

"So we have to go find all these guys?" T-Rex asked.

"Not we," I said. "I have to. And from what Tiberon showed me, having the Jerusalem Stones is the only way I'm getting into the dungeon where my dad is being kept."

"So, it's settled," said Eva. "We'll go for the Jerusalem Stones first, and then your father."

"But, I just said that..." I stammered.

"Sounds good," Will agreed.

"Can we at least have lunch before we go?" T-Rex asked.

"Guys, I appreciate it, but I can't ask you to go," I said. "It's too dangerous."

Eva put her arms around Will and T-Rex. "You don't need to ask us to go, because we're going no matter what. Right guys?"

Will and T-Rex nodded. I grinned, secretly thankful I wouldn't have to face this challenge alone. I felt blessed to have such great friends. "All right," I said. "Let's do this."

"Not without me, you're not," Daniel said, limping out from the Academy gate. "What? You think I'm going to let you have all the glory, Templar? Besides, you're going to need as many swords as you can get."

"And cool gadgets," Xavier chimed in, stepping out from behind Daniel. "Need I remind you that more wars are won because of technological advantages than anything else. That happens to be my specialty."

I could tell that arguing would be futile. We welcomed Daniel and Xavier into our small group. That made six of us. I wondered if and when we were successful with our quest, whether all six of us would survive. Even with this dark thought, I was happy to have these five companions for what was sure to be an incredible adventure. We walked back toward the Academy gates.

"So, which Creach Lord are we going after first?" Eva asked.

"I was thinking the Lord of the Vampires," I said.

"Isn't that Ren Lucre?" asked T-Rex.

"No," Xavier chimed in. "Ren Lucre is the Lord of all the Creach. The Vampire Lord is a different vampire entirely. And, she's technically a vampiress. Don't you guys listen in class?"

"He's right," I said. "And Tiberon gave me a strong image of where I could find her."

"From the sounds of it, we have to go to all five eventually," Daniel said. "I guess it doesn't matter where we start."

"Vampires it is then," said Will happily. "This is gonna be awesome."

"If by awesome you mean filled with incredibly dangerous monsters who want to kill us, then sure," Eva said.

"Yeah," grinned Will. "Like I said, awesome."

"But we're still eating lunch first, right?" T-Rex asked.

We all shared a good a laugh and walked back through the Academy walls. The hunters and Ratlings worked together clearing the debris from the training grounds. Aquinas and Bacho stood in the middle of them, directing the efforts. I still hadn't had a chance to thank Aquinas yet. Her advice that I wouldn't know my true power until I discovered what I stood for had proven all too true. And, just as she had advised, I kept my realization to myself, stored away as my personal touchstone. Even with my new companions signed onto the quest, I knew the trials ahead would be more challenging than anything I had yet faced. I didn't know if I was ready for it, but because of Aquinas, I felt certain I was doing it for the right reason.

Aquinas told me once that a hunter armed with the right *why* could endure any *how*.

I knew the adventure ahead would test that idea to its core. As I looked at my friends and at all the hunters and Ratlings working together to rebuild the Academy grounds, I prayed that she was right, and that we were ready. Because, like it or not, we were about to find out.

A Last Note

As I warned you from the beginning, the act of reading this book makes you part of the monster hunter world. The Creach in your area have already sensed that you have this book, so you must be alert at all times.

I've set up a website to keep you posted on what's happening and to help teach you how to fight:

WWW.JACKTEMPLAR.COM.

The password for the secret area is MONSTER.

See you there. But watch out...there are monsters everywhere!

Do Your Duty, Come What May!

-Jack Templar

From the Author

Thank you for joining me in the world of Jack Templar and the Creach monsters. It's been my honor to get to know Jack and help him get the word out about the dangers that lurk in the shadows of our world.

If you enjoyed the book, I would appreciate a review on any of the numerous online sites where readers gather, particularly Amazon.com. If you are a young hunter, make sure to get your parent's permission first. This helps bring attention to the book and alert others who could benefit from having their eyes opened to the reality of the monster threat.

I look forward to sharing Book 3 with you... *Jack Templar and the Lord Of The Vampires.*

Do your duty, come what may!

Jeff Gunhus

About the Author

Jeff Gunhus is the author of the Middle Grade/YA series The Templar Chronicles. The first book, *Jack Templar Monster Hunter*, was written in an effort to get his reluctant reader eleven-year old son excited about reading. It worked and a new series was born. His book *Reaching Your Reluctant Reader* has helped hundreds of parents create avid readers. As a father of five, he leads an active lifestyle with his wife Nicole in Maryland by trying to constantly keep up with their kids. In rare moments of quiet, he can be found in the back of the City Dock Cafe in Annapolis working on his next novel...always on the lookout of Creach monsters that might be out to get him! Come say hello at...

www.JeffGunhus.com

CPSIA information can be obtained
at www.ICGtesting.com
Printed in the USA
LVOW13s1813260517
535981LV00014B/971/P